Daughter of Starlight

by

Molly M. Hammond

Copyright Notice
This is a work of fiction. Names, characters, places, and incidents are either the product of the author's imagination or are used fictitiously, and any resemblance to actual persons living or dead, business establishments, events, or locales, is entirely coincidental.

Daughter of Starlight

COPYRIGHT © 2025 by Molly M. Hammond

Cover Art by *Teddi Black*

The Wild Rose Press, Inc.
PO Box 708
Adams Basin, NY 14410-0708
Visit us at www.thewildrosepress.com

Publishing History
First Edition, 2025
Trade Paperback ISBN 978-1-5092-6118-5
Digital ISBN 978-1-5092-6119-2

Published in the United States of America

Dedication

To my husband, Jeremy, who has never faltered in his support of my wildest dreams. For that, and for this beautiful life we share, I am forever grateful. You are my refuge, my strength, and above all, my greatest love. Always & Today.

And to my sons, James and William, whose bravery and kindness are a gift to all who know them, and whose steadfast belief in me helped pull this story from premise to printed page. From the bottom of my heart, thank you.

When the stars choose, they never choose wrong.
Their will is etched into stone and carried in the hearts
of heroes long gone.
Invisible threads stretch across the bridges between
worlds
and hover at the edge of sight.
A call must be answered,
What was broken must now be undone,
And the alignment waits for no one.

BOOK ONE

The Call

Chapter 1

Fatigue and fluorescent lighting made Frank appear older than his fifty years. His worn leather briefcase thumped softly as he dropped it on the floor and motioned for Luma to come in. Luma watched him as she stepped into his office. The small hanging placard that read "foster services" swung lazily back and forth as the door closed behind her. Luma allowed her gaze to roam the familiar space. She'd been in this office frequently over the past twelve years but being here now wasn't how she had expected to spend today, of all days.

To Luma's eye, the antique oak desk in the center of the room was too big for the small office. Its curved edges and elegantly carved details stood in stark contrast to the sterility of the gray filing cabinets that flanked it on both sides. Luma pondered where that out-of-place desk had come from—a family heirloom, perhaps? She wondered absently what it must be like to have a family that passed things down through generations or to have a family at all, for that matter.

The knuckles on her right hand still had a bit of dried blood on them, and Luma picked at the flakes while she waited for Frank's reprimand. It wasn't long in coming.

"You can't punch everyone who upsets you, Luma. In the eyes of the state, you're not a foster child anymore;

1

you're an adult. You're just lucky Gabe's nose wasn't actually broken, but from now on, your inability to control your temper will be a matter for the police, not your social worker."

Though her eyes were lowered, Luma could feel the weight of Frank's gaze on her. She started to tuck her hair behind her ears but thought better of it and instead let the unruly dark curls fall back on either side of her face. She had always been self-conscious about her ears.

Luma took a deep breath and tried to keep her voice from cracking as she spoke. "I'm sorry." And she meant it. Frank had been Luma's social worker since the beginning, and she didn't dislike him, at least not as much as she disliked most people. She knew he had done the best he could.

It had been twelve years, but Luma remembered sitting in the child welfare intake office like it was yesterday, a scared six-year-old girl with no memory of parents or family of any kind. The whispers from the other social workers haunted her recollection.

It must have been some kind of terrible accident to leave a child wandering alone in the mountains. Did you see those awful scars all over her palms? So terrible. So terrible and so strange.

Frank's chair squeaked as he shifted his weight, bringing Luma back to the present. She raised her eyes to look at him. His hairline had receded considerably since she had first met him, and what was left was flecked heavily with gray. That comb-over wasn't fooling anybody, and behind his thick glasses, Frank's eyes were tired but kind. A flush of emotion brought heat to Luma's cheeks as she mentally relived the events of earlier that day.

She had been moving the last of her meager possessions into her new apartment when Gabe and his friend had sauntered over, sneering. He had been a foster kid like her, but unlike her, Gabe had a large group of friends. Luma had never been very good at making friends. Making enemies seemed to come easier to her, and Gabe had been the worst of them throughout their high school years together.

But high school was over now. Luma knew that Gabe had also gotten an apartment in that building—it was the only affordable, furnished apartment building in their small western Colorado town, and most of the foster kids wound up there after they aged out of the system. Still, Luma had figured that after graduation, Gabe would just leave her alone. She had figured wrong.

Still, when Gabe began his old standby of insults about Luma's above-average height and the scars that covered her palms, she had tried to ignore him. It was only when Gabe knocked the journals out of her hand as she pushed past him that Luma's famously short temper flared.

The loose-leaf paper held in the journals, each page covered in sketches of the night sky, had fluttered delicately to the sidewalk, but Gabe had landed with a thud, blood gushing from his nose. The well-aimed kick to his crotch while he was down probably hadn't been necessary. Luma was willing to admit that much. But it had seemed worth it at the time.

Gabe had started howling about being attacked while his friend yelled at Luma, calling her a "six-foot freak" and a "psycho." She had been about to punch him, too, when the landlord had come running over. It was sheer coincidence that Frank was driving by at that moment and had come to Luma's defense, helping to defuse the situation before the police were called.

****

Frank shifted again, took off his glasses, and polished them ineffectually on the front of his shirt as he spoke. "Look, I know that for whatever reason, you've never gotten along with Gabe, but you've got to learn to walk away, Luma. As I said, now that you are eighteen…Oh!" Frank smiled and put his glasses back on. "That reminds me." He stepped out of the office for a moment and returned carrying a small cupcake. With a flourish, he plopped it down atop a thick folder on his desk. "Happy birthday, Luma."

The cupcake sagged to the left, looking like it had been forgotten in a hot car for a day or two. A bit of the frosting dripped onto the folder beneath it, the folder that had a small sticker with Luma's name on it and, below that, a stamp that read "closed" in bright red ink. Luma knew what was inside that folder: a stack of papers with her name on them listed under the surnames of various families she had been shuffled to throughout the past twelve years. Papers with notes containing words like *withdrawn, temperamental,* and *unwilling to engage.*

Frank mopped up the frosting drip with a wadded napkin from his pocket. It left behind a grease stain on the stamp so that the red ink on the "c" bled pink. Frank stuffed the napkin back in his pocket and reached out to shake Luma's hand. If the feeling of the raised scars or the moisture on her palm bothered him, he didn't show it.

Frank cleared his throat awkwardly and gave Luma's hand a gentle squeeze. "Please, stay out of trouble. And take care of yourself, okay? I have always felt that there was something very special about you, Luma."

Luma met Frank's gaze and gave him a small smile. She thanked him for the cupcake and for, well, everything he had tried to do for her over the past twelve years. He was a good man, but Luma knew what he had just said was a lie.

There was absolutely nothing special about her.

****

It was the same dream almost every night. Not a nightmare, but not pleasant either. There were flashes of light and color and someone calling her name. All around, Luma could make out the shimmering figures of people. Something in the pit of her stomach gave her the sense that they were in trouble, but whenever she tried to talk to them or get closer, they faded away until all that remained was an unnamed grief.

****

Luma finally gave up on sleep and kicked her feet over the side of her bed. Her one blanket was on the floor, and her thin sheets were in a twisted mess at the end of the mattress. Across the room, her small alarm clock read *5:30 am.*

Luma walked over to her narrow bedroom window and pulled up the shade to reveal an overcast sky and drizzle beading on the windowsill. Still, she got dressed and put on her hiking shoes. Hiking in the nearby mountains was one of the only things Luma truly enjoyed, and she wasn't about to let a few rain clouds keep her from it.

By the time Luma reached the familiar trailhead, it had stopped drizzling, but the heavy clouds remained. She hiked onward into the foothills, her long legs carrying her away from the road and into the stillness of the mountains she loved so much.

Luma smiled to herself and walked higher. The moaning wind through the treetops and the crunching of her shoes on the damp, rocky soil were the only sounds. A strong gust blew behind her, almost as if it were pushing her onward and upward.

Luma.

Had someone just said her name? Luma stopped short. She turned and looked down the trail, then peered left and right through the trees on either side, but she was alone, and now all she could hear was the wind. With a shrug, Luma hiked on, trying to ignore the nagging feeling of unease that had now settled in the pit of her stomach.

A short time later, Luma stopped next to a small stream that gurgled out from between the rocks and stubbornly pushed its way past tree roots and stones on its journey down the mountainside. Across the stream, a large overhang of rock jutted from the hillside, shrouded by pine trees. Luma leaned against the side of a boulder and squinted at the sky. The wind had picked up again, and heavy clouds billowed overhead.

She had just decided to turn back when the first fat raindrop hit her on the side of the cheek. A second later, the downpour started.

A gasp caught in the back of Luma's throat at the intensity of the rain, and she jumped across the small stream and ran for shelter beneath the overhang of rock. Once there, Luma stood in shocked stillness. Weather was notoriously fickle in the mountains, but this downpour was completely unexpected. Her hair and clothing were already soaked, and water pooled on the sandy ground beneath her feet. Dark clouds shrouded the sun, and thunder rolled in the distance.

Luma.

Was that her name again? Luma spun away from the curtain of rain, seeking the source of the sound, and her chest tightened. This was not a shallow rock overhang as she had first thought, but the entrance to a cave.

"Hello?" Her voice sounded small and shaky as it echoed around her. No response.

Heart racing, Luma scanned the sandy ground for other footprints, but the only ones she saw were her own. A brilliant flash of lightning split the darkened sky outside, followed immediately by a deafening clap of thunder, and Luma retreated farther from the entrance. When her eyes adjusted to the gloom, Luma noticed that at the back of the cave, the rocks separated, creating what looked like a narrow passageway deeper into the mountain. Her curiosity piqued, Luma stepped forward into the passageway, trailing her hand along one side as she walked. The rough stone felt pleasantly cool on the jumble of scars that adorned her palms.

After several feet, the passageway took a turn to the right and opened into a wide cavern. Luma blinked, her mouth slightly agape as she stepped into the large space and looked up. High above her, a small opening in the ceiling of the cavern allowed light from the outside to come through. The light wasn't very bright at the moment, given the clouds, but it was enough so it took Luma's eyes a minute to adjust from the darkness of the passageway. Luma removed her hand from the cave wall, her eyes growing wide with amazement that such a grand space lay hidden inside the mountain.

She had just walked to the very center of the cavern

when the ground trembled violently beneath her feet.

Luma!

Luma shrieked and swung her arms wide to steady herself. Her heart pounded as if trying to break free from its cage in her chest.

What is that? Who is calling to me?

Then, as quickly as it had begun, the trembling stopped, and silence filled the cavern once more. Luma took a deep breath of relief just as the ground beneath her gave way, and she was falling.

Chapter 2

She didn't remember hitting the ground, but when Luma regained consciousness, she was flat on her back with her arms splayed out to either side. Her whole body was a mass of sore muscles, and her mind awash in confusion.

With a grunt, Luma rolled onto her side and sat up. She squinted at first, but then her eyes opened wider as her brain struggled to make sense of what she saw. She was in the same cavern. At least, it looked the same, but also...different somehow. High above, sunlight poured through the small opening in the cavern ceiling, shining directly onto Luma's face. Luma looked at the sandy ground to her right and left, the same ground she was sure had collapsed beneath her moments before.

Had it been only moments? Or longer? How can I still be in the same place?

Luma shook her head, trying to clear it, and her stomach twisted into knots as waves of nausea washed over her.

Something isn't right.

Her palms ached, and when Luma turned her hands over, she noted with horror that the old, crisscrossed scars that covered them had become more raised and darker in color than they had been before. The scars throbbed with an intensity that tingled up to Luma's wrists and along her forearms.

Luma stared at both palms, her jaw tight. She had had those scars for as long as she could remember—remnants of some terrible accident that must have befallen her family and left her wandering alone as a child with no memory. They were ugly, and she hated them, but they had never ached like this before.

After a few minutes, Luma dropped her hands and took a deep breath. Judging from the sunlight that now streamed from the hole in the cavern ceiling, the storm had passed. It was time to go home. With another deep breath, Luma pushed herself onto her knees and rose. Once on her feet, she staggered a bit before regaining her balance, and something caught her eye.

Grouped to her right were four standing stones. Luma stared at them, her eyes narrowed. She didn't remember seeing those stones when she had first entered the cavern, and they weren't easy to miss. The stones were massive and spaced evenly apart as if placed there on purpose, and all four of them bore a deep crack from the top down, ending at roughly the middle of each stone.

Acting on impulse, Luma took a step toward the closest stone and reached out her hands. The scars on her palms ached and tingled, and a rush of heat rippled beneath her skin, bringing a flush to Luma's cheeks.

Her fingertips had almost touched the crack in the first stone when a shout rang out from behind her. "Hey! Who are you? What are you doing here?"

Luma spun in the direction of the voice. A young man stood at the entrance to the cavern, his tall body framed by the arch of the narrow passageway, his face cast in shadow. Luma kept her hands in front of her defensively, her breath quick and shallow. She tried to explain herself, but splotches of light danced in her periphery, and the cavern writhed and spun around her. It was all she could do to remain upright as the scars on her palms continued to throb. Her mouth flooded with moisture as nausea churned in her stomach. *Why is it so hot in here?*

"I'm...I'm just...I want to go home." Luma sucked in her breath as her knees buckled. She heard footsteps running toward her, and then everything went dark.

****

It was the same dream again. Flashes of light and color, and in the distance, figures of people she couldn't quite make out, as though she was looking through a foggy window. No shouting this time, just quiet murmurs. The figures moved closer, but she still couldn't see them clearly. In the haze of the dream, Luma's mind flooded with questions, but they drowned on her tongue, unspoken.

****

"You said you discovered her in the Cavern of the Four? Interesting."

Luma's eyes snapped open, and she found herself staring up into the face of a woman who was looking back at her with a concerned expression, her eyebrows knit together and her jaw tight. Luma sat up and looked around.

She was on a narrow bed in what appeared to be a small stone cottage. A fire burned low in the hearth across from her, and sunlight filtered between large tree trunks outside the small window on her left. Luma opened and closed her fists underneath the blankets that covered her, her mind churning. There had been no cabin near the trail she had originally hiked up.

What is this place?

11

The woman at Luma's bedside had long black hair loosely plaited in a thick braid that fell over her left shoulder. The shiny, moonless tresses and smooth skin of the woman gave the initial impression of youth, but there also hung about her the presence of aged wisdom, which gave Luma the strange sense that this woman was far older than she appeared. Luma shifted uncomfortably, keeping her hands tucked beneath the blankets.

"Some tea?" The woman's voice was deeper than Luma expected but had a friendly softness to it. Luma nodded, and from a different room, a young man approached with a kettle and a tray of cups. He set them down on a small table next to the woman, who nodded toward him with a smile. "This is Corr. He was the one who found you in the cavern and brought you here. It appeared you were experiencing some…" the woman paused as if searching for the right word, "…distress." She fixed Luma with an intense stare.

"What were you doing in there?" Corr's voice was also deep and rich but lacked the softness of the woman's.

Luma turned to look at him. He had deep-set eyes, the color of which reminded her of the thick moss that grew along the trunks of dead trees. His hair, like the woman's, was a deep velvet black, but his was cut short, and his exposed ears each came to a delicate but distinct point at the top. Luma stared at them, and one of her hands almost rose to her own ear, but she caught herself and stuffed her hand back under the blanket.

She was about to say something in response to the question when the woman interjected. "Now, Corr, don't be rude. Let our guest have some tea." She gave Luma a warm smile. "My name is Izarre. What is your name, child?"

Luma gave a small smile in return. "I'm Luma."

Izarre tilted her head as if surprised by the name but said nothing and instead offered a cup of tea. Pulling her hands from under the blanket, Luma reached for the cup, but just as she was about to wrap her fingers around it, Izarre let out a small gasp, and the cup slipped from her hands. Luma tried to catch it but missed, and the cup smashed upon the stone floor, splashing tea and scattering shards of pottery.

Luma started to sputter an apology, but Izarre, ignoring the mess, grabbed Luma's hands. Turning them over, she ran her fingers across the scars on Luma's palms, her eyes wide. Startled, Luma looked down and swallowed a cry of shock as she saw that the crisscrossed scars were even darker than before. Now almost black, they stood in stark contrast against the otherwise creamy paleness of her skin.

Luma looked up, her gaze darting between Izarre and Corr, both of whom were standing as if frozen to the spot, staring down at Luma's palms. Embarrassment churned in Luma's stomach, and when Izarre finally looked up at her, Luma was surprised to see her eyes now glistening with tears. When she spoke, Izarre's voice trembled. "Luma. You must come with me."

****

The first thing Luma noticed once they were all standing was how tall the other two were. At almost six feet tall herself, Luma was unused to being the shortest person in the room. Izarre was at least an inch taller than she, and Corr, whom Luma judged to be around the same age as herself, was taller than both of them. Luma realized that, for the first time, she didn't feel self-conscious about her height.

With a sense of urgency that Luma didn't understand, Izarre ushered her and Corr out of the cottage, and the three of them hiked up the mountainside. Luma took in her surroundings discreetly as she walked. This was not the same trail she had hiked earlier that day.

When they reached the cave entrance, Corr announced he would stay back and keep watch. Luma wondered what exactly he was watching out for but decided not to ask. She and Izarre entered the cave together and made their way through the narrow passageway and into the large cavern. The four standing stones loomed silent and still, their cracks half-hidden in shadow.

Izarre approached the stones and gazed up at them, then motioned for Luma to join her. After a few minutes, Izarre spoke, her voice filled with reverence as it echoed slightly in the large cavern. "This is a special place, Luma. A place of great importance to all of us elves. These four stones share a sacred connection, a bond, with the four brightest stars in our night sky. This connection was once what guarded the bridge between this world, Edira, and the neighboring world, Malicath, the world of the wizards."

Luma shook her head and took a step back. "Um, what? Did you say *wizards*, *elves*? This doesn't make any sense."

Izarre nodded patiently. "I know you probably don't remember anything, and this is a lot to take in. But please, let me try to explain."

Luma sighed and raised her eyebrows skeptically but held her tongue.

"There are many worlds," Izarre began, "all existing around each other. Some closer, some farther, but all of them linked. It is through these links, or *bridges*, that it is possible to move between worlds."

Izarre paused, her gaze searching Luma's face as if hoping for a glimmer of recognition. Luma returned her look blankly.

Sighing, Izarre continued. "Malicath is the closest world to this one. So close, in fact, that it didn't take long for the wizards of Malicath to cross the bridge into our world, intent on stealing our world's magic to strengthen their own. That was long ago, and back then, we elves had help. Four powerful beings, the physical manifestations of the four brightest stars in our sky, came to our aid. With their deep magic, they drove the wizards back to their own world, then created these Sacred Stones and filled them with starlight to form a barrier between our two worlds."

Izarre looked reverently up at the stones. "And for many years, the elves of Edira lived in peace. Then, much later, a surprise. A human woman somehow found her way across a bridge and into our world, which is unusual because the world called Earth is so very far from our own, and the bridge link is weak. This woman fell in love with our king and decided to stay on Edira. Eventually, they had a daughter. The baby was born at the exact moment that the Four Stars were in perfect alignment. This imbued the child with the extraordinary power of starlight, and as she grew, her power only increased. But," Izarre shook her head again, her voice heavy with sadness. "We were betrayed by one of our own. The Sacred Stones that protected us were cracked, and the damage to them allowed the starlight inside to spill out, leaving the bridge between our world and Malicath unprotected. Soon, the wizards crossed the bridge with an army. But this time, they came for the child."

Luma's eyes grew wide despite her skepticism. "Why?"

Izarre bowed her head. "The wizards knew that the child born during the alignment was the only one who had the power to stop them once the Sacred Stones were cracked, so they came to kill her. The elves fought fiercely to protect her, but our weapons were no match for the wizard's battle magic. Then, when all seemed lost, the king and queen smuggled her from the capital and brought her to this cavern. We believe the intent was for mother and daughter to escape back to Earth, but it was not to be, and the child, only six years old, was forced across the bridge to Earth alone." Izarre pulled her eyes from the stones and fixed Luma with an intense stare. "That was twelve years ago."

A cold ripple ran down Luma's spine. Goosebumps rose along her arms, and the hair at the back of her neck prickled. "It can't be. It...can't," she whispered, half to herself.

Izarre reached out, took Luma's hands in her own, and gave them a gentle squeeze. "The child was out of the wizards' grasp, but without her, the damage to our four Sacred Stones could not be repaired. The protective starlight in these stones will continue to spill out until the Four Stars come back into alignment. If the cracks are not healed by then, all four stones will crumble to dust. Then, the wizards will have full access to Edira and all its inherent magic."

Luma shook her head. "Um...what exactly does this

have to do with me?"

Izarre smiled. "There is a prophecy. It says that as the alignment draws closer, the Sacred Stones would call out across worlds, seeking the one who has the special power needed to heal them and, in doing so, defeat the wizards." Izarre looked at Luma, her eyes shining. "That is why you, Luma, have been called."

Luma stared back at Izarre for several seconds in stunned silence, then an awkward laugh bubbled up from her throat, and she pulled her hands from Izarre's grasp. "What? Um, no. No." Luma stammered. "There is no way. I don't know how I got here, but I assure you, I am no one special. I just want to get home. I...I can't help you."

"Can't? Or won't?"

Luma jumped at the unexpected sound of Corr's voice. He entered the cavern and strode over. He stared at Luma, his green eyes flashing.

When he spoke, his voice grated with frustration. "Half the elven population gave their lives protecting you twelve years ago. Your parents gave their lives to get you to safety. And now that you are finally back, you just want to leave us again? How could you be so selfish when so much is at stake?"

Luma stared at him, the shock at his accusations keeping her words prisoner at the back of her throat. But soon, that shock dissipated. She took a menacing step toward Corr, her eyes narrowing and her fingers curling into fists as her temper broke free and took control of her tongue.

"I'm selfish? How dare you! You don't know me! You don't know anything about me or about what I've been through! My *parents?* What are you talking about?"

Luma's breath was coming faster now, and her vision blurred around the edges. Shooting pains ran from her palms up her forearms, and she loosened her fists, still glaring at Corr as she tried desperately to steady her breathing. Anger raised the pitch of her voice. "None of this makes any sense. I don't know what, or who, you are talking about, but it's not me! I don't owe you, or anyone else, *anything!* Got it? I just want to go home!"

Izarre stepped forward and placed herself between Corr and Luma. She glanced over at Corr and motioned with her head toward the cavern entrance. "Enough, Corr. Please, go keep watch."

Wordlessly, Corr spun on his heel and stalked off toward the passageway. Izarre turned and looked at Luma with great sadness reflected in her large, dark eyes. Then, without a word, she grasped Luma's wrists and pulled them upward, palms facing the stones. Luma was about to jerk her hands away when, all at once, a symbol began to glow at the base of each stone. A jumble of short, straight lines, crisscrossed over each other— mirror images of the scars on Luma's palms. Flashes of light danced in Luma's periphery, and whispers swirled around her mind. A voice, soft and gentle, filled her ears. *Luma.*

Izarre released her grip, and Luma stumbled backward, watching with wide eyes as the carvings faded.

Izarre nodded. "It is as I expected. When the stones forcibly transferred you out of this world and into another, they left their mark."

Luma's hands trembled uncontrollably, and a wave of nausea crashed into her. Her mind churned with questions as weakness clawed at her limbs and heat simmered beneath her skin. She fell to her knees just as Corr dashed back into the cavern, his face flushed and his voice breathless from running.

"Wizards! I just saw a group of them crossing the valley on horseback. They are headed this way." He stared at Luma as she knelt on the ground, her entire body shaking and her face ghostly pale. Then he turned to Izarre, his voice steady but strained. "She isn't strong enough to fight them now. If the wizards find her here, they will kill her."

Chapter 3

Luma only caught snippets of the hurried conversation between Corr and Izarre as she stumbled after them on shaking legs out of the cavern and back toward the small cottage.

"You must take her," Izarre was saying, "it's the only way, and she cannot get there alone." Though Luma couldn't make out his response, Corr's dark brows were knit together, and whatever he had said had been through clenched teeth.

****

A short time later, Luma's nausea had mostly dissipated, and she was reluctantly following Corr on a narrow trail through a thick pine forest. Izarre had given them each a small satchel with food and flasks of water. Corr had a bow and a small quiver of arrows slung across his shoulders and a dagger belted to his hip.

Luma was worried about Izarre and had asked why she didn't come with them, but Corr had only shrugged in response. "She won't leave the cottage until the time is right. But she'll be okay." His voice dropped, and he said, almost to himself, "As long as there aren't too many of them."

Luma didn't like the sound of that at all, but the look on Corr's face told her not to press the matter. Her head was still swimming with all that had happened in the last several hours. This morning, she had woken up in her small apartment. Now, she was apparently fleeing for her life through a forest in some unknown world with a sullen companion who was taking her to an unknown place.

For the second time since they had started, Luma tripped on a tree root and stumbled onto one knee, cursing under her breath. Corr didn't look back or slow down. "Keep up, little girl. We have a lot of ground to cover before nightfall."

Luma rubbed her bruised knee and glared at the back of Corr's head. She brushed the hair out of her eyes and took a few jogging steps to catch up with him.

"Who are you calling 'little girl'? You can't be much older than I am."

Corr only grunted in response and kept walking, picking up his pace so that he remained in front of her. From behind him, Luma piped up again, annoyed at being dismissed. "Where are you taking me, anyway? I already told you—I want to go home!"

Corr's broad shoulders tensed, but he remained stubbornly silent, and the anger at being ignored brought a flush to Luma's cheeks. She clenched her jaw. *Fine.* She stopped walking. Corr noticed the lack of footfalls behind him and also stopped.

He spun back to face her. "I said, keep up."

Luma met his glare unflinchingly and squared her shoulders. "Tell me where we are going. I know you are taking me somewhere, and if it's not back home where I belong, then I want to know where!"

Corr stalked over, covering the distance between them in a few long strides, and stopped just inches from Luma's face. Luma's breath caught in her chest, and her stomach did an unexpected flip-flop. *His eyes really are*

21

the color of moss.

Luma's first instinct was to take a step back as Corr leaned into her space, but instead, she lifted her chin defiantly and held her ground.

Corr's eyes narrowed as he spoke. "I am taking you to the Inland Sea to find the mage so you can learn how to channel that starlight power of yours and heal the Sacred Stones before it's too late. Because otherwise, the magic will be sucked dry from this world, and everyone I care about will die at the hands of the wizards." He paused, and grief flitted across his face before it was quickly masked. "You've made it clear that you don't care about anyone here besides yourself, but I do." He leaned in a little closer, his voice dropping to a dangerous whisper. "So. Keep. Up."

****

The wizards arrived at her door faster than Izarre had expected. She took a steadying breath as the pounding on the cottage door intensified.

The moment she turned the knob, Izarre was swept aside as several wizards pushed into the room, all with short white hair and carrying polished wooden staffs. Izarre took a few stumbling steps backward, then turned to glare at the group when someone else entered.

Like the other wizards, her hair was pure white, but hers fell in thick waves down her back, resembling a field of wind-swept snow. There was a palpable air of strength about her, and Izarre watched with caution as she moved with cat-like grace into the main room of the cottage. Her eyes landed on Izarre, eyes that were a striking, deep, royal blue and ringed with heavy, black lashes. Her mouth smiled. Her eyes did not.

"Hello, Izarre." She arched a silvery eyebrow. "All

alone?"

Izarre raised her chin, her fists clenched at her sides. "What are you doing here, Vell?"

Vell gave a short, mirthless laugh. She tossed her head, and the waves of white hair shimmered as the strands caught the afternoon light through the small cottage window. "You know better than to play dumb with me, Izarre. And I know as well as you do that with the next alignment approaching, the Sacred Stones have been calling out across the worlds." Her mouth curled into a smirk, and her blue eyes glowed with a wild light. "And just this morning, there was a pulse of magical energy from the cavern. I could feel it."

Izarre clenched her jaw and said nothing.

Vell raised her left arm, did a small flick of her wrist, and a staff materialized out of the air and into her hand. It was made of beautiful black wood and polished to a low sheen.

Vell wrapped her fingers around it and smiled her joyless smile. "Cracking those Sacred Stones almost killed me, you know. But thanks to my agreement with the wizards, I have become stronger than I ever could have imagined. In a few short weeks, the Four Stars will finally come back into alignment. When that happens, your precious Sacred Stones will crumble, and my power will be solidified. You may still be clinging to some far-flung hope, some ridiculous prophecy, but the truth is, there is no one in this world, or any other, that can stop me now."

Izarre's cheeks flushed, and she stared at Vell with unguarded hostility. When she spoke, her voice shook with rage. "Just because your hair turned white, and you have a shiny new stick doesn't change what you are—a traitor!"

Vell's eyes flashed, and she raised her hand. Izarre let out a strangled gasp as she was lifted a few inches off the floor and held there, unable to move. Vell took a step closer and smirked into Izarre's face, reveling in the power of her holding spell. She shook her head in mock pity, then, with a flick of her wrist, sent Izarre slamming against the opposite wall of the cottage. Vell held her there for a moment before casually lowering her hand and dropping Izarre to the floor, where she collapsed in a heap, gasping for air.

Vell regarded her for a moment, a look of passive indifference on her beautiful face. "The lack of magic you elves wield is pathetic." She turned to the other wizards in the cottage. "Someone recently bridged into this world through those Stones. Whoever it is, I want them found. Send out a raptera. They can't have gone far."

With that, Vell turned and swept out of the door, leaving Izarre on the cottage floor, her limbs trembling with the exertion of trying to move while under the holding spell. Izarre's breath came in ragged gasps, and she struggled to sit upright as the sound of horse hooves receded into the forest.

****

The sun had begun to dip in the western sky when Corr decided they should take a few minutes to eat and rest. Loath to show her exhaustion, Luma stifled a groan as she lowered herself down at the base of a spruce tree and propped her sore feet onto an exposed root. Corr unslung the quiver and bow from his shoulders and sat a short distance away, pointedly avoiding her gaze.

Just then, a large tawny owl swooped soundlessly

down from between the branches of the spruce tree and landed softly on the ground between Luma and Corr. It fixed its huge, amber eyes on Luma, tilting its head as it regarded her. Luma stared back in shocked surprise, her water flask held suspended in front of her open mouth.

The owl held its unblinking stare for a moment longer, then swiveled its large head to look at Corr, clacking its beak.

"I have just come from Izarre's. She told me the news, but I had to see for myself. Though, I must say, this isn't a bit how I pictured her. Are you sure she is *The One*, after all?"

A shriek escaped Luma's mouth at the sound of the owl's voice, and she lurched backward, bumping her head painfully against the tree trunk and sloshing water across the front of her shirt.

The owl glanced at her again, then turned back to Corr, clearly unimpressed. "Like I said. I am not at all convinced. A lot of trouble to go through if she turns out to be useless."

Luma's shock quickly turned to annoyance. She glared at the owl as she tried to discreetly wipe the spilled water from the front of her shirt. "Um, excuse me. I am not useless."

The owl ruffled his feathers haughtily and flexed his impressive wings. "Well, that remains to be seen. Now doesn't it."

Luma opened her mouth to retort, but Corr held up a hand for silence. "Luma, this is Trill. He is a friend and a valuable ally against the wizards. Trill, this is Luma. I found her in the Cavern of the Four. She has the markings, and Izarre says she has the power. She just doesn't seem to remember anything from…before."

Trill took a couple of ungainly steps across the ground toward Luma, who leaned back and watched the large owl approach with caution.

Trill tilted his head from side to side and inspected Luma's palms, then raised his orb-like eyes to stare skeptically into her face. "Well, well, you do indeed have the markings. But what of the power? The Sacred Stones won't heal themselves, you know! Time runs short! What exactly is the problem here? No power or no will to wield it?" Trill puffed up his downy chest feathers as he fired off questions.

Luma shrank back under the onslaught of his interrogation. "I…I don't know, I…"

"Just want to go home?" Corr interrupted her, a mocking tone in his deep voice. Luma flushed red and scowled at him. Corr smirked at her for a moment, then turned his attention to the owl. "Izarre is convinced that Luma has the power. She just doesn't know how to channel it effectively. I'm taking her to the mage."

Trill ruffled his feathers again. He turned away from Luma and hopped back to Corr, bobbing his head thoughtfully. "The mage is in exile across the Inland Sea these twelve years. Still, he is probably your best bet if she doesn't know how to wield her power. But you must move quickly. A group of wizards had just left Izarre's when I arrived there. No need to worry, she's fine." He added, noting the concerned expression on Corr's face. "But," the big owl continued, "they know that someone came across the bridge, and they are searching as we speak." Trill paused and blinked slowly at Corr, his amber eyes glinting in the low, filtered sunlight. "Vell is with them."

Luma didn't understand why Corr suddenly tensed

when Trill said that name, but she knew it wasn't a good sign. Corr grabbed his quiver and arrows. "Thank you, Trill. We will move out immediately." He looked at Luma. "Pack up, we need to go."

Luma, her feet still aching, was about to argue, but something about the look on Corr's face made her decide against it. She was repacking her bag when a sparrow fluttered onto the branch just above her head.

Luma looked up at the small bird and smiled. "Oh, hello, friend. What is your name, little one?"

From across the way, there was a loud snort followed by a round of poorly stifled giggles. Luma turned to see Corr clutching his sides as his body shook with laughter while Trill pinned her with the look of snobbish disapproval that owls have so wonderfully perfected.

Luma threw up her hands in exasperation. "What? I was just trying to be friendly!"

Corr took control of his laughter long enough to choke out a few words to Trill. "She thought sparrows could talk! *Sparrows!*"

Confused, Luma looked at Trill.

He shook his large, feathered head and peered down his beak at her severely. "Only *owls* talk, my dear. Oh goodness. No memory, Corr said. I didn't realize it was this bad." With a flap of his large wings, Trill rose into the air and settled on a low tree branch. "Well, Corr, if you can get her there, the mage certainly has his work cut out! I'll leave you to it. Do move quickly. I will be in touch when I can."

With that, Trill pushed off the branch and soared upward, but not before Luma heard him mutter to himself, "The fate of our world is in her hands, and she's trying to talk to sparrows…"

****

They walked for several minutes without speaking. Largely because Luma was still fuming about her recent embarrassment, and Corr was still taken by random fits of laughter and head shaking. Luma wondered briefly if punching him in his stupid, laughing face would be worth the momentary satisfaction if he ended up abandoning her in this unknown forest.

Finally, they emerged from the trees onto a fairly well-traveled dirt road. Corr stopped and stared down the road to the right, as if trying to make up his mind.

Luma stopped too, and glanced at him moodily. "What's the matter? You lost?"

Corr turned and arched a single dark eyebrow at her. "No. But you certainly would be if I wasn't here."

Luma glared at him, unwilling to admit that he was right.

Corr checked the position of the sun, then sighed and nodded, his decision made. "I'd rather not travel in the dark. We can stop over in Aquaea for food and supplies and leave again at first light."

"What's Aquaea?" Luma regretted the question almost immediately after it passed her lips for fear that Corr would start laughing at her again.

But to her surprise, Corr didn't laugh; he just looked back at her with a bemused expression on his face. "You really don't remember anything, do you?"

Luma returned his gaze, somewhat confused by his response but still on her guard. "Obviously not. I already told you! What, you thought I was faking this whole time? I'm not even sure I believe any of this elf, wizard, *war stuff*." The last two words came out more harshly than Luma intended, especially since Corr's expression changed to one of such grief.

There was deep pain behind his mossy green eyes, but the tone of his voice now took on a hard edge. "The war was real. I promise you that. Whether you choose to believe it or not."

Luma felt her cheeks flush. Corr adjusted the bow across his shoulders and took a few steps down the road before turning back to her, his tone slightly softer this time. "Aquaea is, well, was, the elf capital before the war. Come on." He started walking. For several minutes, Luma stood and watched him, trying to reconcile the flood of emotions swirling through her.

Can this really be happening?

Corr was getting farther ahead. In a few minutes, he would be out of sight around a bend in the road. Sighing, Luma shouldered her pack and trudged after him. He obviously wasn't going to wait for her.

The low sun still felt hot on the top of Luma's head, and the trees on either side of the road were stunted and shrubby and didn't offer much shade. Luma squinted ahead and saw a grove of taller trees farther on where the road curved. Maybe there she could find some relief from the heat.

Then, suddenly, the sun was gone. A deep shadow fell across Luma's body and stretched outward, darkening the dusty path in front of her. Luma stopped and looked upward just as a deafening screech rent the air, followed by a flash of yellow talons. The air hissed painfully from her lungs as Luma hit the ground.

Landing hard on her back, Luma instinctively raised her forearms to shield her face, then a scream of agony ripped from her throat as thick, curved talons raked across her skin.

Blood from her torn forearms dripped onto her face, and Luma peeked around her arms to see the head of a huge bird, something between an eagle and a vulture, staring down at her. Its savage black eyes blinked once, and then it lunged, its hooked beak aiming for her head. Luma curled her body and rolled to one side, flinching as the beak thudded to the earth exactly where her head had been a second before.

Panic coursing through her body, Luma tried to scramble away, but the creature quickly adjusted, slamming a foot down onto Luma's torso. Luma wrenched her arms free as the talons sank into the earth, pinning her against the ground. Twisting her head as far as she could, Luma saw a large stick lying in the dirt nearby. She grabbed for it, and just as the bird's beak descended again, Luma swung the stick in an upward arc with all her might. With a satisfying crack, the stick struck the side of the creature's face. The impact knocked the attack off course but also sent painful shockwaves down Luma's injured arms. She screamed and dropped the makeshift weapon.

Tears poured from Luma's eyes, and she struggled weakly, gasping for breath as the weight of the monstrous bird's foot pressed down on her rib cage. Light burst along the edges of Luma's vision as her lungs begged for oxygen, but just as she began to slip into unconsciousness, there was a screech, and the crushing weight lifted off her chest.

Luma rolled out from under the foot, gulping huge breaths of air. Her forearms were trembling, bloody, and covered in dirt. Another screech from the bird rang in her ears, and through watering eyes, Luma saw the creature shift its massive body, turning to face a new foe.

Corr was running back up the road, nocking another arrow in his bow as he went.

The arrow lodged in the huge creature's torso, just above where two other shafts already protruded. The bird lunged at Corr, who dodged to one side and loosed another arrow. The barbed shaft skimmed the top of one of the bird's massive wings, and a splash of blood ran down the inky feathers to splatter on the ground. Screeching in pain and anger at being denied its intended prey, the bird crouched and, in a rush of wind, took to the air, spiraling upward with thunderous beating wings.

From the ground, Luma's wide eyes followed the creature's ascent. She felt a hand on her shoulder and looked up to see Corr bending toward her. His mouth was moving, but it took Luma's shocked mind a few seconds to comprehend what he was saying.

"Get up, Luma! You've got to get out of here. *Get up*!"

Luma struggled to her feet and with Corr half supporting her, made her way as fast as she could down the road.

"Get to the tree line!" Corr was shouting in her ear. He pointed ahead to the grove of tall trees Luma had seen earlier. "Run before it..." The shadow fell across them once more. In one fluid movement, Corr swung Luma behind him. He reached for another arrow as the giant bird plunged at them from above, but before he could aim, the bird's talons crashed into him.

Corr fell with a loud grunt but still managed to loose the arrow. It narrowly missed the bird's neck as the creature lurched to one side and took to the air again, preparing for another dive.

Blood pouring from several deep lacerations across his chest, Corr scrambled to his feet, and Luma noticed with a rush of horror that his quiver was empty.

Above them, the monstrous bird had finished its wheeling ascent. With another ear-splitting screech, it dove. Corr unsheathed his dagger and turned to Luma, pointing urgently toward the grove of trees in the distance.

"Luma, *run!*"

But Luma remained rooted to the spot. She stared wide-eyed at Corr while her panicked heart galloped in her chest.

When the creature had first attacked her, Corr had already been a safe distance away. He could have hidden in the trees. But he hadn't. He had come running back. And now, there he was, standing protectively in front of her, wounded and bloody, with nothing but his dagger against a monster.

He wouldn't survive this. *Why was he doing this?*

Luma raised her eyes skyward at the descending creature, its vicious curved beak and razor-sharp talons aimed downward. Its fierce black eyes were locked on her. She was clearly the intended target of this attack, and yet Corr was willing to trade his life to give her the chance to flee.

Emotion, unlike anything Luma had ever known, surged through her: wild panic, yes, but also something else. It was as if a fire had ignited in her blood—fire and a turbulent, chaotic fury.

Faster than thought, Luma jumped in front of Corr and raised both her hands upward at the descending creature. She locked her elbows as a wild, guttural scream ripped from her throat. Not the scream of fear or pain but of defiance.

Heat rose to a simmer beneath her skin, followed by a powerful pulse of energy that rolled through Luma's body. The scars on her palms tingled and ached just before a blinding white light burst from her upraised hands. The light streamed upward and crashed into the huge bird head-on, sending it careening backward.

Hands still raised, Luma watched its trajectory as the creature arced through the sky and then began a flailing descent in the distance. Only then did Luma lower her hands. Sweat ran down the sides of her neck, and her chest heaved as nausea churned in her stomach. She doubled over and vomited onto the dirt of the road.

After a moment of heaving, Luma took a shaky breath and looked up to find Corr standing at her side. His eyes were like saucers, and his mouth hung open as he stared at her. In a daze, Luma wiped her mouth and straightened her back. The blood from the wounds on her forearms ran in small rivulets across the still-throbbing scars on her palms.

She tried to say something to Corr but couldn't find the words. Her vision blurred in and out, and she swayed wildly on her feet. Strong, steadying arms encircled her waist, and Corr's face swam in front of her vision.

"I told you to run, Luma. Why didn't you run?"

Luma blinked up at him and tried to focus. She opened her mouth, and this time, her words crawled out in a hoarse whisper, answering his question with a question of her own. "Why didn't you?"

Then she collapsed.

****

"We found the raptera. It's...it's dead."

Naro was a strong wizard, high-ranking among his

peers, and powerful in his own right. Still, he found himself taking an involuntary step backward when the one he was addressing turned around. Despite an unorthodox rise, Vell was now the most powerful wizard their world had seen in a thousand years.

Vell fixed Naro with an icy stare and arched a single, silvery-white eyebrow. "Dead? Impossible. No elf can kill a raptera with their sorry excuse for weapons."

Naro nodded. "We did find some elf arrows in the body, but that's not what killed it. It was killed by…something else…" his voice trailed off, withering under Vell's intense gaze. Her fingers drummed impatiently against the staff in her left hand, her nails making soft clicking noises against the beautiful black wood.

She sighed, her long white hair glinting as she strode past Naro. "Okay then, show me."

A short time later, Vell was circling the huge body of the creature that had attacked Luma and Corr. The fierce eyes were closed, and the deadly beak hung slack. After a short inspection, Vell stopped walking and stood silently, her head cocked to one side and her deep blue eyes narrowed. Several other wizards milled nearby. She ignored them and continued staring at the carcass of the beast.

When she finally spoke, Vell's voice was soft and calm, like dark ocean waters hiding the circling sharks beneath. "This raptera was killed with starlight magic. *She* has returned, and I want her alive. Find her and bring her to me at the White Keep."

Chapter 4

Luma's eyes fluttered open, and she stared upward, mesmerized by the shifting patterns on the stone ceiling above her. Then, her gaze flitted to the right and left, taking in more of her new surroundings.

She was lying on her back amongst a pile of blankets in a small room. Or was it a cave? The walls and ceiling were made of stone. Not chiseled, nor roughly cut by a craftsman's hands, but smooth as if worn away by the persistent running of water. In fact, a small stream of water gurgled along one edge of the room through a shallow canal carved into the stone floor. Short, thick candles were placed at intervals along the canal, and it was their comforting light that flickered upon the ceiling.

Luma pushed herself up and flinched. Both her forearms were heavily bandaged, and the sudden movement brought with it shooting pain. Luma's attention refocused on the dark scars that crisscrossed her palms, remembering the intense white light that had burst from them back on the road. Her mind reeled. *What is happening to me?*

The side of her shirt felt stiff, and Luma looked down and realized it was covered in dried blood. With a grimace, she brought her hand to her torso, fingers gently probing, but felt no wound beneath the heavy stain.

"That's not your blood. It's his."

The voice belonged to a young woman who had

appeared noiselessly at the entrance to the room. Her straight, dark hair skimmed the top of her shoulders, and she wore the front pulled into a high ponytail that bounced up and down as she walked over. Both edges of her pointed ears were thickly adorned with small rings and studs.

With a friendly smile, the woman placed a tray of food on the floor next to where Luma was sitting. Then she picked up a small pitcher, walked over to the stream, and dipped it in. Luma's gaze followed her movements.

"Whose blood is it?" Luma asked cautiously.

The woman walked back with the pitcher and set it down next to the tray of food. "Corr's, of course. That raptera really tore him up, but he still managed to carry you here. Well, most of the way here. Elas and I got you both the rest of the way."

She looked at Luma's blank expression and giggled. "Hi. I'm Aire. Elas is my brother. He's with Corr now. You'll meet him later."

Luma smiled. "Hi. I'm Luma."

Aire tilted her head, her high ponytail bobbing. "I know who you are. You're the one who has the power to heal the Sacred Stones and…" She rolled her eyes upward and made a dramatic sweeping motion with her arms. "Save us all." Then she looked back at Luma and winked, a mischievous glint in her large, dark eyes. "No pressure, though."

Luma laughed nervously. "Well, um, I'm not so sure about all that, but…yeah. No pressure." Despite the terror of what she had been through and all the questions that swirled in her mind, Luma found something strangely comforting about Aire's light-hearted approach.

Aire sat down and handed Luma the small pitcher, which Luma took with a smile of thanks. The water from the stream was cold and sweet, and Luma gulped it down, just then realizing how parched her throat was.

It was only after she had quenched her thirst that the flood of questions came tumbling out. Aire, in her flippant manner, laughed and flung herself dramatically onto the blankets, pretending to be bowled over by Luma's nonstop questions. Luma took the hint and quieted down, but she still wanted answers and looked at Aire expectantly.

Noting Luma's expression, Aire sighed and sat up. She tucked her legs beneath her and arranged the blankets into a comfortable seat.

"Okay, okay." Aire ticked off her fingers as if mentally trying to keep track of it all. "So, the first one. Yes, we are in Aquaea, the capital city of Edira. Of course, during the battle, it was pretty badly burned. Many of the elves who survived the battle fled, but some of us stayed. Now, we mostly live in these underground dwellings below the main buildings. It's not the most luxurious," she glanced around the small room and shrugged, "but better not to draw too much attention to ourselves nowadays."

Luma broke off a piece from the small bread loaf that Aire had brought in on the tray. She munched on it and took a few more gulps of water, waiting for Aire to continue. Aire tapped another finger. "Others? Well, yes and no. So many died during the wizard invasion and subsequent fighting twelve years ago. Elas and my parents among them. There are surviving elves scattered around Edira, I believe, deep in hiding if they know what's good for them. Honestly, I'm not even sure how many of us are left."

Luma studied Aire's face. She could tell that this woman was a master of hiding her true, deepest emotions, but so was Luma, and she recognized it immediately when the flicker of deep sorrow broke through the façade and ran across Aire's pretty features. But there was something else too: anger? Then Aire blinked once, and it was gone behind the mask.

Aire shrugged and ticked another finger, marking the next of Luma's questions. "That thing that attacked you was a raptera. Awful creatures. They're basically impossible to kill and totally ruthless once they have a target. The wizards brought them from their world to assist in hunting down rebellious elves. You're lucky, though; sometimes, the wizards coat a raptera's talons in poison before releasing them. If that had been the case, you never would have made it. You or Corr."

Aire paused and fixed Luma with a curious stare. "But poison or not, normal elves don't survive raptera attacks. They just don't."

Luma felt a weight in the pit of her stomach as the memory of Corr telling her to run while preparing to face the raptera alone rose in her mind.

"Well, I think it's safe to say that she is no normal elf."

Luma and Aire turned at the sound of the new voice. The speaker stepped into the room and nodded politely. "Hi there, Luma. I'm Elas."

Elas and Aire were twins, and they were remarkably similar in look, though in manner, where Aire tended to favor the dramatic, Elas was more subdued. Luma found that she liked them both instantly, something she was not accustomed to with others.

The three of them ate the food together, and then Aire took Luma into another small, subterranean room and gave her some new, blood-stain-free clothes, remarking that the pants might be a little long because, "well, you're kinda short." Luma scoffed and shook her head. That was a first—she had never been called short in her whole life.

Luma followed Aire back into the other room to find Corr sitting there. He had also changed clothes, and his shirt hung open, revealing a thick bandage that crisscrossed his bare chest. He stood up when Luma entered the room, hurriedly buttoning the shirt. Concern creased his forehead, and he took a step toward Luma, looking as if he wanted to reach out to her, but quickly changed his mind.

"Luma." His voice was soft and slightly hoarse, and he paused to clear his throat. "Are you okay?" His green gaze searched her face with a genuine worry that brought a lump to Luma's throat. She swallowed hard.

"I'm okay. Are you okay?" Her gaze flitted across his broad chest, where the bandage was now hidden under his shirt.

Corr nodded quickly. "I'm okay." He offered her a small smile and a dimple appeared on his left cheek that Luma hadn't noticed before.

Luma nodded and looked down, shifting her weight awkwardly. Then she raised her eyes back to Corr. He was still staring at her with that concerned expression, and her stomach did a little flip-flop. Her pulse quickened, and she looked away.

"You...carried me here? After..." Luma's voice trailed off, and she swallowed again.

"Yes." Corr's answer was gentle and barely above a

whisper. His gaze collided with hers and remained.

Luma nodded and crossed her arms over her chest, then dropped them to her sides, suddenly unsure of what to do with her hands. *Why is he looking at me like that?*

"Thank you."

"Of course."

Corr finally dropped his gaze, and an uncomfortable silence hung between them, during which Corr picked at an invisible thread on the cuff of his shirt sleeve, and Luma shuffled in her too-long pants.

From behind Luma, Aire looked at Elas and rolled her eyes. Then she cleared her throat loudly and suggested that they go to ground level and make a fire. Corr, obviously grateful for the distraction, quickly agreed and led the way out of the cave room, followed by Luma.

Aire turned back to Elas and arched an eyebrow as they went up. "Yikes, that was awkward."

Elas cringed and shook his head. "So awkward!"

****

A short tunnel led upward and into a sparsely furnished room at the back of a larger building that looked like it had once been a grand manor house. The roof was now partially missing, and the fire-blackened oak beams stood out like the ribs of some long-dead behemoth.

At one end of the room, beneath what remained of the roof, was a wide fireplace. A few rickety chairs and a small pile of blankets had been placed in front of it, and yesterday's embers still glowed faintly red under a layer of white ash. Luma walked closer and looked at the thick stone mantelpiece that arched over the fireplace. Tilting her head and squinting in the dim light, she ran her fingertips along the intricate carvings made in the stone: figures, animals, stars.

"Look familiar?" Corr's voice brought Luma out of her reverie, and she turned to find him, Aire, and Elas watching her.

Luma felt heat rising in her cheeks, and she hoped fervently that the others wouldn't notice her flush in the low light. She dropped her hands and shifted uncomfortably under the expectant weight of their combined gaze. "No."

And there it was again. Luma could feel it. The palpable disappointment. It had emanated from everyone she had met here so far when they discovered that she, their supposed *last hope*, didn't know anything about anything.

The heat in Luma's cheeks increased. She had tried to tell them that this was a mistake, that she wasn't anyone special. Luma's palms felt sweaty, and she tried to discreetly wipe them on the sides of her borrowed shirt. It didn't help.

Elas stepped toward the fireplace. He picked up a small bag for kindling and inspected its meager contents. "Well, this won't do to start any fire," he said, breaking the awkward silence. "We need more kindling before it gets too dark to see anything."

Her cheeks still burning, Luma reached over and took the bag from Elas's hands. "I'll do it."

Corr pointed to a large, curved doorway at the opposite side of the room. "Out there is the courtyard, and just beyond that, the edge of the woods. There should be plenty of kindling sticks around there. I'll go with you."

Luma shook her head and tried her best to sound

casual. "No need for that. I can do it alone."

Corr started to protest, but Aire interrupted. "Of course, Luma, that would be great. We'll get the larger pieces and meet you back here in a few." She shot a warning glance at Corr in case he planned to say anything else. Luma nodded and headed across the room, determined not to show the insecurity she still felt clinging to her body.

Corr watched Luma with worried eyes as she passed through the doorway arch and disappeared into the semi-darkness.

"She shouldn't be out there alone." He glared for a minute at the empty doorway, then he threw up his hands, turning back to Aire and Elas. "I don't get it. She has the power. I've seen it, and it's…incredible, but it's like she has no control over it. I was with her in the Cavern of the Four. She got dizzy when she got too close to the Sacred Stones, and then after the raptera…" Corr's voice trailed off, and he shook his head in frustration. "It's like…it's like the starlight power itself is making her sick." He ran a hand through his hair and glanced again at the darkened doorway.

Aire sighed. "Give her a break, Corr. Can't you see how hard this has been for her? The bridge from Edira to Earth is a long and dangerous one, and it obviously took its toll. She was just a little kid back then for Stars' sake! You can't expect her to be called unexpectedly back to Edira after twelve years and immediately know exactly who she is and what she must do."

Elas walked over to the back edge of the room where cut logs had been neatly stacked under the remaining roof to keep them out of the weather. He gathered a few up in his arms and set them down in front of the fireplace, talking as he worked. "During the alignment eighteen years ago, pure starlight from the Four Stars poured directly into her at the moment of her birth." Elas shrugged and brushed woodchips off his hands. "That amount of starlight magic in one person is extremely unstable. Even with years of intense training, it's a lot for a body to take. No wonder it is making her sick."

"He's right," Aire chimed in. "And as the next alignment gets closer, it will be harder and harder for Luma to safely control it. And it's going to take a huge amount of control to channel that much power long enough to heal the Sacred Stones."

Corr nodded, his face grim. "The next alignment is expected to take place in just a few weeks. Izarre was right. There is only one elf who can teach her to control and channel the starlight within her."

Aire arched an eyebrow skeptically. "Corr, the mage hasn't been seen since before the Sacred Stones were cracked. And besides, he may not be willing to train another after…" her voice trailed off.

Corr shrugged. "What choice do we have? Vell and the wizards are too powerful, and Luma's starlight is the only thing strong enough to stop them. I've got to get Luma to the Inland Sea and find the mage before the alignment."

Aire and Elas looked at each other, and then Aire spoke what was on both their minds. "It will take several days for you and Luma to recover from your wounds. But when you are ready, we go together."

****

Luma returned with a bag full of kindling sticks just as true darkness settled over the ruined city. Soon, Elas had a fire crackling in the large fireplace, and the topic of whether Luma remembered anything was pointedly avoided. The weather was fair, with a soft, cool breeze blowing gently, so the small group decided to stay above ground to sleep.

Luma lay on her back, snuggled under a blanket farthest from the fireplace, and gazed past the burned-out roof beams and into the darkness above.

A multitude of stars twinkled throughout the night sky, but she quickly noticed that four of them were far brighter than the rest. Forming a slightly jagged line in the center of the sky, these stars shone so brightly that they appeared to dim the others nearby, creating a halo of velvety darkness around them.

A shiver ran down Luma's spine as she stared up at those four nearly aligned stars, and at her sides, the scars on her palms began to tingle. The world she had left, the life she had known, seemed so fresh in her mind and yet, at the same time, so distant now. Would she ever make it back there? And, in truth, did she even want to?

Luma curled her fingers into loose fists beneath her blanket and a warmth spread from the scars on her palms through her hands and up her bandaged forearms. And when she finally closed her eyes to sleep, the images of the four bright stars shone on behind her eyelids.

Chapter 5

Corr and Luma remained in Aquaea as they recovered from their encounter with the raptera. After several days, Elas removed each of their bandages and was pleased to see their wounds had healed over nicely.

****

The once-thriving elven capital city was built along the banks of the wide and fast-flowing River Aque. In a testament to elvish engineering, many city buildings were seamlessly constructed on top of, and incorporating a wide-ranging network of natural water-worn caves that honeycombed the riverbank. It was in one of these water-level caves that Corr and Aire stood one morning as a brilliant sunrise painted the sky outside with a multi-hued brush.

Aire balanced deftly on a small ledge above the fast-moving river. She tugged on the net she had set out a few days before and gave a small whoop when she saw several large fish inside. With Corr's help, she pulled the net free of the water and eagerly collected her slippery prey.

****

While Aire and Corr were checking the nets, Elas and Luma were above ground, outside of the manor house courtyard at the edge of the forest. Luma had the kindling bag over her arm and was once again on the hunt for small sticks while Elas moved deeper into the forest, collecting edible plants and berries. He was almost done, and turned as Luma approached through the trees, toting a full bag of kindling, a smile on her face.

Elas's grin in response quickly faded as he saw Luma veer slightly left, off the path he had carefully followed through the trees. His cry of warning came too late. Luma's hands and forearms brushed through a clump of tall, broad-leafed plants growing in the shade of a large evergreen tree.

Luma's response was immediate, and her gasp of surprise was soon followed by screams of pain. Luma dropped the kindling bag and stared down through watering eyes as huge, red blisters erupted across her arms. Her skin felt like it was on fire, and her breath came in ragged sobs as agony scorched through her body.

Elas rushed to Luma's side and pulled her away from the clump of plants, taking great care to avoid being touched by them himself. He sat her down at the base of another nearby tree, whose low-hanging branches were adorned with brilliant white leaves.

Moving with calm efficiency despite Luma's agonized sobs, Elas circled the trunk of the tree until he found a small flat mushroom growing out of the bark. Delicately, he tugged the mushroom free from the trunk and ripped it in half, allowing a sticky substance to begin flowing. Returning to Luma, Elas gently slid one-half of the mushroom along the blistered skin of her left arm, then repeated with the other half along her right arm.

Luma gasped as the effects of the mushroom sap immediately quelled the burning pain on her skin. She slumped against the tree trunk. "Thank you."

Elas breathed a sigh of relief and gave Luma a wry

smile. "And that's why we never touch the leaves of the Fireburn plant."

Luma sat up and gingerly moved her arms. Under the thin layer of mushroom sap, the angry red welts had already begun to shrink. "Fireburn plant?"

Elas nodded. "Yes. It's called that because when the leaves come into contact with bare skin, it burns," he arched an eyebrow at her, "like fire."

Luma snorted and rolled her eyes. "Wow, clever name. Very clever."

Elas laughed and shrugged. He pointed toward the plants, their leaves rustling innocently in the early morning breeze. "They grow mostly in the shade of the big evergreens, but not always, so it's best to learn to identify them quickly. Tall, thick stalk, broad leaves that indent in and out along the edges like a flame. If the burns from the plants are left untreated, they will spread quickly throughout the body and ultimately lead to a very uncomfortable death."

Elas paused and held up the two halves of the mushroom for Luma to see. "But in all things: balance. These mushrooms are the antidote. They grow on the bark of the Everwhite tree." He pointed up at the tree they were sitting under with its beautiful snow-white leaves.

Luma gazed up at the tree, then looked back at Elas and nodded. "Got it. Thank you."

Elas smiled and offered her a hand up. "Sure thing. Now, let's head back. Corr and Aire should have gotten enough fish by now."

At the mention of food, Luma's stomach rumbled loudly. "Lead the way, Elas. And this time, I will follow your path exactly as you walk it!"

****

The combination of the freshly cooked fish with the plants and berries that Elas had gathered was delicious.

Luma took a final sip of cold water and sat back, fully contented. The blisters on her arms were already almost gone, and she took Aire's gentle teasing about her mistake in stride, smiling and laughing in a way she had never done with other people.

Corr put down the flat plank of wood he had been using for a plate and nodded decisively. "I think Luma and I are recovered enough, and the alignment waits for no one. We must continue our journey to the Inland Sea." Aire and Elas looked over at Luma, and she nodded her agreement.

Aire turned back to Corr. "Let's spend the rest of today gathering as many supplies as we can. We leave tomorrow at first light."

****

Later that afternoon, while Corr, Aire, and Elas were down in the caves sorting through supplies, Luma explored on her own outside. She had walked all around the large manor house and was now wandering through the woods that encroached on the north side of the building, opposite the courtyard where she had been before.

The trees were huge, and obviously very old, the girth of their trunks and the width of their spreading limbs a testament to their longevity. Luma circled one such behemoth, her left hand trailing along the knobby bark as she walked, staring upward in awe.

If he hadn't made a grunt of pain, Luma would have walked right into him. The man was leaning against the far side of the huge tree, bent double in agony, his breath rasping through gritted teeth. Luma shrieked and jumped backward, which only then caused the man to look up and see her.

His eyes were bloodshot and watering, and his face was nearly as pale as the silvery white hair on his head. Luma stared at him and then gasped when she saw what was causing this stranger so much pain. Large blisters, bright red and angry looking, covered the front and back of the man's hands, spreading up his wrists and encircling his forearms below his elbow-length tunic.

Luma immediately recognized the blisters, and her stomach dropped. "Oh! Oh no! Um, don't worry. I...I can help you."

Luma looked frantically around, trying to remember what Elas had told her about the antidote to the Fireburn plant. Then she saw it, a tree a few feet away with beautiful, snow-white leaves.

Scanning the ground to make sure no Fireburn plants grew nearby, Luma darted to the tree and circled the trunk. It took her two times around before she was able to spot the small mushroom growing out of the bark just above her head. Standing on tiptoe, Luma reached up and pried the mushroom loose from the trunk.

Dashing over to the man, who now had sunk to the ground, Luma held the mushroom in shaking hands, trying to remember what Elas had done to get the sap to flow. After squeezing it a few times with no success, Luma finally ripped the mushroom in two and gave a small cry of victory as sap started to ooze from the torn sides.

"Don't worry. Hold still." Luma knelt and began gently rubbing the mushroom halves along the man's arms and hands.

The man let out a long sigh as the antidote took effect, and his shoulders shook with relief. "Thank you." His voice grated hoarsely from his throat.

Luma breathed a sigh of relief but still looked at him with concern.

"Glad I could help. Those Fireburn plants pack a punch!" She gave a rueful laugh. "I thought I was the only one who didn't know to avoid them, but hey, I guess not! I'm glad I found you when I did!" She smiled at him. "I'm Luma."

The man looked up as Luma tossed the mushroom halves aside and brushed off her hands. His still bloodshot gaze came to rest on Luma's scarred palms, and a strange expression flickered over his face. Luma shifted awkwardly, and the man quickly averted his gaze. He stood up.

"I should go." He avoided her eyes.

Confused at his abruptness, Luma nodded slowly. "Oh, okay. You sure you're good?"

The man looked at Luma again with that strange expression on his face. "I'm…I'm good. Thank you again. Really. You…saved my life."

Luma's smile widened. "Of course! I'm so glad I was able to help you."

Still smiling, she watched as the stranger made his way through the trees, then she shrugged and walked off in the other direction, back the way she had come.

It was only after Luma was out of sight that the man stopped and retrieved what he had previously dropped into the undergrowth: a tall, polished wooden staff.

****

That evening, Corr, Luma, Aire, and Elas gathered near the fireplace with their supplies. The food that could be carried was packed up, and Corr had found enough arrows to refill his quiver.

Luma sat awkwardly to one side, having neither a weapon to contribute nor a skill to offer. At least, not one she could control. While Aire and Elas debated the benefits of a short sword to a bow and arrows, Corr shifted closer to Luma and held out the dagger he had brought with him when they left Izarre's cottage.

Luma shook her head, but Corr was insistent. "Just take it and put it on your belt tomorrow when we leave. You never know—might come in handy." He smiled at her, and the dimple on his cheek showed up again.

Luma looked at the weapon skeptically but finally accepted the dagger with an embarrassed nod of thanks and placed it down next to her small bag of supplies.

The sun hovered just above the western horizon when everything was finally ready, and then the debate about where to sleep began.

Aire said that since the weather remained clear, they should do as they had done before and sleep on ground level by the fireplace.

Corr argued that it wasn't safe, and that they should sleep down in the caves. "The wizards could be nearby— we know they are searching for Luma. It's too exposed up here." Corr gestured around the room, with its burned-out ceiling and doorless entrance to the dark courtyard beyond.

"Lighten up, Corr." Aire rolled her eyes. "We've been around this area for days and haven't seen any sign of wizards."

"That doesn't mean they aren't close." Corr retorted.

Aire sighed and turned toward Elas. "You were out in the woods earlier. Any wizards?" She cocked her head, and her high ponytail bounced.

Elas shot Corr an apologetic glance before answering. "No."

Aire then turned to Luma. "What about you?"

Not wanting to cause upset, Luma didn't reply but merely shrugged. She didn't even know how to recognize one of these "wizards" if she saw one, but she didn't want to admit that out loud.

And so, in the end, Corr was overruled, and as darkness crept over the forest, the four of them settled down to sleep in front of the fire.

Aire and Elas were soon breathing deeply in the rhythmic cadence of slumber, but rest was not as forthcoming for Luma. She sat where the shy light from the fireplace gave way to darkness, her arms wrapped around her knees and her chin raised, staring up at the four bright stars. The line they made in the night sky looked less jagged than it had just the night before, but maybe she was imagining it.

A cool breeze gusted through the open roof, and Luma shivered. Groping around in the semi-darkness, her fingers found the edges of a small, thin blanket, which she started to pull up over her knees.

"Here, use this one."

Luma startled at the voice to her left. She hadn't realized that Corr was also still awake. He walked over carrying a thicker blanket, which he draped gently over her shoulders. An instant warmth spread through Luma's body, and she smiled at Corr as he sat down beside her.

"Thanks."

Corr shrugged. "No one was using it. And...you looked cold."

Luma nodded gratefully and then returned her gaze

upward to the jagged line of stars. "Are those…them?" She hated how her voice sounded so small and hollow.

Next to her, Corr's answer came softly out of the darkness. "Yes. Those are the Four Stars." He paused and took a breath before continuing. "And their power resides in you."

An uncomfortable weight settled in the pit of Luma's stomach, and she shook her head, still grappling with the whole situation, unwilling to fully accept that she had any sort of real power.

She looked down and spread her fingers wide, staring through the dim light at the tangle of dark scars that covered her palms. She hated the way everyone looked at her like she was something special when, deep down, she knew the terrible truth—that she would surely disappoint them all in the end. The back of her eyes burned, and she blinked, sniffing loudly.

Corr reached out a calloused hand and his fingers lightly traced the dark web of scars on her right palm in a way that made Luma's breath catch in her throat.

Corr's voice was still soft. "You don't have to be afraid of it."

Luma's cheeks flushed hot, and she jerked her hand away. "I'm not afraid."

Corr lowered his hand and shifted to face her more directly. The light from the fire glowed behind him, casting his face in shadow. Still, Luma could feel his gaze boring into her, and she stubbornly turned her head away.

"I didn't mean it like that," Corr sighed. "I just meant that…you don't have to fight it. Once we find the mage, he can teach you to channel your power, but you are already a lot stronger than you think you are, Luma."

Luma made a small derisive snort and kept her head turned away from Corr. Her cheeks still felt hot. "You don't know me." Her words came out harsher than she intended, and she swallowed hard, desperate to keep back the tears that burned in her eyes. Then she spoke again, cringing inwardly as her voice trembled. "I...I keep trying to tell you. I'm *not* special. I...I have no idea what I'm doing."

Luma felt a weight as Corr placed a hand on her shoulder. She tilted her head toward it just as a fat teardrop rolled down the side of her cheek and landed on the back of Corr's hand. Embarrassment flooded through her, and Luma tried to pull away, but Corr gave her shoulder a gentle squeeze. He inhaled like he was about to say something, then decided against it. He paused, then spoke again.

"Get some sleep, Luma. We leave at first light tomorrow."

Sniffing, Luma nodded wordlessly, not trusting her voice. Sighing softly, she lay down and was immediately asleep.

****

The hand over her mouth was heavy and rough.

Luma's eyes flew open in the darkness, and she immediately tried to twist away but was met with the unsettling sensation of not being able to move her limbs. Her gaze roamed madly, searching the shadows, but from where she lay, she couldn't see Corr, Aire, or Elas. Panic surging through her veins, Luma tried again to move her arms enough to reach for the dagger Corr had given her, but it was as though her limbs were made of lead weight. Feebly, she twisted her head, desperate to get out from under the heavy hand that covered her mouth. The scars on her palms began to ache, and her fingertips twitched.

Then, a face loomed into view. It was a man, several years older than she. His silvery white hair and neatly trimmed goatee stood out against the surrounding darkness. In one hand, he was holding Corr's dagger, which he waved mockingly back and forth in front of Luma's face.

"And what, exactly, did you plan to do with this, anyway?"

Chuckling nastily to himself, he picked up one of Luma's limp hands and inspected her palm, his light blue eyes wrinkling at the corners as he smiled in an unfriendly way that made Luma's skin crawl.

He glanced to his left and spoke to someone that Luma couldn't see. "It's her all right. Give her a dose, and let's go. I can sense the starlight trying to break free already, so make sure the spell holds, especially around her hands."

Luma gave a muffled cry from under the man's hand as she felt a sharp prick in the side of her neck. Then, everything went black.

Chapter 6

Named for its façade of creamy marble, the White Keep was once the seat of elven power, set high in the cliffs above the winding River Aque. It had fallen to the wizards quickly after the initial invasion, and now the multi-functional building served as their home base.

****

Luma's eyelids fluttered. Floor-to-ceiling windows flooded the large, rectangular room with light from the rising sun that glinted off the polished stone floor.

With a soft groan, Luma licked her parched lips and squinted down, grimacing from the glare of the sun in her eyes. Her head throbbed. She was slumped in a wide chair with her arms in front of her, palms resting on opposite wrists and bound together tightly with some sort of silvery rope. She tried to pull her hands loose, but the strange rope gave no quarter.

Just then, at the opposite end of the room, a door banged open, and the man Luma recognized from the night before strode toward her. He was dressed in dark pants and a tunic with fine silver stitching along the elbow-length sleeves. He carried a polished wooden staff in his left hand, and the dagger Corr had given her swung from his belt.

"Well, well. Look at you." He chuckled.

Luma scowled up at him, still straining against the bonds that held her wrists.

The man smiled his unfriendly smile and stopped directly in front of her, leaning down into her space. He looked her up and down appraisingly and arched a white eyebrow, his deep voice dripping with sarcasm. "Well. For the long-foretold *Daughter of Starlight*, you sure don't put up much of a fight."

The tone in his voice made Luma's blood boil. Gritting her teeth, she leaned back in her chair and kicked out in one fast, savage movement. Both her feet struck the man directly in the stomach with a force that pushed Luma's chair backward. The man's eyes bulged, and the air left his mouth with an audible *whoosh* as he crumpled forward onto the stone floor.

Hands still bound, Luma leaped from the chair and spun, searching for any means of escape. She immediately ruled out the windows, all of which overlooked a sheer cliff, dropping straight to the river below.

Luma turned her attention to the door on the other side of the room. She darted past the man, who was still struggling to catch his breath, his mouth gaping open and closed like a landed fish. Luma was almost to the door when it swung open once again. She skidded to a stop as the most strikingly beautiful woman she had ever seen entered.

The woman held her tall frame with an air of regality. Her large eyes were blue, not light and watery like the man's, but a richer shade like deep ocean water. Waves of thick, silvery white hair fell in cascades down her back, and she cocked her head to one side and looked at Luma with a bemused expression. Her blue gaze slid over to the man on the floor, then back to Luma, and her wide mouth curled into a sly smile. "Well. I see that the poison wore off rather more quickly than we anticipated."

Luma stared at the woman and took an involuntary step backward. "You poisoned me?"

The woman gave a short laugh and nodded. "Only a very little bit of poison. Nothing you couldn't handle, Luma." She glanced again toward the man, who was slowly getting to his feet, then she looked back at Luma with a playful wink. "Obviously."

Luma took another step back, her gaze darting around the room, her breath shallow. "Where am I? How do you know my name? Why am I tied up? What have you done with my friends?"

The woman's smiling expression changed to one of pity. "Your *friends*? Is that what you think they are? Oh, my dear." She clicked her tongue. "But not to worry. Now that you are here with me, I will answer all your questions, and I will share with you the *real* truth. But…" She raised her eyebrows and tilted her head. "There must be a semblance of trust between us."

Luma narrowed her eyes at the man who had just picked up his staff and come to stand nearby, glaring murderously at her from over the woman's shoulder. The woman sighed and waved her hand dismissively toward him. "Naro, leave us."

Naro continued to glare at Luma for a moment but then nodded deferentially toward the woman and exited the room, slamming the door behind him.

The woman turned back to Luma, her voice light and friendly. "Like I said. I will explain everything, and I will release the bonds on your hands, but you must promise to behave and listen to what I have to say. Yes?"

Not seeing that she had much of a choice, Luma

nodded, and the woman smiled warmly. "Good. Welcome to the White Keep, Luma. My name is Vell, and I've been expecting you."

****

The three cells beneath the White Keep had been chiseled directly into the cliff face, each with a heavy metal gate across the opening. In the cell at the far end, a bright shaft of sunlight filtered through a small, high window slit cut into the stone for ventilation.

Aire sat with her back against the rock wall of the cell, her dark gaze following Corr as he paced in and out of the light shaft in front of her. Finally, she blinked and shook her head. "Can you stop that, Corr? You're giving me a headache."

Corr stopped walking and spun to face her. "I can't believe they were able to sneak up on us like that. And now they have her!" He clenched his fists, his shoulders shaking with anger born of guilt. "We should have been more careful." He glared at Aire and started pacing again.

Aire sighed and hung her head. "I know, Corr. I'm sorry."

Elas, who had been standing off to one side of the same cell, walked over and put his hand on Corr's shoulder, squinting as the shaft of light fell across his eyes. "I'm sorry too, Corr, but pacing and regret won't help us. We need a plan."

Corr was about to respond when suddenly, the shaft of light from above them was gone. Corr and Elas looked up and caught a glimpse of amber eyes peeking down at them. Corr called upward. "Hello? Trill? Is that you?"

The large eyes blinked slowly as Trill's voice answered. "It is indeed."

****

Upstairs, a small table had been brought in, and Luma was once again seated in the wide chair. Her hands were still bound with the silvery rope, and she watched with narrowed eyes as Vell conversed in low tones with a small group of others near the door.

Finally, the others left, and Vell turned back to Luma with a disarming smile. "We will have some food shortly. I'm sure you are hungry. Now, let's get you out of those bonds."

Vell did a slow flick of her left wrist, and a beautiful wooden staff materialized out of thin air. Luma's eyes went wide, and Vell smirked as her slender fingers curled around the smooth, polished black wood. "Only the best wizards are able to call their staffs to hand. And, of course, I am the best."

Luma held Vell's gaze, determined not to let her face betray her inner emotions. "And…I'm still tied up."

Vell laughed. It was a soft, tinkling sound that caught Luma off guard with its gentleness. "So you are." Vell's voice still had a trace of laughter in it when she spoke again. "I promised I would free your bonds, and so I shall. Hold still."

She lifted her staff and angled it slightly toward the silvery rope encircling Luma's wrists. Just then, the door at the other end of the room banged open once again, and in walked another man carrying a tray of food.

Vell sighed and lowered her staff. "What timing! Over here, Ruvyn."

The man walked over with the tray, and Luma had to bite her tongue to keep from gasping aloud, for she recognized him immediately. It was the same man she had helped in the woods after his encounter with the

Fireburn plants.

Luma's heart dropped as realization crashed into her. All the wizards she had now seen had one thing in common: they all had distinct, silvery white hair. Surprise gave way to roiling anger that churned in Luma's stomach. The man she had helped was a wizard, and he must have told the others where to find her.

The man kept his head lowered, but his eyes flicked up and met Luma's as she glared back at him with a combination of rage and indignation. The man quickly lowered his eyes and turned away. He nodded respectfully to Vell as he hurried past and shut the door behind him.

Luma felt blood rushing to her cheeks, but she swallowed hard and took a deep breath, not wanting to let on. She cocked her head at Vell and raised her still-bound arms. "Now. Where were we?"

Vell raised her eyebrows at Luma with a smug smile. "You've got a little fire in you. I like that."

The bonds that encircled Luma's wrists disappeared with a twitch of Vell's staff, and at the same time, the scars on Luma's palms began tingling. Luma curled her fingers into gentle fists under the table.

Vell pulled up a chair across from her and smiled. "Better?"

Luma nodded and plucked an apple from the tray of food, taking a small bite. "Yeah. Thanks."

Vell fixed Luma with an intense stare, her dark blue gaze roving Luma's face, taking in every feature and causing Luma to shift uncomfortably.

When Vell spoke again, it was slowly, as if she were weighing each of her words carefully. "Luma, I know that the elves you have met, your so-called 'friends' have told you a tale about our two worlds, but I promise, that is not the whole story."

Luma swallowed her bite of apple and shrugged in what she hoped was a casual, confident manner. "Look, I don't know how I got here, and everyone keeps telling me I'm all sorts of *special*, but I don't really get any of it."

Vell looked slightly surprised, then nodded. "Of course, I understand, Luma. I'm sure this is all very confusing after your long absence. What you need is someone strong to guide you, which is why I am here to offer you a partnership."

Luma was about to take another bite of apple but paused, her mouth open, hovering over the fruit in her hand.

Vell gave a short laugh and nodded. "Does that come as a surprise? It shouldn't. Whether you believe it or not, my dear, the starlight inside of you, the power it has, is no small thing. The elves say you are special, and in that, they are right. But know this: they will never allow you to wield that power to your full potential. Only I can help you do that." Vell leaned forward and stared hard at Luma, her large, beautiful eyes blazing with an intensity that caused a shiver to run up Luma's spine.

Vell leaned closer, and when she spoke again, her voice was barely above a whisper. "Together, we would be unstoppable."

Luma remained silent, though her mind churned with questions. Vell studied her for a moment, then reached across the table. Luma recoiled, but not fast enough. With a flick of her wrist, Vell brushed the thick dark hair away from Luma's face and tucked it behind her softly pointed ear.

Vell smiled. "Ah. There they are. Not as distinct as most elves, naturally, because of your human mother. I never really liked humans, I must admit. For so young a species, they are extremely arrogant and stubborn. I suppose you were compelled to hide your ears during your time in the human world. How unfortunate."

Luma's face flushed, and Vell leaned back once again, still looking at her. "They are nothing to be ashamed of, my dear. All elves have ears shaped like that. See?"

Vell reached up and pulled her long, silvery hair back with both hands, revealing ears that tapered to a tall, slender point, each decorated with small, shiny blue studs that ran down the outer sides.

Despite herself, Luma gasped. "Wait…you're an…elf? I thought you said you were a-a wizard?"

Vell chuckled. "Luma, my dear child. I am both. And you could be, too."

Luma drew her eyebrows together skeptically, still unable to make sense of what Vell was saying. She started to open her mouth to ask another question, but Vell held up a hand for silence.

"Just a moment, dearie. I said I'd explain everything, and I will. But I fear I've gotten ahead of myself. Allow me to go back to the beginning."

Luma closed her mouth and settled back in her chair, waiting.

Vell took a sip from a mug of tea and swallowed thoughtfully before she began. "I'm sure you've already been told that elves are not a naturally magical race. And that is true, but not entirely. Every now and then, an elf is born with certain qualities that, if fostered correctly, can become the ability to channel magic. And I was one of those." There was pride in her voice. Vell paused and took another sip of her tea. Luma watched, her mind spinning, but she held her tongue.

Vell put down the tea and continued. "From a very young age, my budding magical ability was apparent to everyone. But instead of encouraging me to grow in my power, King Tarak, his human queen, and the Elders Council focused on trying to make me control it. *Limit* it. As a teenager, I was sent to study with Eldamarr Rinn, the elf mage, but he, too, sought only to stifle my magical potential. And then a few years later, you, my dear, were born during the Alignment of the Four." Vell cocked her head at Luma. "You see, Luma, both of us have access to incredible power. But while yours was merely an accident of birth, mine is innate—it is in my blood. But suddenly, that didn't matter anymore."

Luma started to feel uncomfortable under the weight of Vell's gaze. The tiniest hint of malice flickered behind Vell's beautiful royal blue eyes as she spoke.

"The elves, my own kind, chronically underestimated me. They turned their back on me and my abilities. They were willfully blind to how truly special I was. So, I found others who saw me as I was meant to be. The wizards of Malicath recognized my powers and offered to help me. You see, Luma, elves may not be naturally magical, but the elf world itself is."

Luma furrowed her brow, not understanding.

Vell smiled, but her eyes blazed. "Yes, Luma, this world, Edira, is the most inherently magical world in the cosmos. But the elves that are native to it refuse to take advantage of its vast magical resources, preferring to live simply and without. Stubborn fools." Vell shook her head in frustration. "The wizards could take the raw, magical power of this world and use it for greatness, but the elves never allowed it, and those four Sacred Stones aided them in their refusal. Until I came along." Vell smirked and raised her chin, her fingers drumming lightly on the polished wood of her staff.

Luma narrowed her eyes, trying to remember what Izarre had told her in the cavern. "So, you, um, cracked the four Sacred Stones and let the wizards pass through into this world?" she asked.

Vell nodded. "Yes. I did. And doing so took nearly all my strength. In fact, it almost killed me. But look at me now. Once I fully embraced their ways, the wizards of Malicath showed me how to enhance my innate magical powers in ways that the elves never would have allowed." She smiled haughtily.

Luma shook her head. "A lot of elves died because of what you did. And...And..." Luma paused, trying to collect her swirling thoughts. The scars on her palms ached. "They told me you were trying to kill me!"

Vell's smile faded, and her face took on a look of injured pride. "No, no, my dear. You've got it all wrong. I was trying to save you."

Chapter 7

Trill had just left the tiny window slit above the cells when a man's face appeared at the bars, his silvery white hair standing in stark contrast to the surrounding gloom.

Aire looked up from where she was sitting on the cold stone floor, her eyes narrowing to a glare. "What do you want?"

The man glanced quickly back over his shoulder and then leaned forward, his voice low but urgent. "My name is Ruvyn, and I want to help you get out of here. But we must hurry."

Elas walked over and stood in front of the wizard, who had to raise his chin considerably to look into Elas's face. "Why should we believe you, wizard?" Elas challenged. "None of *your kind*," he spat the words out as if they left a bad taste in his mouth, "has ever wanted to help an elf."

The wizard squared his shoulders and stared up at Elas. "Nor has any elf ever sought to help a wizard with no thought of their own benefit," he cocked his head to one side, "But Luma helped me. She almost certainly saved my life, and now I return the favor."

Corr was instantly at Elas's side, facing Ruvyn through the cell bars. "Where is she? Where is Luma? If you've done anything to hurt her, I swear…"

Ruvyn again glanced over his shoulder, interrupting. "Keep your voice down, elf. She is in the meeting hall with Vell. She is unharmed as of now, but we all know that will change quickly if Vell doesn't get her way."

Ruvyn pulled a set of keys from his pocket. Holding his staff in his left hand, he selected one key and slid it into the bolt on the door of the cell. "At the east end of this hallway, there is a hidden door carved into the rock. The passage ends at the river, where a small boat is docked. Wait there, and I will bring Luma to you."

Corr snorted and shook his head. He folded his arms across his chest and glared at Ruvyn with unmasked hostility. "No way, wizard. We aren't going anywhere without her. And how do we know this isn't some kind of trap?"

Ruvyn sighed and stepped back to allow the cell door to swing open. "Fine. If you don't want to wait at the river, then wait here. I'll bring Luma as soon as I can, but after that, you're on your own."

Then he spun on his heel and stalked up the stairs without looking back.

****

Upstairs, the tension that followed Vell's last statement hung thickly in the air between her and Luma. Underneath the table, Luma slowly clenched and unclenched her fists, trying to get the throbbing in her palms to stop. Her head was beginning to ache, and she turned away from Vell and gazed toward the tall windows overlooking the cliff. Her eyes unfocused slightly, and she blinked several times, trying to clear her thoughts.

A soft clinking noise pulled her attention back, and she turned around to see Vell had poured her a cup of tea. Vell placed the cup delicately on a saucer and slid it across the table with a sweet smile. "I know this is a lot to take in, Luma. But time is of the essence, and decisions must be made."

Luma nodded. "I know, I know. The alignment."

Vell leaned forward. "Yes, Luma. The alignment waits for no one. It will come, and without interference, the work I started on the Sacred Stones will be completed. Once they are destroyed, the full might of Malicath can enter this world. Don't you see? The wizards of Malicath can help you, as they did me, to grow your power like never before. We could rule as allies—not only Edira and Malicath, but Earth, as well, and why not the rest? There are dozens of worlds we could bridge to and conquer easily. With your starlight and my magic, there would be no one who could stand in our way."

Luma noticed that Vell's knuckles were white with tension as she gripped her staff. When Vell spoke again, her voice quivered slightly, and she leaned forward. "The last alignment made you, Luma. But this next alignment has the power to remake the cosmos."

****

Luma leaned back into her chair. Images flashed before her eyes: standing in front of the four monolithic stones. The hopeful, pleading look on Izarre's face. The glowing carved lines at the base of each stone and the faintest whisper of someone saying her name, reaching out for her.

Your parents gave their lives to get you to safety, Corr had told her in that cavern. And then, he had told her to run and leave him to face that monster, that raptera, alone.

Clarity rolled over Luma like dawn across the horizon. She pushed back her chair and stood up. "No."

Vell also rose to her feet, her eyebrows raised, and her voice incredulous. "No?"

Luma squared her shoulders defiantly and nodded once. "I may not know how yet, but I plan to heal the Sacred Stones. I will not let them be destroyed."

"Well. That's very *disappointing*." Vell gripped her staff and took a menacing step toward Luma. "And I *hate* being disappointed."

Luma's heart raced, and she retreated a step just as the door to the room creaked open, and Ruvyn approached Vell's side. His voice cut through the tension between them.

"A moment, Vell. A moment. Perhaps a little time of 'reflection' down in the cells will cool her off and help change her mind." He glanced at Luma, who glared back at him. Ruvyn stepped forward and took hold of Luma's arm. "I will take her there myself."

Luma twisted backward and struck out at Ruvyn, knocking his hand away. "Touch me again, and I promise you'll regret it." She growled. Then she turned back and faced Vell, her voice rising with her anger. "Where are my friends? What have you done with them?"

Vell glanced at Ruvyn. "Leave us."

Ruvyn shuffled and held out his hands appealingly. "Vell, don't you think some time in the cells…" his voice trailed off when Vell fixed him with an icy stare. When she spoke, her voice was dangerously soft.

"I said. Leave. Us."

Ruvyn looked at Luma and then with a sigh turned and left the room, leaving the door slightly ajar. Vell smirked as she slowly circled Luma, her staff pointed toward Luma's chest, the end of which was now glowing a soft blue.

"No need to worry about your friends, my dear. Their destiny is to die with the rest of the elvish race that oppose me, and now, so is yours."

A bright, blue light shot from the end of the staff and struck Luma hard in the shoulder. She cried out and stumbled backward, gasping as searing pain radiated through her body. Vell gave a short, mirthless laugh and circled again. "That was just a very minor taste of what I can do. The power of my battle magic is unsurpassed by any wizard."

Luma threw herself to the side as the next blast shot from the glowing end of Vell's staff. She hit the hard stone floor and rolled, gritting her teeth as waves of hot agony raced through her body from the wound on her shoulder.

Through watering eyes, she looked up and saw Vell approaching, smug malice written on her beautiful face. Luma had seen that look often enough before from her old bully, Gabe, and rage churned in her stomach.

Scrambling to her feet, Luma ran for the door, but Vell sprang forward and blocked her path, leveling her staff at Luma's head. Panic rising in her blood, Luma threw up her hands and a pulse of energy rolled through her.

The surge of white light from Luma's palms hit the blast of blue from Vell's staff in midair. Taken aback by the impact, Luma shrieked and staggered backward, crashing into a wooden stool near the table and breaking off one of its legs. Vell's battle magic blast whizzed past her ear and exploded against a wall column, leaving a deep, black mark on the white stone.

Vell continued to advance as Luma struggled to sit

up, nauseated and gasping for air. "You are much weaker than I thought." Vell chuckled as she lowered her staff in line with Luma's head. "This will be pitifully easy. Arrgh!"

Vell's cry of surprise mingled with a grunt from Corr as he hit her arm from behind, knocking the staff out of her grasp.

The staff clattered loudly to the floor and slid to the opposite end of the room. Aire and Elas rushed in and helped Luma to her feet as Vell spun around to face Corr. She whispered a short incantation, then reached her arms in front of her and clenched her right fist. Corr's body went rigid and was suspended just above the ground. Sweat beaded at his temples as he tried in vain to fight the holding spell.

Her jaw clenched, Vell crossed the room in a few strides, dragging a helpless Corr with her as if by some invisible tether. She stopped in front of one of the huge windows and peered down over the steep cliff edge to the churning river far below.

With her right hand still clenched in a fist, Vell flicked her left wrist, and her staff materialized back into her hand. She smirked up at Corr, who was still suspended and struggling weakly. "You look somewhat familiar, but I can't quite put my finger on it." She shrugged. "Oh well." Vell pointed her staff at the window, and Luma flinched as the air filled with the sound of shattering glass.

Wind swept up and into the room from the broken window, and sparkling shards of glass rained down on the sides of the sheer cliff like edged diamonds. Vell stepped forward and moved her arm in a wide arc, swinging Corr around to teeter on the edge of the open window. Vell's silvery white hair blew around her face as she turned back toward Aire and Elas, who were now standing defensively in front of Luma, their eyes wide.

Vell raised her voice to be heard above the wind. "Sorry, Luma, but you chose the wrong side. And wrong choices have consequences for everyone."

In one swift, savage movement, Vell opened her fist and pushed. For a single, terrifying moment, Corr's green eyes locked with Luma's, then his arms flailed once, and he disappeared backward, out the broken window and over the edge of the cliff.

"No!" Luma, Aire, and Elas's distraught voices rang out as one.

The three of them rushed to the window ledge just in time to see, far below, a splash as Corr hit the churning water and was immediately swept away in the fast-moving current.

Aire and Elas remained peering desperately over the ledge, but Luma spun around and faced Vell. Eyes blazing and breath coming in ragged gasps, she let out a hoarse scream and raised her hands.

Vell raised her staff just in time to deflect the blast of starlight but was pushed backward by the force of the impact. Quickly regaining her balance and composure, Vell smiled wickedly and pointed her staff at Luma's chest.

Breathing heavily, Luma raised her hands again to meet Vell's challenge, and this time, when the two magical powers clashed in mid-air, it was Vell who stumbled. Setting her feet, Luma kept her arms locked straight out in front of her, her rage activating pulsing waves of starlight that rolled through her body, down her arms, and out through the scars on her palms.

The intensity of the white light streaming from her hands was almost blinding, and it felt to Luma as if her very blood was on fire. Gritting her teeth and trying desperately to quell the nausea roiling in her stomach, Luma took one step, then another on shaking legs that threatened at any moment to give out beneath her. Still, she took another step. Vell continued to give ground until her back was nearly against one of the large stone pillars that framed the far end of the room.

Fierce blue eyes finally showing a tinge of fear, Vell gripped her staff with both hands as she used her considerable might to force more battle magic from her staff, all of which was needed to protect her from the deadly concentration of starlight. But Vell could also see that Luma was beginning to falter. Moisture beaded across Luma's forehead, and small streams of dark red blood began to trickle from her ears and mingle with the sweat from her temples. Behind her, Aire and Elas stood transfixed by the scene, unsure of what to do.

Luma's chest heaved as she struggled for breath, and her arms began to shake. Realizing that Luma couldn't keep this up much longer, Aire darted forward and grabbed the broken stool leg.

Concentrated as she was on Luma, Vell didn't see Aire swing the heavy piece of wood until it slammed into her ribs.

Vell lurched sideways from the intensity of the impact and dropped her staff as the side of her head struck the stone column behind her. She collapsed into an unconscious heap on the polished floor at the same moment Luma's exhaustion overcame her.

Aire flipped the stool leg in the air once before catching it again. "Ha! Who needs starlight power when you've got a broken stool leg?" She smiled triumphantly over at Luma, who swayed on her feet, her arms hanging limp at her sides. Blood continued to trickle from her ears and down the sides of her neck.

Aire's smile faded. She dropped the stool leg and dashed forward. "Luma!"

Luma looked back at Aire with bloodshot eyes. "Corr. We need to find Corr."

Her eyes rolled back in her head, and Elas ran over and helped support her body, gently tapping her on the cheek. "Luma, stay awake. Luma!"

Luma's eyes fluttered slowly as she struggled to hold onto consciousness. Her face had gone ghostly pale.

From the door at the other end of the room, the wizard Ruvyn called out, beckoning them urgently with his hand. "The others are coming; you can't fight them. We've got to get Luma out of here. Follow me!"

Aire and Elas, supporting a semi-conscious Luma between them, followed Ruvyn as fast as they could out of the large room and down to the cells. The hidden door at the far end swung slowly open, revealing a winding set of stairs carved into the stone. Ruvyn held the door as the three of them passed through.

Elas stopped and looked back. "Are you coming with us?"

Ruvyn shook his head. "No. But go quickly. Find the boat at the bottom of this staircase and get her away from here."

Elas nodded and turned away, but Aire reached out her hand and placed it on Ruvyn's forearm as he held the door. "Thank you."

Ruvyn nodded. He pulled off a small canteen of water that was slung over his shoulder and passed it quickly to Aire. "You must hurry."

Aire looped the canteen over her shoulder and smiled in thanks as Ruvyn backed up and allowed the heavy door to swing closed. The stairway was immediately enveloped in darkness, but it wasn't long until Aire and Elas could make out the flickering patterns of light reflecting on water below them.

At the base of the stairway, they emerged onto a small stone ledge in a wide cavern half filled with water from an inlet of the river. At the far end of the ledge, a sleek, wooden rowboat was tied to a ring driven into the rock.

With Elas's help, Luma crawled feebly into the boat, followed by Aire. Elas untied it from the mooring before jumping in. He pushed off from the ledge and grabbed the wide paddles, handing one of them to Aire. The boat bobbed outward and then was quickly picked up by the current flowing past the small inlet.

Luma slumped in the middle of the boat and closed her eyes, her entire body aching. Elas leaned forward and tried to speak to her, but Aire stopped him. "It's okay, Elas. Let her rest. Keep an eye out for any signs of Corr, but let's focus on getting Luma away from here as fast as possible." Her gaze roved over Luma's limp form. "The mage is the only one who can help her now."

Chapter 8

Back in the White Keep, Vell grunted and slowly sat up. The fingers on her left hand curled around her staff, and she grimaced, her right hand carefully massaging a large bump on the side of her head. Naro offered her water, but she waved him away.

"Where is she?" Her voice was dangerously calm.

Ruvyn stepped forward, his head hung low. "She's gone, Vell. She and the two others escaped to the river; they must have discovered the staircase down to the boat."

Vell turned slowly and fixed Ruvyn with a hard stare. "They did, did they? That is unfortunate."

Ruvyn nodded, his head still low and his eyes downcast. "Most unfortunate."

Vell stared at him for a moment longer, then shrugged airily and smiled. She stood and walked to the broken window and peered down at the rocky cliff and the churning water far below. "A minor setback. Nothing I can't handle." She turned back around, her white hair shimmering. "Ruvyn, go and see to the horses." With a nod, Ruvyn departed, closing the door behind him.

Vell turned her attention to Naro. "Send out a raptera to search the river. Luma is very weakened at the moment, but she won't remain so for long, not with the alignment approaching. She has chosen wrong. I want her dead before nightfall."

Naro nodded darkly. "Right away, Vell."

He turned to leave, but Vell reached out and caught him by the arm. She leaned forward and spoke in a low voice, her deep blue eyes flashing. "And Naro, watch yourself. It seems we have a traitor in our midst."

****

A large sun, partially obscured by thick, ominous clouds, looked down on the rowboat and its three occupants.

The swift current was moving them so quickly that Aire and Elas stowed the two oars. Luma lay curled in the bottom of the boat, her eyes squeezed shut and her skin a pallid, sickly white.

Elas watched her, his shoulders tense. "She doesn't look so good."

Aire had been facing forward, her eyes raised, staring at the thick clouds building overhead. She turned back and glanced at Luma's pitiful form, then nodded in agreement with her twin brother. "No, she does not. Corr told us that using her starlight power made Luma sick, but I didn't think it was this bad." She sighed and gnawed on her lip, worry creasing her forehead. "Let's hope Trill was able to alert the mage because, unfortunately, there is nothing more we can do for her."

The two of them lapsed into grim silence as the little boat skimmed down the river under an increasingly dark sky.

****

"Luma."

The voice was soft and melodic, seeming to come from close by and far away all at once. Darkness surrounded her except for a shaft of light from high above. And in front of her...the Sacred Stones.

In the bottom of the boat, Luma twitched in her sleep as she sank further into her dream.

There was a noise from the narrow entrance as three people, a man, a woman, and a small child, entered the cavern. The man looked like he had come from battle; his handsome face was smeared with dirt and blood. The woman's tousled blonde hair was streaked with soot.

The man urged the woman and child forward toward the Sacred Stones, but the woman stopped and threw herself on him, clutching him tightly. When she spoke, her voice was strained with grief. "I never wanted to leave you, Tarak."

The man wrapped his arms around the woman and held her close, his face the picture of sorrow. "I know Seren. I know. But it's too late, and there is no other way. We cannot let them get to her."

Seren released her hold on Tarak, and he knelt before the child and gently stroked her curly, dark hair. "You are very special. Never forget that. And you will come home one day."

A boom rent the air from just outside the cave entrance. Tarak spun and drew a sword from the scabbard slung across his back. "They've found us. You must hurry!"

Seren grabbed the child's hand, and they rushed toward the Sacred Stones as Tarak cautiously edged near the entrance to the cavern, his large sword held in both hands.

Another loud boom and particles of rock dust floated down from the cavern ceiling.

Seren stood before the first of the Sacred Stones and placed her palms along the deep crack that ran down it, then bade the little girl to do the same. The girl, much shorter than her mother, placed her palms lower down. Seren closed her eyes, and the carvings at the base of the stone began to glow beneath the child's hands until it radiated outward, slowly encircling them both in warm, glittering light.

Tarak moved to the entrance of the cavern. He took another step forward just as a blast of blue hit him in the upper shoulder, throwing him backward.

"Tarak!" Seren's anguished scream filled the air. Two men, both with silvery white hair and holding staffs with glowing blue tips, charged into the cavern.

Tarak struggled to his feet and managed to cut them down with his sword before they could raise their staffs again, bellowing as he did. "Go, Seren! Get her away from here!"

Wielding his sword skillfully despite his wound, Tarak dodged another blast of battle magic and rushed to block the narrow passageway that led into the cavern.

In the very close quarters of the narrow passageway, the wizards were at a disadvantage, unable to aim their staffs effectively to use their battle magic. Tarak fought with a ferocity born of desperation, wreaking havoc with his sword in the small entrance. Then, a brilliant flash of blue lit up the passageway and crashed violently into Tarak's chest. With a final grunt of pain, he fell, his sword clattering to the cavern floor.

"Don't let her escape!"

A woman, her silvery white hair billowing as she ran forward, leveled her staff at the woman and child in front of the Sacred Stones.

"No! Leave her alone!"

The cry echoed through the cavern as a young boy burst from the narrow passageway.

Dodging battle magic blasts from the wizards behind him, the boy pulled a dagger from a sheath at his hip and lunged at the white-haired woman.

The woman turned and side-stepped to avoid the awkward attack. In one savage, graceful movement, she brought her staff crashing down across the boy's outstretched right forearm and was rewarded by the subtle snap of a bone breaking.

With a sharp cry of pain, the boy dropped the dagger and stumbled to one side, cradling his arm as tears streamed down his face.

The light around the Sacred Stones was growing brighter, and the white-haired woman spun back toward them, raising her staff once more.

Seren, now partially covered in the glittering light, threw her body in front of the child, taking the full blast of battle magic that had been meant for her young daughter.

With a scream, Seren collapsed to the ground, and the light from the Sacred Stones seeped away from her like scattering droplets of water. The child, who was already fully covered in the light, cried out and tried to reach for her mother, but her palms remained locked onto the carvings at the base of the Sacred Stone as if glued there by some powerful, unseen force.

Behind her, the woman smiled cruelly and aimed her staff again.

The boy, his right arm hanging limp at his side, darted forward and grabbed the hilt of the sword from near Tarak's lifeless body. The king's weapon was far too big for the young boy, but he gritted his teeth and hefted it in one hand from the cavern floor.

"I said, leave her alone!"

Mustering his strength, the boy jumped forward and swung the sword. The woman with the staff turned and side-stepped again, but slower this time, and the keen edge of the blade caught her in the upper arm.

Grunting, the woman glanced at her arm as blood began to seep from the wound. She leveled her staff at the boy, her blue eyes blazing.

"You'll pay for that."

Just then, from the cavern floor, Seren reached up and, with great effort, placed one palm on the bottom of the Sacred Stone in front of her. The light around the child immediately intensified into a swirling vortex, from which a soft buzzing emanated. And above the sound, Seren's voice came through, barely more than a whisper.

"You must go alone now, but at least you will be safe. My Luma. My Daughter of Starlight."

The cavern filled with blinding white light, the core of which swirled around the child. It glittered and swirled faster and faster, culminating in a massive pulse of energy that reverberated outward from the Sacred Stones, blasting through the cavern, and blowing the attacking wizards backward.

Then, all at once, the light was gone. And so was the child.

****

"Aahhhh!"

Luma surged upright, tears streaming down her face and her body shaking uncontrollably. Gasping and wild-eyed, she flailed right and left, causing the small boat to rock precariously in the swift current.

Aire cried out and clutched the side of her seat while Elas grabbed onto Luma's shoulders. "Luma! Luma! It's okay! You're safe, but you've got to stop; you'll capsize us!"

Luma's eyes focused on Elas, and she took several deep breaths, trying to shed the remnants of the dream that clung to her like cobwebs. Elas stared back at her, his eyebrows knit together in worry. Luma wiped her eyes with a trembling hand as Aire's voice cut through the fog in her mind.

"Hey, Luma. Welcome back to consciousness and all that, but we've got a problem!"

A shadow fell across the boat. At first, it appeared to be another passing cloud until the tell-tale screech split the air.

The raptera circled once, then dove.

Luma, Aire, and Elas threw themselves flat in the bottom of the boat. The huge bird's talons raked the bow, and water splashed over the sides and onto the back of Luma's shirt as she lay face down. Huge black wings beat the air as the raptera rose and began circling for another attack.

Aire scrambled up and grabbed one of the oars, her jaw clenched in determination. Gripping it tightly, she swung with all her might as the creature dove. The raptera flared its wings at the last second and swerved to avoid the oar, then banked in the air and attacked again. Aire hurled herself to one side, and the bird's razor talons missed her shoulder by a hairsbreadth.

The current was still moving swiftly, but the repeated attacks had knocked the small craft out of the middle of the river. It veered close to the water's edge and bumped violently off the large rocks in the shallows.

At the opposite end of the boat, Elas grabbed the other oar, ready to defend against the next attack. He shouted to Aire and gestured to the rocky shoreline that ran along this portion of the river.

"We need to get into some cover!"

Aire took her eyes off the beast wheeling above them long enough to give Elas a quick nod.

Luma, weakness clawing at her body, looked ahead and pointed with a trembling hand. "Up there!"

Ahead, amidst a pile of boulders, a large rock sloped downward from the shore and into the river, and the little boat was headed straight for it. Luma glanced at Aire and Elas and they nodded their understanding. Above them, the screeching cry of the raptera rang out. Water churned around the sloping rock where it entered the water, and Luma, Aire, and Elas held their collective breath as their little boat raced toward it.

"Now!"

At Elas's shout, the three friends launched themselves from the boat.

Elas hit the rock highest up, his feet struggling to find purchase against the damp surface. Aire and Luma landed lower down and immediately slipped back toward the water.

Finding his balance, Elas spun and scrambled down to help them. Aire grabbed Luma's hand. Then she reached her other toward Elas, and he hauled them up farther onto the sloping rock.

"Get among the boulders! Quick!"

Elas pushed Aire and Luma ahead of him, toward the safety of the jumble of large rocks, just as the raptera dove once again.

With Elas on their heels, Aire and Luma threw themselves into a small opening between two large boulders, then spun back to urge Elas in as well. Elas had just reached the mouth of the opening when he cried out, arching in pain as the talons of the raptera raked across his back.

Aire screamed, and Luma grabbed Elas's hand and heaved him into the space between the rocks, where he immediately collapsed.

"Get back, get farther back!" Luma's voice was hoarse as she grabbed one of Elas's hands and pulled with all her might.

Aire, tears streaming down her face, helped drag Elas underneath the jumble of rocks, leaving a bloody trail on the sandy soil.

A loud scratching from directly above her caught Luma's attention. She screamed and ducked as the vicious hooked beak of the raptera shoved its way into the cracks between the boulders, snapping the air where Luma's head had been just a moment before.

Heart pounding in her chest, Luma grabbed a large stone from the ground near her feet and, with a cry of rage, smashed it into the searching beak as hard as she could. There was a loud crack and a squawk as the beak withdrew.

Smiling with grim satisfaction, Luma clutched the stone and kept her eyes raised, circling slowly. She didn't have long to wait until the raptera tried again, this time raking its huge talons along the top of the rocks above Luma, causing a shower of rock dust to drift down over her head. Clenching her jaw, Luma shook the dust from her hair and waited.

High above, the clouds continued to gather. In the near distance, thunder rolled, and rain began to splatter down on the rocks.

There was a screech directly to her left, and Luma spun just as the vicious beak broke through again. Luma jumped forward and bashed the stone into the side of the beak twice before it retreated. This time, when she pulled the stone back, a portion of it was covered with a dark stain of blood.

Thunder rolled again, closer this time, and the rain poured down in sheets.

Breathing heavily, Luma blinked away the rainwater that dripped through the cracks in the rocks as she continued to circle and stare upward, clutching the stone, her knuckles white with tension. She jumped at another scratching sound from above, but only silence followed. Cautiously, Luma crept forward and peeked out of a space between the rocks just in time to see the raptera launch itself upward and wing back along the river through the driving rain.

Luma's sigh of relief died in her throat as she turned and saw Aire, huddled under an overhang of rock, cradling Elas's head in her lap.

With shaking hands, Aire pulled the canteen strap over her shoulder and tried to get Elas to drink. The little bit of water that poured from the canteen ran uselessly down the sides of Elas's mouth to dampen the sandy soil on either side of him.

Aire looked up at Luma. Her eyes were red-rimmed, and her cheeks were stained with tears.

Luma dropped the stone and rushed forward, falling to her knees next to Elas. His face was ghostly pale, and dark tendrils spread out just under the skin of his upper shoulders. Luma stared at them in confusion until the memory of something Aire had told her when they first met flashed in her brain. She looked up at Aire, who nodded, seeming to understand Luma's unspoken question.

"Poison." Aire's voice was a hoarse whisper made raw from crying.

Luma's heart dropped. "No."

She stared back down at Elas. His eyes were half open, his breathing labored and shallow. "No!" Luma said again, more forcefully this time.

She reached forward and carefully turned Elas over onto his stomach while Aire continued to cradle his head.

The back of Elas's shirt was torn in three jagged rips across his back. Luma carefully pulled the shirt up and had to swallow a small gasp when she saw the wounds underneath. Three deep gashes, each with dark, menacing tendrils that twisted outward from the wounds and spread across the skin. Luma reached out and gently touched Elas's back. He made no movement in response, and his skin was hot and clammy under her fingertips.

Luma shook her head, her heart pounding. "This can't happen. He cannot die from this! I won't let it happen!"

"Luma, there is nothing we can do." Aire's voice was choked with sobs. "There is no antidote for the wizard's poison."

Luma shook her head again, unwilling to accept what Aire was saying. The scars on her palms began to ache, and she opened and closed her fists, her mind desperately seeking a solution. Then, on an impulse, Luma placed both her hands on Elas's wounded back.

The aching of her scars continued, and she pressed them down harder against Elas's torn skin, spreading her fingers wide, heedless to the blood that seeped from the wounds.

"Hold on, Elas!"

The aching in Luma's palms intensified, tingling

across her hands and up her wrists, but instead of trying to fight it, like she usually did, Luma took a deep breath. As she exhaled, she relaxed her shoulders and focused on the weight of her hands pressing onto Elas's back.

A pulse of energy rolled through Luma's body, and heat simmered beneath her skin. She pushed down harder and closed her eyes. From what seemed like far away, she heard Aire gasp. Luma didn't open her eyes but kept her focus on the contact between her palms and the wounds on Elas's back.

Luma winced as the energy rose from her center, up her shoulders, and down her arms, cascading like waves out through her palms. Over and over, the waves rolled through her as Luma held still, her eyes squeezed shut and her mouth forming a thin line. Beads of sweat appeared on her forehead as heat began to build in her body.

Across from Luma, Aire sat gaping open-mouthed at the scene in front of her.

White light began to radiate from the underside of Luma's palms. In response to the light, the dark tendrils on Elas's skin writhed and withered like worms in the sun. Slowly, the tendrils began to pull back, retreating toward the wounds themselves and then farther still, twisting up around Luma's fingers.

Aire held her breath as the dark tendrils continued to pull away from Elas's skin and snake upward around Luma's wrists. A deep, scarlet flush came to Luma's cheeks. She took another breath and, with eyes still tightly closed, slowly, slowly, began to lift her palms off Elas's back.

As her hands lifted upward, so too came the last of the dark tendrils.

Suspended by the scars on Luma's palms, they dangled briefly in the air before being pulled upward until both of Luma's hands and wrists were covered in a web of twisting tendrils. Luma snapped her hands closed into fists, and a blinding flash of white light filled the small space. Aire recoiled, throwing her arm up to shield her eyes.

When she lowered her arm a second later, Luma sat before her, chest heaving, and her hands, with no dark tendrils in sight, hanging limply at her sides. From Aire's lap, Elas opened his eyes, groaned, and tried to push himself up.

Luma immediately leaned forward and put a cautious hand on his shoulder. "Don't move too much, Elas, you're wounded."

Elas shifted to look at her, grimacing in pain at the movement.

"Luma. Are you okay?" He turned back in the other direction. "Aire? Are you okay? What's the matter?"

Aire was bent over her lap, her hands covering her face and her shoulders shaking with uncontrolled sobs. Slowly, she lowered her hands and took a few ragged breaths. She stared at her twin brother through eyes that were red-rimmed and puffy.

"I'm okay, Elas. But I thought I lost you." She was forced to stop, momentarily held captive under a wave of fresh tears. Wiping the heel of her hand across her cheeks, Aire looked over at Luma, her voice trembling. "Thank you. How…how did you do that?"

Luma gazed down at the mass of scars that covered her palms and shook her head. "I don't know."

Elas stared back and forth between them, confused.

Luma raised her eyes. "We are not out of danger yet.

We need to find Corr and get away from here. I don't think Vell will give up hunting me so easily."

Aire cocked her head, a glimmer of her former, irrepressible self shining through. "Oh! I didn't realize what we just went through was supposed to be 'easy.'"

Despite her exhaustion, Luma laughed. She rolled her eyes and used one hand to flippantly toss her hair over her shoulder and affected a high, breathy voice. "Oh, that? That was, like, a piece of cake, my dear!"

Aire gave a watery giggle and wiped away the last of her tears.

Above them, thunder rolled again, followed by a brilliant flash of lightning. The rain continued to beat down, seeping between the cracks in the boulders.

Aire scooched backward to allow more room underneath the rock overhang, then waited for another crash of thunder to fade before giving voice to what they were now all thinking. "It'll be dark soon. Best wait here for the storm to pass."

Chapter 9

The sun set, and the relentless downpour continued. The rain pelted the surface of the rock overhang until thin rivulets flowed over the edge and seeped into cracks between the boulders to dampen the ground at the feet of the three friends sleeping underneath.

Farther down river, the rain also pelted upon the upturned face of Corr.

****

Roused to consciousness by the watery onslaught, Corr sputtered and coughed, groaning as he raised one arm in a vain attempt to shield his face. His upper body was lodged between shoreline rocks and the trunk of a fallen tree that was half submerged in the river, while his lower body bobbed in the shallows. Corr bent his knees and tested his legs, grimacing as the blood circulated through his cold limbs, bringing with it aches and tingles. Using the tree trunk as a guide, Corr pulled himself from the water and then slowly up onto the bank.

Exhausted and soaking wet from both river and rain, Corr took mental stock of himself. No broken bones and no apparent large injuries, though his ribs ached painfully with every breath, and his head throbbed. Gingerly, Corr reached back and felt a large knot at the base of his skull, probably thanks to the tree trunk.

He looked up the bank to where the night-darkened forest crept down to meet the rocky shore and wondered with a sense of dread what had happened to Luma, Aire, and Elas. Corr raised his chin and squinted upward, blinking away the rain. Even through the cloud cover, the Four Stars could be seen. There was nothing on Edira that could dim their light, part of the reason they were so special. The Four twinkled down at him from their jagged line high above, and Corr shivered. The alignment was just a few weeks away, and without Luma, the world as he knew it would fall to the exploitation of the wizards, and all would be lost.

Corr hung his head, his failure to protect Luma settling over him like a heavy, wet blanket. He leaned against the trunk of the fallen tree and allowed the rainwater to run in a stream over his forehead and down between his feet. Deep fatigue clawed at Corr's battered body, and his shoulders slumped as he closed his eyes.

Sleep had almost overtaken him when the butt of a spear jabbed between Corr's shoulder blades. His eyes flew open, and he jerked to one side, his right hand instinctively reaching for the dagger on his belt—the dagger that was no longer there.

Groping around him in the dark, Corr's hand closed on a large river rock. He crouched defensively, his gaze searching the darkness around the fallen tree. A figure rose from behind the tree trunk, and then others materialized out of the shadows of the forest, their weapons glinting in the starlight.

"Who are you?" Corr squared his shoulders as he stood and raised his voice to be heard over the driving rain.

The figure from behind the tree trunk stepped forward, spear held at the ready. "I'll be asking the questions. Who are *you?* What is your purpose here?"

Corr was about to respond when another voice interrupted. "Oh, relax, Haryk, he's clearly not a wizard." The owner of the voice walked closer, shaking water from her long hair. She thrust her hand toward Corr. "Greetings, friend. I'm Emalet."

Haryk, the elf who had spoken first, pushed Emalet's hand away before Corr could reach for it. "Just because he's not a wizard doesn't make him a friend."

Emalet fixed Haryk with a hard stare, her voice deceptively calm. "Do that again, Haryk, and you'll lose that hand."

Corr, unsure of what to think, slowly bent and put the rock he had been clutching back on the ground. Straightening up, he held his hands out wide. "My name is Corr. I am unarmed, and I am not your enemy."

Emalet shot Haryk a smug, sideways glance and once again extended her hand. Corr reached forward, and they clasped opposite wrists in the elvish greeting. Haryk tilted his head and looked Corr up and down appraisingly while thunder rolled and lightning sporadically brightened the inky night sky.

Emalet smiled and nodded at Corr. "You look like you've been through it, Corr. Like I said, I'm Emalet, and this," she jerked her head to her right, "is Haryk. And we," she gestured to the others that still lingered in the shadows, how many there were exactly, Corr couldn't tell. "We are the ERC."

Corr shook his head, not sure he had heard correctly. "The what?"

Emalet gave Corr a wink as she ushered him toward the tree line. "I'll explain later. Why don't you come with us, friend."

****

Several hours later, the rain finally stopped, and Luma shifted in her sleep. Grimacing at the stiffness in her neck, she fluttered her eyes open and found herself staring straight into two wide amber orbs.

"Yaahha!" Luma reeled backward, smacking her shoulder on the edge of the rock behind her.

At her side, Aire and Elas also startled awake. Quickly recovering from her initial shock, Luma rubbed her bruised shoulder and glared at the large owl in front of her.

"Trill! You scared me. I didn't hear you fly up."

Trill preened his tawny breast feathers, scattering a few remaining droplets of rainwater across Luma's legs. He fixed her with a snobbish look.

"No...of course you didn't." He flexed his huge wings as if to prove his point.

Then he cocked his head from side to side, slowly blinking at Aire and Elas. "So, you are out of the dungeon and into the river. An improvement, I suppose, but not by much. We have no time to waste. Where is Corr?"

The back of Luma's eyes pricked, and she exchanged pained glances with Aire and Elas. When Aire spoke up, her voice was strained with emotion. "He...he was thrown into the river from the White Keep. We don't know where he is now."

Trill shifted from foot to foot atop the small boulder he was perched on. "I see. Well, I have delivered Corr's message to the mage, and there is no time to waste. No time at all. We must get Luma to the banks of the Inland Sea. The mage will take it from there."

Luma shook her head. "What about Corr? We need to find him first."

Trill ruffled his feathers and clacked his large, yellow beak impatiently. "After we get you to the mage, I will fly out and see if I can find him. But *you* are the priority here, not Corr."

Luma's jaw twitched. She shook her head again. "Trill! How can you say that? Corr was thrown from a high window! He might be injured! He might be…" her voice trailed off as a lump formed in her throat. She took a breath and glared at the owl. "I thought Corr was your friend."

Trill met her gaze levelly with his immense eyes and pulled himself up to his full height. "That is true, all true, but *you* are the Daughter of Starlight, and if the alignment comes and you are not ready, none of that matters. Not for Corr. Not for any of us."

Trill's words settled over the three of them like a dense fog. Luma glanced at Aire and Elas, both of whom nodded in agreement with Trill but distinctly avoided her eyes. A hollow ache formed in Luma's stomach.

Trill, practical as always, was back to business. He clacked his beak again. "Right. It is already an hour past dawn. The Inland Sea is still miles away, and you three will be traveling on foot. We must be going."

The wounds on Elas's back had already begun to heal overnight, a pleasant surprise that Aire attributed to whatever Luma had done to remove the poison. A few minutes later, Luma, Aire, and Elas emerged from their shelter amid the boulders, squinting in the sunlight that blazed down from a sky now devoid of clouds.

Trill flew farther down the river and came back with good news. Their little boat had been caught on a sandbar not far away. After a quick inspection, they determined that the craft was still in good enough condition to carry them, though Aire shuddered at the deep scratches along its sides, remnants of the raptera's claws.

Going by river some of the way would save time, and Trill was pleased, well, as pleased as owls allow themselves to be. Soon, he was winging high above them in the clear blue sky as the three friends navigated their boat into the swift current of the River Aque once more.

Chapter 10

When Corr awoke the next morning, it took him a few moments to remember where he was. The stone walls of his room were rough-hewn, not smooth and undulating like the ones carved by water that he was used to.

Corr sat up in the small bed, nursing his bruised ribs as the memory of the night before came back to him. He had been brought to some kind of secret stronghold, built right into the craggy cliffs that dominated the far edge of the forest bordering the Northern plains. When he had arrived last night with Emalet and Haryk, it had been too late, and he too exhausted for formal introductions.

Just then, Emalet poked her head around the corner of the doorway. "Hey there, Corr. Come with me. There are some elves I want you to meet."

****

Trepidation simmering in his mind, Corr followed Emalet through winding passages and down a flight of rough stone steps. They emerged at the base of the cliff and into a small clearing surrounded by tall trees. Dappled sunlight filtered down to the mossy forest floor through the leafy canopy. Milling around the clearing were about two dozen elves, and they all turned as Corr and Emalet approached.

In the light of day, Corr immediately recognized the group as Northern Plains Elves, and his trepidation grew.

He had lived in the Southern forests near the capital his whole life and was well aware of the political and cultural tensions between the Forest Elves in the south and the clan from the Northern plains. Though the capital of Aquea, with the king and Elders Council, technically ruled over all elves, the Plains Clan kept their distance, choosing isolation over political discourse and largely maintaining a sense of autonomy.

From the perspective of the Forest Elves, Plains Elves were uncivilized at best, downright savages at worst. Their blond hair and light eyes, such a contrast from the black hair and dark eyes of Forest Elves, were regarded with suspicion. And while Forest Elves wouldn't dream of marking their bodies, the pale skin of Plains Clan Elves was often covered in a myriad of colorful tattoos.

Corr shifted uncomfortably under the weight of the group's silent stares. Then, the one he recognized as Haryk strode forward. Haryk stopped a short distance from Corr and extended his hand. "Hello again, Corr. Sorry about last night. One can never be too careful when out on patrol."

Corr grasped Haryk's wrist in greeting and nodded his understanding. "Thank you, Haryk," he said. "I'm grateful for your hospitality. What is this place?"

Haryk puffed out his chest and smiled. "Corr, welcome to Northhelm. Built in secret by the hands of Northern Plains Elves centuries ago as a place of safety. And now, once again, it has proven helpful in these troubled times. We are warriors all, and together, we make up the ERC—the Elvish Resistance Council."

Corr raised a skeptical eyebrow. Emalet stepped forward and placed a hand on Corr's arm. "Twelve years ago, when the wizards invaded, the capital fell."

"I know," Corr interrupted her, his dark green eyes flashing. "I was there."

Emalet lowered her eyes and nodded sadly. "We in the North may not have been at the initial battle, but the wizards didn't stop at the capital. They continued hunting down all elves, and we fought, too. We fought to protect our land and our world. Those who didn't lose their lives, scattered, forced to live in fear and in hiding. But over the years, that fear has been replaced with resolve! We are coming back together, getting strong again! Ready to take back our world."

Corr looked around at the group of elves in the clearing. They were all well-armed with bows and spears and admittedly looked like a group of disciplined fighters. But he still shook his head.

"That sounds great, Emalet," he protested. "But Plains Clan or Forest Clan, it doesn't matter. Not anymore. We have no weapons that can withstand wizard battle magic, at least not for long. Elves can't win against wizards in an open fight."

"Who said anything about an open fight?" The voice came from behind him, and Corr turned to see who had spoken.

The elf was young, barely more than a child. She was whisper thin and several inches shorter than the other elves, but she strode up to Corr with an air of assertiveness that belied her youth and small stature. Her skinny, exposed arms were covered in what Corr immediately recognized as the dark red scars of battle magic. She had a bow across her shoulder and a large knife at her hip, but she looked up at Corr with a face that still bore the soft roundness of childhood. Despite this, there was something behind her pale eyes that told Corr not to underestimate her.

Emalet stepped forward and threw a heavily tattooed arm around the young elf's shoulders. "Corr, this is Figg. She runs our guerilla operations."

Corr raised his eyebrows as he looked back and forth between Emalet and this child. "Guerilla operations?" He didn't even try to keep the skepticism out of his voice.

Figg cocked her head to one side and flashed a smile up at Corr. "You said it yourself, forest-dweller. We can't beat the wizards in an open fight. But there is more than one way to fight a war. And this one, we intend to win."

****

The methods of the Elvish Resistance Council were genius in their simplicity, as Corr soon learned.

Through careful surveillance, they had discovered that Vell and her wizards were focusing a lot of their time and energy on the quarry from which the Sacred Stones had originally been taken before their placement in the cavern. The quarry was a particularly potent source of the naturally occurring magic on Edira, magic which the wizards were bent on stealing to exploit for their own ends.

So, the ERC went to work quietly, disrupting the process as much as possible. They stole and destroyed the supplies that the wizards used to extract the raw magic for transport back to Malicath. They felled trees to block pathways and they even carefully laid traps of Fireburn plants in any areas that were known to be heavily used by the wizards.

They used their weapons too, arrows mostly, strategically picking off any wizards they could without drawing too much attention, firing with deadly accuracy, and then disappearing like smoke on the breeze. The rules of engagement were simple, clearly laid out to everyone by Figg. Never get caught, never give the wizards a chance to use their battle magic, and never let up.

Corr was intrigued with these ongoing resistance efforts and impressed with Figg's knack for guerilla warfare. But the fate of Luma and his friends weighed heavily upon him. For whether or not the Plains Elves wanted to believe it, Corr knew that while the Sacred Stones remained cracked, Edira remained at risk. And if the Sacred Stones were destroyed during the coming alignment, the wizards would be unstoppable, and all this would have been for nothing.

He brought this concern to Haryk, Emalet, and Figg the next day as they shared a meal in one of the meeting rooms inside Northhelm. Haryk had already told him that they were out on patrol tracking a raptera attack when they had found him by the river. So, Corr thought it was likely that Luma, Aire, and Elas had managed to escape the White Keep. Whether the monstrous bird had been successful in killing its quarries, Haryk couldn't say, but he had seen it flying away that night through the storm.

Corr got up from the table and paced, his agitation at so many unknowns making it impossible for him to keep still.

"We've got to find them."

Figg's pale eyes moved back and forth as she watched Corr. Then she lowered them back down to her work at hand, fletching a small pile of arrows. She kept her eyes lowered as she spoke.

"Why? For all we know, they've already been killed

by that raptera. I mean, those things have a pretty high success rate when it comes to killing elves." She glanced up, then raised her eyebrows at Emalet, who was giving her a shocked look like she had said something insensitive.

"What? They do!" Figg continued. "We all know it. And pretending otherwise doesn't help anyone. Besides, if this Luma is who you say she is, then sending out a patrol to look for her is dangerous. We know that Vell must be searching for her, too."

Corr stopped pacing and spun to face Figg.

"That's exactly *why* we need to find her! Don't you see that she is the key to stopping this war once and for all? Luma is the Daughter of Starlight. She is the only one who has the power to heal the Sacred Stones during the alignment. I pledged to get her to the mage, and I will go alone to find her if I must."

Haryk shook his head. He looked back and forth between Emalet and Figg, then over at Corr.

"If what you say is true, and your friends did manage to escape the raptera, then they will be headed toward the Inland Sea, which is at the far border of the Northern Plains. You won't go alone. We leave tomorrow."

****

The River Aque, wide and fast-moving near the capital, slowed and narrowed as it wound out of the thick Southern forests and into the expansive plains.

For a while, Luma, Aire, and Elas managed to coax the little boat along, using the oars to push off the ever-increasing sandbars. Soon, however, it became clear that their journey by water had come to an end. They got out and waded a short distance, dragging the craft behind them, then finally hauled it out of the water and into a small dip in the land where it was partially obscured by the tall grasses.

Having lived surrounded by mountains all her life, or at least all the life she could remember, Luma was transfixed by this new landscape.

The plains before them stretched nearly unbroken to the horizon and were covered in thick grasses that undulated in the wind like waves on the ocean.

The last two days had remained clear, and Luma squinted in the unfiltered sunlight. A shadow zipped overhead, and Trill landed silently nearby, shuffling impatiently from foot to heavily-feathered foot. Aire and Elas made sure that the boat was securely beached and then came over to stand on either side of Luma.

The big owl looked at the three of them and blinked slowly before he spoke. "Not much farther now. Not much. The Inland Sea is another day's journey for you from here. Due north. I will go on ahead and inform the mage of your progress."

Without offering further explanation or waiting for a response, Trill launched himself back into the sky and was soon out of sight. Luma turned to her two companions.

"For a talking owl, he's not much of a talker."

Aire shrugged and handed Luma the canteen of water. "Owls are like that." She cocked her head to one side. "Are they different in the human world?"

Luma, who had just taken a sip of water from the canteen, snorted and then coughed, wiping her mouth. "Um, yeah…different in the fact that on Earth, owls, or any animal for that matter, don't talk!" She giggled and then raised her eyebrows at Aire and Elas, who were looking at her in confusion.

"None? Not a single one?" Elas shook his head in disbelief.

Luma laughed again and nodded. "No! Not a single one! Well, I guess some parrots can learn to speak, but even they only repeat or mimic what they have heard before from humans, not actually talk, like, on their own."

Aire and Elas looked at each other and then back at Luma, both obviously trying to determine if she was joking. Luma nodded at them earnestly. "It's true."

Aire smiled. "Only mimic, huh? That's got to be annoying."

Luma shrugged, a wry smile tugging at the corners of her mouth. "Well, I've never actually owned a parrot, but yeah, I think it probably is."

Elas reached for the canteen and took a sip, then trudged off through the thick, waist-high grass, heading north, calling over his shoulder as he went. "We'd best get a move on. It's another day's journey before we reach the Inland Sea. And if we keep the mage waiting, we are bound to get a stern lecture from our very own talking owl."

****

The three friends continued to follow the river, or what was now more of a stream, so they could quench their thirst as needed. Elas was uniquely skilled at foraging for food, a talent that proved applicable even in this unfamiliar area, and for which Aire and Luma were very grateful. They walked for the remainder of the afternoon and then decided to camp for the night at the crest of one of the small rolling hills that dotted the plains landscape.

"Better to be higher and able to see anyone who tries

to sneak up and attack," Elas said, and he was only partially joking. The fact that they were most likely still being hunted by Vell and her wizards was at the fore of all their minds.

Maintaining a cautious approach, they decided to sleep in shifts. When it was Luma's turn, she sat with her knees hugged into her chest and stared upward at the bright starlight shining down from the Four, whose jagged line in the night sky was now unquestionably less so, even to the untrained eye.

The scars on her palms ached ever so slightly, and Luma remained gazing upward as she felt the heavy weight of expectation on her shoulders, along with the deep and familiar sense of inadequacy churning in her stomach.

****

The next day dawned bright and clear. They set off early, but the going was slow, and the sun was hot. Luma wiped the back of her hand across her forehead for what felt like the hundredth time and gratefully accepted when Elas offered her the canteen of water. She paused for a moment and took a sip while Aire and Elas trudged on ahead.

At first, Luma thought it was the elf siblings that she heard talking in low tones, but she soon realized that the voices were coming from behind her. Luma ducked below the top of the grass, her heart pounding. Keeping her head low, she darted forward to catch up with Aire and Elas. She tapped them both on the arm and put a trembling finger to her lips.

It didn't take long for the sound of the voices to reach Aire and Elas as well, and they stared at Luma with wide eyes, frozen with fear.

Aire was first to recover. Silently, she crouched and wound carefully through the grass to their left. Elas and Luma followed until they reached the base of another small hill. Moving to the far side, the three friends crawled slowly toward the crest and then lay on their bellies, concealed by the surrounding grass. Soon, the voices rang out again, more clearly this time.

"It was another trap. I don't know how they are doing it, but it's getting worse," one voice said.

"Are you sure? Those plants grow all over this cursed world. Maybe it was an accident," another voice responded.

"An *accident?*" the first voice retorted sharply. "A pile of those plants all laid out in a concealed pit across the main route to the quarry is no accident. It was a trap set by the elves. You weren't there, but I was, and I saw it. Everyone was covered in burning red blisters. Ugh, you should have heard the screams."

From their hiding place atop the small hill, Luma exchanged glances with Aire and Elas, the same question on all their minds: *elves were fighting back?*

The voices were closer now, and the three friends held their collective breath.

Another voice now joined the conversation. "And a few days before that, a bunch of horses were turned loose during the night, and a good amount of our extracting supplies were destroyed. Vell was livid. I'll tell you one thing: I'd hate to be any of those elves if they get caught."

The first voice responded. "Oh, they will get caught eventually, that is for certain. Besides, the alignment is only a few weeks away, and once those Sacred Stones are destroyed, we can extract as much magic as we want."

Luma glanced once again at Aire and Elas. There was fear and anger in their eyes, for they knew that the wizards spoke the truth. Without the protection of the Sacred Stones, Edira would be completely overrun and sucked dry of its magic by the wizards.

By the sound of it, the voices seemed now to be moving farther away, and the three friends relaxed slightly.

After another minute, Luma pulled her knees underneath her and cautiously raised her head to look around. It was a mistake. The second her head cleared the grass, she locked eyes with the wizard in the front of the group as he turned to check on something behind him.

Stifling a gasp, Luma ducked back down, but it was too late.

A cry rang out from the wizard. "Hey!"

They had been spotted.

Chapter 11

Cursing under her breath, Luma raised a finger to her lips as she, Aire, and Elas scrambled backward down the other side of the hill, hoping to make their escape through the tall grass. Once at the bottom, they remained crouched and circled one side of the hill and straight into the group of wizards.

Leaping forward, one of the wizards grabbed for Luma's arm, but Elas grabbed her instead and pulled her backward.

"Run!"

Abandoning all pretense of stealth, the three of them dashed off through the tall grass with the four wizards close on their heels.

The grass was tall and grew densely together, marring their progress. Aire chanced a quick look over her shoulder, then jumped to one side as a blast of battle magic hit the ground next to her and left behind a patch of scorched earth. A second later, Luma felt a wave of heat streak by her left ear, and another blast exploded in front of her. Dodging to one side, her eyes watering and her breath coming in ragged gasps, Luma checked to make sure Aire and Elas were still next to her and then forced herself onward.

A few minutes later, the grass began to shorten and thin, which Luma realized was better for running but also made them easier targets. There was a whoosh behind her, and she jumped to the left, barely avoiding another blast of battle magic. Her panicked mind whirled, desperate for a solution that didn't end with them being captured or killed, but nothing came up.

A quick glance at Aire and Elas running beside her confirmed that they had no solutions either except to try and outrun their pursuers.

But suddenly, running wasn't an option anymore.

The grass now became sparse in the rocky soil, and just ahead, the land itself disappeared completely over the edge of a steep ravine. Luma skidded to a stop and jumped backward. Pebbles pushed forward from her feet flew over the edge, bouncing erratically off the jagged rocks that protruded from the sheer sides of the drop.

Dizzied by the height, Luma spun around. On either side of her, Aire and Elas had also stopped, their faces flushed and their chests heaving as they frantically looked for another way to escape. Behind them, the four wizards slowed and fanned out in the short grass, hemming them in against the edge of the ravine.

They were trapped.

Luma clenched her jaw and put her arms out defensively, her fingers trembling. The wizards closed in, their staffs held menacingly in front of them, their faces smug with the knowledge that the three elves had nowhere left to run.

Trying, and failing, to keep her voice from shaking, Luma called out, "I'm Luma. Take me and let the others go."

"Luma! No!" Elas's voice hissed from beside her.

Luma ignored him and spoke again louder this time. "I'm the one that Vell wants. You will leave the others alone."

The wizard in the middle chuckled mirthlessly. "Yes, Daughter of Starlight. You are the one that Vell wants. She wants you dead, along with all other elves that try to stand in our way!"

The end of the wizard's staff began to glow blue, and his eyes glittered wickedly as he aimed it at Luma's chest. Heat simmered beneath her skin, but just as Luma braced herself, a small cry gurgled from the wizard's mouth. His eyes bulged, and he stumbled forward, a long, slender arrow protruding from the center of his back.

Luma's scream of surprise mingled with the shouts of the three remaining wizards, who spun around just in time for three more arrows to find their mark. In a matter of moments, all the wizards were on the ground, their staffs falling from lifeless hands before disappearing.

Arms still held outward, Luma stood frozen with shock, her eyes wide and her mouth agape. From the tall grass, another group emerged, led by a small, fair-haired elf with a bow in her hand and a quiver slung across her narrow shoulders. She was followed by two others with similarly light hair and then another who was taller and had darker, close-cropped hair.

"Corr!"

The sound of Aire's joy-filled cry startled Luma out of her stupor. She let her arms drop and watched in stunned disbelief as Aire and Elas dashed forward.

Corr's face creased into a wide smile at his friends, and then he looked down at the smaller elf beside him. "Just in time. Nice shooting, Figg."

Figg cocked her head and gave him a crooked smile in return. "You too."

Aire and Elas had already thrown themselves at

Corr. The sound of Aire's shrill laughter echoed around them as she wiped tears from her eyes with the heel of her hand. Elas thumped Corr on the back, grinning broadly.

After a few moments of chaotic reunion, Corr disentangled himself from the twins and gestured around to the other three elves he was with. "This is Haryk, Emalet, and Figg. They are part of the ERC—the Elvish Resistance Council—and they have been fighting back against the wizards."

Haryk stepped forward. "We are Plains Clan."

Aire glanced at Elas, then back at Haryk, her dark gaze roving from Haryk's light hair to the brightly colored tattoos that covered both his bare arms. "Yeah. I could tell."

In the awkward silence that followed, Luma watched the two groups of elves regard each other with open suspicion. She didn't know why these other elves looked different from her friends or why that mattered, but she could sense a strong air of tension between the two groups.

Finally, she stepped forward on legs still weak from the departing adrenalin. "Hi. I'm Luma. Thanks for your help back there."

All eyes now upon her, Luma shifted uncomfortably.

Corr stepped forward, and before Luma could respond, he wrapped his arms around her, pulling her against his chest in a tight embrace.

"Luma, thank the Four Stars you are all right." His breath felt warm against her ear.

Completely caught off guard, Luma stood rigid, her arms hanging limp at her sides. After a second, Corr released her, and Luma took a step back, flushing. Corr also stepped back and shuffled awkwardly.

Aire looked at them both and rolled her eyes. "Okay then. Well, we should probably get out of here before more of *them* show up." She cocked her head toward the slain wizards.

Luma looked back over her shoulder at the bodies of the four wizards, lying prone in the sandy soil amid the scrub grasses, and her stomach knotted and twisted. She glanced back at the group questioningly. "So…what do we do with them?"

The small elf that Corr had introduced as Figg crossed her arms and shrugged, her eyes hard as she stared at Luma.

"Do with them? We leave them. They won't bother you anymore."

Luma was taken aback by the callous response, especially from one so young, but she was also more than a little annoyed at the patronizing tone Figg used to answer her question. She arched an eyebrow at the small elf.

"Um. Yeah. They're dead. I know they won't *bother* me anymore. But still, shouldn't we…bury them, or…something?"

Figg snorted and rolled her large, pale green eyes dramatically. Then, she glared back at Luma. "You think they would have shown you the same courtesy? Or them?" She gestured to Aire and Elas. "I think not, *Daughter of Starlight*." She spat the words out like they left a bad taste in her mouth. Then continued, sarcasm edging into her tone. "Maybe you shouldn't be telling us how to handle wizards…you're new here."

Luma clenched her fists, her quick temper flaring.

"New here? What is that supposed to mean?"

Figg took a step forward and jutted out her chin. "It means that when the Sacred Stones cracked and the wizards invaded, you were whisked off to safety, sent far away, to the human world, so I'm told. But not us. We were here. And we were *dying*."

Corr stepped forward, trying to edge himself between Figg and Luma. "Come on, Figg, it's not her fault."

Figg turned to Corr and raised her eyebrows, her tone mocking. "No. No, of course not. All these years, she's been safe and sound, and thank the Four Stars for that." She once again fixed Luma with a cold stare. "And all these years, we have continued to fight and sacrifice for you. And what have you done? What have you sacrificed? What are you *willing* to sacrifice?"

With that, Figg shouldered her bow, turned on her heel, and began walking off along the edge of the ravine, pausing only to wrench the arrows free from the wizards' bodies as she went. Haryk and Emalet gave Luma and Corr apologetic glances, then followed Figg.

Luma watched them go as a blanket of deep shame draped itself over her shoulders. Aire and Elas edged closer to her, and Corr caught her eye and tried to give her a small, encouraging smile, but Luma turned her face away, the back of her eyes burning.

"I...I don't remember. I didn't have a choice. At least, I don't think I did. I don't know. I'm...I'm sorry." Her voice caught in her throat, and she lapsed into embarrassed silence.

Corr put his hand gently on her forearm. "It's okay, Luma. Come on, let's get you to the mage."

****

The three of them walked off together, following Figg, Haryk, and Emalet from a distance.

It took them a while to skirt the top of the ravine, and to Luma's mild surprise, the three elves in front of them seemed to know exactly where they were going. Finally, they were clear of the ravine. A plain of scrub grasses spread out in front of them and then dropped away in a steep cliff. Luma watched intently as Emalet, Haryk, and Figg walked ahead a short distance along the edge of the cliff, then stopped. With a small jump, they disappeared over the edge.

Luma shrieked and ran forward. Quickly covering the distance, she peered cautiously down over the lip, her heart pounding.

The three elves looked back up at her, and Luma's eyes grew wide. Figg, Haryk, and Emalet were standing on a narrow ledge, which, upon closer examination, was the beginning of a staircase that had been skillfully cut into the rock. Cleverly camouflaged against the cliff face, the stairs descended to where Luma could see a narrow, pebbly beach with water gently lapping the shoreline. The edge of the Inland Sea.

Chapter 12

Haryk, Emalet, and Figg descended the staircase. Luma glanced over her shoulder as Corr approached, followed closely by Aire and Elas.

Corr nodded to her. "Go ahead."

Figg, who was behind the other two and already about halfway down, paused and looked back up at Luma. Not wanting Figg to see her hesitation, Luma crouched and made the small hop onto the narrow ledge, swallowing hard as her stomach churned from the height. Still, she took a breath and began slowly descending the stairs, dragging her left hand along the cliff side for balance. Behind her, Aire, Elas, and Corr followed.

When her feet finally crunched onto the pebbled shore, Luma let out a long sigh of relief, which caused Figg to roll her eyes. Luma was about to make a retort to Figg's expression when Emalet gave a cry and pointed. All eyes turned seaward, and Luma squinted from the glare as she gazed beyond Emalet's pointing finger across the glittering waves. Then she saw it, a small smudge on the horizon. As she watched, the smudge grew steadily larger until it was not a smudge anymore but the distinct outline of a small ship.

Luma watched anxiously as the ship drew closer, and then something else caught her eye. Flying just above the single mast was Trill. His huge, silent wings barely moved as he soared on upward currents of air. As the ship drew closer to the beach, Trill folded his wings and dove, flaring them wide at the last second to land soundlessly, as usual, on the beach.

He swiveled his large head and blinked upward at Luma. "So. You have arrived."

Luma nodded at the stoic owl, amused at how simply he had summed up her long and perilous journey to this place. "I have."

Trill ruffled his feathers. "Good. That is good."

Luma smiled down at him, and then the sounds of stones crunching pulled her gaze up. The ship had come aground on the beach in front of them, and a figure descended the small walkway to the shore. He stepped onto the pebbles and walked toward her while the others moved respectfully aside.

Luma studied him as he approached. Like most of the elves she had met so far, he was tall and long-limbed. He was dressed simply in pants and a dark gray tunic, not exactly the image she had conjured in her mind of the powerful elf mage that Corr had told her about. His hair was dark and not as closely cropped as Corr's or Elas's, though not as long as Haryk's, and what Luma noticed immediately was that on the left side of his head, running through the surrounding dark tresses was a streak of brilliant, silvery white. The same silvery white color of Vell's hair and the hair of the other wizards. Luma's scars tingled, and at her sides, she slowly clenched and unclenched her fists.

The mage stopped in front of her, then reached out and took both of her hands in his. Luma stood rigid as he slowly turned her wrists so that her palms were facing up, exposing the tangle of dark scars that crisscrossed them both. He stared down at her palms for what seemed like a long time while Luma's stomach twisted into anxious knots. Finally, he gently folded Luma's fingers over her palms and let go of her wrists, allowing her hands to drop back to her sides. Then he looked up at her, his wide, gray eyes studying her face and twinkling with a strange light.

When he spoke, his voice was deep and soft, like a feather bed. "Luma. Welcome. I am Eldamarr Rinn."

Luma swallowed, trying to dislodge the nervous lump that had formed in her throat. She nodded, unsure of what to do or say since this elf, along with everyone else she had met so far, already seemed to know who she was. And not only knew who she was but expected great things from her. Powerful things. And yet, she had never felt weaker in her life.

Eldamarr Rinn shifted his gaze over to Corr. He smiled and took a step forward, placing a hand on Corr's shoulder and nodding with approval.

"Corr. Izarre was right to send you with her here. Thank you." He turned to face the others. "It has been twelve long and desperate years since the Sacred Stones were cracked, but now we truly have hope. Still, there is much work to be done." He looked over at Luma. "The alignment is closing in and will bring with it opportunities, as well as great challenges for you, Daughter of Starlight. We must begin your training."

Luma glanced around, shuffling awkwardly. She hated the way everyone was looking at her. "Um. Here? Now?" She had no idea what he meant by "training," and the feeling in her scars had moved from tingle to ache.

Eldamarr Rinn gave a small chuckle and shook his head. "No, no. Not here. We will go back across the Inland Sea, where the wizards cannot interfere."

Figg, who had been uncharacteristically quiet until this point, readjusted her bow across her shoulders and spoke up. "Well, okay then. You two have fun. Meanwhile, the wizards are already extracting Edira's magic from the Quarry of the Four, so we'd best be going." She started walking back toward the cliff staircase.

Corr reached out and caught Figg by the elbow as she passed him. "And you're going to stop them?"

Figg looked at him with raised eyebrows and tugged her arm loose from his grasp. "Someone's got to."

Eldamarr Rinn walked over and put a hand gently on Figg's shoulder. "Your bravery and determination are admirable." He looked from Figg to Haryk and Emalet. "The elves of the Plains Clan have always been fierce fighters, and we will need all the fighters we can get when the time comes."

****

The hard soles of Vell's boots clicked softly as she walked, the sound reverberating off the polished stone walls. The windows on either side of this hallway in the White Keep were tall but very narrow and didn't let in much sunlight. Not that there was much sunlight today. The clouds were heavy and dark, having thickened since midmorning, bringing with them a brooding, dangerous atmosphere.

It matched Vell's current mood perfectly.

When she reached the heavy double doors, Vell took hold of both handles and wrenched them open. She passed quickly inside, allowing the doors to close behind her with a bang that echoed back down the long hallway.

The room itself was not very large, and Vell strode past the sparse but comfortable furnishings at the far end, where in a corner, atop a wooden pedestal, was a wide bowl made of brushed copper and filled with liquid. Vell placed her hands on either side of the bowl and stared down at her reflection. A few seconds later, her reflection in the liquid began to ripple and blur, and the face of another slowly appeared.

The features of the face were misty and hard to make out, but the voice that echoed up from the bowl was clear. "Well?" the voice said impatiently. "Make your report. Where is she?"

Vell continued to stare into the bowl, her fingertips gripping the edges tightly. "She made it to the Inland Sea. We found the bodies of the wizards that were patrolling the grasslands, all killed by elf arrows. It was an ambush. She must have had help."

The voice from the bowl spoke with a soft but harsh tone. "So you failed. If she is across the Inland Sea, we cannot reach her. The Sacred Stones are still intact enough to prohibit it. And her starlight power will increase as the alignment approaches."

Vell set her jaw, her beautiful dark blue eyes flashing with temper. "I have not failed. My army is already working to extract magical resources from the Quarry of the Four to strengthen Malicath. In fact, we already have enough to transfer in the next few days. Did you forget that I am also an elf, born here on Edira? The movement of the stars into alignment benefits my natural magic as well. And unlike Luma, I have had years to understand it, to learn how to use it as a weapon."

A cold chuckle rippled from the bowl. "Powerful as you are, Luma's starlight, whether she knows it now or not, cannot be matched. Malicath needs all of Edira's magical resources if it is to become the most powerful world in the cosmos, and now, because of our bargain, so do you. Until the Sacred Stones are completely destroyed, we will not be able to access all of what we need. Luma must not be allowed to heal them during the alignment."

Vell took a deep breath, the fingers on her left hand absently rising to scratch at the long scar running down her upper arm. Twelve years later, and that sword wound still itched occasionally.

Pursing her lips, she cocked her head to one side as she looked at the misty face staring up at her from the liquid. "Do not underestimate me as the elves once did. I will draw her out before the alignment, and I will kill her."

****

At the edge of the Inland Sea, it was time for goodbyes. Trill hopped over to Luma. "I shall go now, as I have other matters to which I must attend."

Without waiting for a response, Trill beat his huge wings and launched himself into the air. In a moment, he was up over the lip of the cliff and out of sight, but the others were not as eager to leave.

Corr, Aire, and Elas had all offered to go with Luma and the mage, but Eldamarr Rinn shook his head. "Luma will need all her focus to accomplish what must be done during the alignment. You have journeyed far together, but this part, she must do alone."

After a brief consultation with Figg and Emalet, Haryk stepped forward and suggested that Corr, Aire, and Elas join them at Northhelm. Despite their reservations about Northern Plains Elves, Aire, and Elas were curious to learn more about guerilla warfare, and all three of them accepted, though Corr's gaze kept returning to Luma, his forehead creased with worry and his shoulders tight.

Eldamarr Rinn thanked them all again, then reboarded the boat to make ready to sail. Luma started to follow him, then turned back. She looked at Corr, Aire, and Elas, the back of her eyes burning.

She blinked several times and cleared her throat. "Stay safe, okay?" Her voice shook despite her best efforts to keep it steady.

Corr stepped forward and placed his hand on her shoulder. Luma's head automatically tilted toward the comforting warmth and weight of it, but she caught herself and stopped.

Corr smiled down at her, but sadness shone in his moss green eyes as they roved across Luma's face, as if trying to memorize every detail. "We will keep doing what we need to do, and you learn what you need to learn. When the alignment comes, and we see each other again, we will all be ready."

Luma nodded, trying to feign confidence that she did not feel. "I will be ready." Then, without another word, she turned and walked up the small plank to the ship's deck on shaking legs.

****

Emalet, Figg, and Haryk had already begun climbing the stairs to the top of the cliff, with Aire and Elas following a short distance behind. But Corr remained on the beach. He stood as if rooted to the spot, watching the ship become small as it skimmed across the glistening water of the Inland Sea.

Corr's jaw ticked as his mind flashed back to that night twelve years ago when the smoke had filled the air, and the sounds of war raged through the capital. After he had helped smuggle them out of the besieged city, Corr had watched as King Tarak, Queen Seren, and his friend, their young daughter, disappeared on horseback into the dark forest bound for the Cavern of the Four.

But just when he had thought they had successfully escaped, Corr's relief had turned to horror as he had watched from his hiding place as Vell and a group of wizards followed in pursuit. With no plan and no weapon other than the dagger at his hip, Corr had taken off after them, determined to do anything he could to keep Luma safe.

****

Lost in thought, Corr absently ran his fingers along his right forearm. Twelve years later, and his now-healed bone still ached occasionally. Twelve years later, and here he was again, watching Luma travel away from him as he helplessly hoped for the best. For the future of their world, the stakes had never been higher.

So now, with his heart tight in his chest and his eyes burning, Corr murmured a farewell as he watched the mage's ship, with its precious cargo, recede into the distance. "Protection of the Four go with you, Luma. Until you return."

BOOK TWO

The Question

Chapter 13

Luma stood on the deck of the ship, her hands lightly gripping the railing as she watched the shoreline and its one remaining occupant grow smaller. Luma raised one hand to wave at Corr, but she was already too far away for the gesture to be seen from shore.

Still, she watched until the shoreline was lost behind the softly rolling waves, and a strange feeling that vacillated between excitement and anxiety washed over her. There was no turning back now. What if everyone was mistaken? What if, as she feared, she wasn't their promised hope, the solution that they all thought she was? Or worse, what if she had the power but lacked the strength and courage to do what was required when the time came?

Luma's stomach churned, and her head ached along with the scars on her palms. The waters of the Inland Sea were not salt but fresh and cold, and Luma leaned out over the railing and closed her eyes, relishing the refreshing light spray of water across her face.

Feeling slightly better, Luma opened her eyes and peered into the rushing water below, squinting from the glare. The water was clear and brilliant blue, reflecting the sunlight that sparkled and shimmered over the waves. Then suddenly, the water next to the ship darkened.

Luma leaned farther out, tilting her head for a better look. From just under the waves, a black shape had moved alongside the ship and was keeping pace easily with the fast-moving vessel. Luma's gaze darted back and forth, and a small gasp escaped her lips as she realized that whatever it was beneath the water, it was nearly twice as long as the ship and easily as wide.

Luma gripped the railing with both hands, but as quickly as it had appeared, the black shape dove and, without any disturbance to the water above it, disappeared completely from view. The water alongside the ship returned to its formerly brilliant hue, and the waves rolled on calmly as if nothing had ever been there at all.

Luma turned from the railing just as Eldamarr Rinn approached. She tried to smile, but the churning in her stomach had returned, and the expression she offered was more of a grimace.

The mage looked kindly at her, the corners of his gray eyes crinkling. He reminded Luma of Izarre in the way that he had the aura of someone much older than his physical body suggested. She wondered if all elves were like that. How long did elves normally live, anyway? Were they extremely long-lived, as the storybooks on Earth suggested, and if so, what did that mean for her, being supposedly half-human? Just then, the sound of the mage's voice pulled her back from the brink of becoming lost in her own thoughts, and Luma realized she hadn't comprehended what he had said. The wind picked up around the ship, and a loud rushing sound filled the air.

"Sorry, what did you say?" she asked, raising her voice to be heard over the sound.

Eldamarr Rinn leaned closer so she could hear him.

"I said, we are almost there."

He pointed over her right shoulder, and when Luma turned to follow his line of sight, a small shriek flew unbidden from her mouth.

Just ahead, the crystalline blue waters of the Inland Sea fell away into a thundering waterfall that stretched as far as the eye could see in either direction. And the little ship they were on was careening straight toward the edge.

Luma spun back to face the mage, her eyes wide with panic. Her mind whirled, and she opened her mouth to speak, but the idea that they were about to plunge to their deaths stole her words and kept them beyond reach. Luma gripped the ship's railing with both hands and squeezed her eyes shut as the vessel teetered on the edge of the abyss, and the deafening sound of the falling water filled her ears.

Then she felt the weight of Eldamarr Rinn's hand on her forearm. The thundering sound of the waterfall was gone. Luma opened her eyes and blinked several times.

The mage had a slightly apologetic look on his face. Luma stared at him for a moment, then looked around. The little ship was once again bobbing on calm, clear blue water, slower than before but still moving steadily forward.

Luma turned back to the mage, her eyes wide. He shrugged. "I was going to tell you about that, but we made good progress and got here a little faster than I anticipated." He looked at Luma's shocked expression and smiled apologetically. "Sorry."

Luma regarded him incredulously for a moment before she trusted her voice enough to speak. "What...what *was* that?"

Eldamarr Rinn's smile broadened. "That…oh. That was just a bit of base magic, nothing fancy. An optical and auditory illusion."

Once again, he pointed over Luma's shoulder. She turned skeptically, bracing herself for another shock. Instead, she saw land looming up from the blue water in front of them. An island, both foreboding and beautiful.

A wide beach made of fine black sand, dark as midnight, contrasted with the blue waves that lapped placidly along its edge. Rising directly above the beach was a high, rocky cliff atop which Luma could make out a structure, a large dwelling, or something like it. To the right and left of the beach, vegetation grew—small, scraggly trees surrounded by bushes and the kind of thick, saw-leafed grass that thrives in sandy soils.

A few minutes later, the ship's bow ground to a halt in the shallows of the beach below the cliff.

Luma removed her shoes and stepped onto the beach for the first time. The powder-like black sand shifted beneath her weight and clung stubbornly to the soles of her bare feet. Luma lifted her eyes from the sand at her feet to the sky, where the Four Stars, in their softly jagged line, twinkled down on her.

She took a deep breath. Now, the real work was about to begin.

****

Twilight had settled over the mountains when Trill landed noiselessly in front of the small cottage. Izarre sat cross-legged on a soft mat to the left of the door, her eyes closed, her hands in her lap.

"Hello, Trill." She didn't open her eyes or turn her head.

Trill, having been denied the startled surprise that he

normally elicited with his silent arrivals, preened his chest feathers moodily.

"Luma is with the mage."

Izarre took a deep breath and released it slowly into the gathering darkness. Her shoulders slumped with relief. She opened her eyes and looked gratefully at the large owl.

"Thank you, Trill. There is no one better than Eldamarr Rinn to prepare Luma for what is needed. I only hope that there will be enough time. More of the protective starlight leaks from the Sacred Stones with each passing day. I can feel it."

Trill blinked his amber eyes as he looked back at Izarre. "A group of Plains Clan Elves are fighting a war of disruption against the wizards' efforts to extract magic at the quarry. Corr, Aire, and Elas have joined them, but I fear it is not enough."

Izarre raised her eyebrows at this news. "Corr, Aire, and Elas, with the Plains Clan?"

She paused and turned to face Trill fully. "Of course. It is high time we elves put aside our differences and unite against our common enemy. Many elves on Edira are still scattered and afraid. They need to know that the Daughter of Starlight has returned, that there is hope! That there is, once again, something to fight for."

Trill clacked his large, hooked beak in agreement and flexed his enormous wings. "I will gather the other owls, and we will spread the word." A moment later, he was gone into the night.

Izarre, alone once more, folded her hands back in her lap, but this time, her eyes remained open, and she stared through the darkness up the path that led to the mountain cave.

Deep inside the cavern, the four Sacred Stones stood silent and waiting, bathed in moonlight from the small hole in the high ceiling—their cracks gaping like open wounds.

Chapter 14

"Well, that was awkward." Aire took a bite of flatbread and washed it down with a swig of water from a small cup. "I'm not sure this is such a good idea, Corr."

She, Corr, and Elas were gathered around a rough wooden table in one of the larger rooms in Northhelm that served as a dining room. When they had first arrived, the introductions to the Plains Clan fighters had involved suspicious stares from both parties. There had also been a significant amount of low grumbling on the part of the Plains Elves about these new outsiders taking residence within their secret fortress. Now, a week in, tensions still simmered.

Corr looked up from the bowl of stew he was eating. "They are fighting against the wizards and doing a pretty good job of it. Figg is a natural when it comes to this guerilla warfare stuff." He paused at the look on Aire's face: her lips were pursed, and one of her eyebrows arched skeptically.

Corr shrugged. "I know they are Plains Clan, and I know the rift between the Forest Clan and the Plains Clan runs deep. But I, for one, don't want to sit in hiding and wait for the alignment while the wizards steal Edira's magic. We may not have the power to heal the Sacred Stones like Luma, but we can do something, and this is it."

Aire's eyebrow remained arched for a moment

longer, clearly unimpressed with Corr's speech. She sighed and turned to Elas. "And what do you think, little brother? Can we find common ground with these Plains Clan weirdos?"

Elas shot Aire a reproving look. "Probably not if you keep calling them weirdos." Aire rolled her eyes, but Elas continued. "Forest Clan and Plains Clan have never been great at working together, but in the end, Edira belongs to all of us, and the wizards are trying to exploit it, as they've already done to so much of their own world. If there is a way to fight back until Luma can heal the Sacred Stones and get rid of the wizards for good, then I'm in. And hey," he thrust an accusing finger toward Aire. "Don't call me 'little brother'. You know we're twins, right?"

Aire playfully pinched Elas in the upper arm. "You know full well I was born first. I am a solid three minutes your senior. Older I am. And wiser, too."

Elas batted away Aire's pinching fingers. "Older, maybe. But definitely *not* wiser!" He thought for a moment, then continued. "That Plains Clan Elf, Emalet, she's a good archer. I might ask if she has an extra bow I can use."

Aire smirked and batted her eyelashes dramatically. "Ooh, *little* brother, if you love the Plains Clan so much, you can ask them to give you a tattoo like they all have. Riiiight…here!" She pinched Elas's arm again.

Elas grunted and twisted away, trying to get out of range. "Hey, no way. Never!"

Just then, the door to the dining room bumped open, and Figg walked in, accompanied by Emalet. Corr, who had been trying his best to ignore Aire and Elas's banter, swallowed the last of his stew and looked up. Aire and

Elas looked up as well, and the flush that came to Elas's cheeks when he saw Emalet was not lost on his sister.

Figg, as usual, got right to the point. "Sun's almost down. You coming?"

****

The sunset painted a masterpiece of orange and gold across the western horizon as Corr, Aire, and Elas joined a small party of Plains Clan Elves and set out for the quarry.

They moved silently through their surroundings with the grace that comes naturally to all elves, and before long, the group had settled undetected amongst the rocks and bushes that ringed the quarry edge.

Figg peered down into the quarry basin, where a large number of wizards had gathered. Her keen gaze roved right and left, carefully taking in the scene below. Gathered in the center of the wizard group was a cluster of about a dozen crystal canisters. Inside each canister was a substance, not quite liquid, not quite solid, but slowly shifting and glowing a creamy white—raw magic extracted from Edira's core.

Figg's eyes narrowed, and her fingers strayed toward the hilt of the dagger at her hip. Then she felt a light pressure on her arm and glanced backward. Her gaze collided with Emalet's, who shook her head warningly. Figg took a deep breath, and her fingers retreated from the dagger hilt. She turned back toward the wizards, who were conversing with each other in low tones. Figg motioned to the group to get closer.

Slowly, carefully, the elves descended the hill, taking care to remain undetected by the wizards below. They concealed themselves once again amongst the rocks and bushes, this time close enough to hear.

"I'm not sure it's going to work," one wizard muttered.

Another wizard to his left shrugged and tilted his head from side to side as if weighing options. "It could work. I think it's doable, but we need to make sure that we can sustain the connection to Malicath long enough to make the transfer."

A wizard from across the group chimed in. "There are enough of us to force a bridge to Malicath." He gestured toward the cluster of canisters. "And with Vell's power, we can hold it long enough for a transfer."

"That's right, Naro. My power can easily hold a bridge long enough to transfer this magic."

Vell walked over with grace and confidence—her polished staff held loosely in her left hand. Coming to a stop in front of the crystal canisters, she stooped and picked one up, admiring its softly glowing contents.

"Beautiful, isn't it? And such a waste to allow raw magic like this to simply exist, untapped in the ground." Vell shook her head as if in sadness. "But now that it has been freed from its prison here on Edira, it will soon be put to good use, strengthening Malicath."

Carefully she placed the canister back on the ground with the others, then turned to face the rest of the group of wizards. "This quarry has the strongest potential bridge link outside of the Cavern of the Four. We will gather here at dusk in three days to make the transfer. In the meantime, collect more if you can, and put a lock spell on these canisters so they can't be tampered with before we start the transfer. Naro, you come with me." Vell turned and headed back in the direction of the White Keep, with Naro following obediently behind.

Figg motioned with her hand, and the small group

of elves melted silently backward into the surrounding darkness, away from the gathering of wizards and the canisters of stolen magic.

Once they were back up the hill and out of earshot, Figg gathered the others around, her voice strained with suppressed anger. "They've already extracted more of Edira's magic than I had anticipated. The approaching alignment must make the magic easier to get to." She shook her head. "We can't get past the lock spell, so we will have to wait. Still, we know what their plan is, so that's good."

Aire's voice piped up from the back of the group. "Yeah, we know their plan, but what are we going to do?"

Figg's mouth curled into a smile. "We are going to stop them."

****

It was fully dark when Vell and Naro arrived back at the White Keep and walked into the large room where Vell had interrogated Luma.

The window that Corr had been thrown from was still broken, and Vell stood in front of it, staring into the night, while the sound of the rushing River Aque far below filled the room. Her silvery white hair blew up and around her face. Naro came and stood near her, not too close, but near enough.

After a moment, Vell turned toward him, and her lovely, deep blue eyes flashed in the light of the torches that burned from wall brackets around the room.

"Those elves continue to make things difficult. What news do you have for me?"

Naro tried his best to sound confident. "I believe we are getting closer to figuring out where their hiding place is. Shouldn't be long now."

Vell prowled back and forth in front of the open window. "Good. We don't have long. I want that group of troublemakers found and made an example of before the alignment. We can't get to Luma now that she is across the Inland Sea, but if we can get to her new 'friends,' that'll be good enough. That way, we stop their disturbance of our work and potentially bring their precious Daughter of Starlight out of hiding and back where she is vulnerable." Vell's fingertips made a soft clicking noise as she drummed them along the edge of her staff.

Naro nodded. "We are investigating possible locations of their home base. Once we find it, I will report back to you immediately."

****

Back at Northhelm, Figg briefed the other elves about the wizards' plan to force open a bridge and transfer stolen magic from Edira to Malicath. The news was met first with surprise, then anger, and plans for how to stop it lasted well past midnight.

Still, Figg, Haryk, and Emalet were up early the next morning, Figg with a smile on her face and a glint in her eye, her small body practically radiating with the potential for violence.

Elas was up early too and watched Figg as he filled a quiver with newly fletched arrows. He caught Emalet's attention as she walked past.

"She's an eager one," Elas remarked, nodding toward Figg, "for one so young."

Emalet glanced at Figg, then returned her gaze to Elas and shrugged.

"That one is older in spirit than she is in years. It has

made her a fierce fighter, and we are glad for it, but a childhood lost is no blessing."

Elas cocked his head to one side, not quite understanding, so Emalet took a seat next to him and picked up another quiver to be filled, sighing sadly.

"It was not long after the capital fell, and the wizards were still hunting for the child—the Daughter of Starlight. The bodies of King Tarak and his human queen were found in the Cavern of the Four, but the child wasn't, so the wizards thought it was all a distraction, and perhaps the child had been hidden amongst the Plains Clan. At least, that was their excuse for killing so many of us."

Emalet shook her head, her shoulders drooping under the weight of grief and loss, still heavy after twelve years. Elas was about to place a comforting hand on her arm but changed his mind at the last minute. He fumbled awkwardly with his quiver.

Glancing at Elas again, Emalet continued, keeping her voice low.

"The wizards attacked a small Plains Clan settlement. Afterward, we found Figg amidst the ruins of what had been her family home. She was clutching a knife and sitting beside the bodies of her father, mother, and older brother, all of whom had been killed by battle magic. She was so young, so small, and she had battle magic wounds all over her body. With injuries like that, she should have been dead too, but a need for revenge does wonders for one's will to live." She cocked her head at Elas. "There were two wizards also in the home when we arrived. They had been stabbed to death."

Emalet nodded at the stunned look on Elas's face. "Ever since then, Figg has been uniquely driven by her hatred of wizards. I mean, we all want them gone, and we've all lost loved ones, friends, and homes since the Sacred Stones were cracked. But, for Figg...she was so young to have seen and done such things. It's just..." Emalet paused as if searching for the right word but couldn't find it. She sighed. "It's different for Figg. Not all wounds are physical, and sometimes those wounds are created too early and inflicted too deeply to be healed. She has a brilliant mind for strategy and is one of the fiercest fighters I have ever seen. But for that, she paid, and continues to pay, a bitter price."

Emalet put down the now full quiver of arrows next to the one that Elas had been working on. Then she placed her slender, tattooed hand atop his, and Elas's heart thumped erratically in his chest.

Emalet smiled at him. "Soon, we will put our plan into action at the quarry. Let us hope Figg's 'eagerness,' as you put it, will see us through the day."

Chapter 15

"Again."

For the third time in ten minutes, Luma pushed herself up from the beach, wiping black sand from the side of her cheek. Eldamarr Rinn stood a short distance away, a slender, smoothly polished wand held loosely in his right hand. When he saw her rise, he raised his arm and pointed the wand at her.

"Focus."

"I am focus-aargh!"

Luma's breath rushed from her lungs as another small blast hit her in the side of the rib cage. Flailing her arms, she stumbled backward but remained standing until another blast sent her sprawling once again into the sand.

This time, instead of waiting for her to rise, the elf mage advanced. Luma grunted in surprise and scrambled backward, her heart pounding at the possibility of taking another hit, this time at close range.

"Wait! I'm not ready!" Luma hated how scared her voice sounded in her ears.

Eldamarr Rinn kept advancing. "The wizards will not wait. If you fall, they will never allow you to get back up." The wand was pointed directly at her chest, and Eldamarr Rinn's normally soft voice cracked like a whip. "Focus!"

"I...I..." Luma continued to scramble backward on

all fours, her hands and feet slipping awkwardly on the shifting sand.

The end of the wand glowed menacingly, and cold fear coursed through Luma's body. Just as another blast launched from the end of the wand, she threw up one hand in front of her. A sharp crackle split the air as the light that streamed from Luma's palm hit the pulse of base magic from the wand and deflected it to the side. Eldamarr Rinn stopped advancing.

Luma, still sitting on the sand, clutched her stomach as familiar waves of nausea rolled through her. Her vision blurred in and out, and her hands shook violently. Eldamarr Rinn placed his hand on her trembling shoulder.

Luma looked up at him, blinking several times in an effort to clear her vision.

"I did it."

The mage nodded slowly. "Yes, Luma, but fear is not the same as focus. The reason you feel sick after using your starlight is because you are actively working against it. There is so much power in you, but with that also comes much chaos. Starlight is extremely volatile, so you must learn to channel it calmly for your own sake. Only then will you be strong enough to stand against the wizards and heal the Sacred Stones."

Luma lowered her eyes, her shoulders slumping. "I didn't ask for this."

Eldamarr Rinn offered his hand to help Luma up, his voice gentle once again. "No, my dear. But know this: you said that Vell told you your power was an accident of birth, but that is not true. The Four Stars chose you for a reason, and they are *never* wrong."

Luma made a quiet, derisive snort and avoided the

mage's eyes as shame brought an ache to her heart. "I am not strong enough. And I have never been."

The mage tilted his head as his eyes sought hers, but Luma kept them downcast. "You are much stronger than you think. And remember, Luma, strength comes in many forms."

Luma took the mage's hand and stood up on shaking legs, then paused to wipe the fine, black sand off her pants and the back of her tunic.

Eldamarr Rinn gestured toward the building atop the cliff. "Shall we go and have some lunch?"

Luma smiled but shook her head. "You go ahead. I want to walk for a bit."

The mage nodded and, tucking the wand back into his pocket, began the hike up to the top of the cliff. Luma watched him go for a moment, then turned and began trudging down the beach. Stopping after a short distance to remove her shoes, Luma walked along the shoreline, gasping as the icy cold water of the Inland Sea reached out to lap the edges of her bare feet.

She walked farther than she had before during the week she had been on the island, and as always, Luma enjoyed exploring. After a while, the black sand ended, and a jumble of boulders crowded together amidst the trees and shrubby bushes along the shoreline. Luma put her shoes back on and climbed onto the rocks, careful not to slip on the ones that had been dampened by the splashing waves. As she scrambled up and farther inland, the rushing sound of a waterfall in the distance caught her attention.

Jumping skillfully from boulder to boulder, Luma made her way farther into the interior of the island. A short distance in, the jumble of boulders gave way to scrubby grass surrounded on three sides by high rocky cliffs, over one side of which a wide waterfall poured down into a small pool below.

It was a beautiful scene, but the waterfall itself was what caught Luma's eye, for though at first glance, it appeared to be normal, the more she looked at it, the more she realized it wasn't normal at all. The water cascading over the cliff did not do so in a flowing rush, like regular free-falling water, but in an organized pattern. Individual streams of water fell in nearly straight rows so that altogether, the water itself resembled the bars of a cage. Luma tilted her head and took a step closer, the sound of her shoes muffled by the thick, scrubby grass. Then, her focus shifted from the waterfall itself to the area immediately behind it.

It was dark behind the falls but with more depth than the walls of the surrounding cliffs. A cave, perhaps? Luma took another step. Then, there was movement from within the darkness. A glint of reflection on the water and a large something shifted in the shadows, just behind the bar-like water of the falls. The scars on Luma's palms began to ache and throb in a way that they had not since she had first been called back to Edira.

Caught off guard by the intensity of the aching, Luma stumbled backward, gritting her teeth. She clenched her hands into fists, her nails biting into the flesh of her palms, as she continued to retreat away from the waterfall until, finally, the pain in her scars began to ebb.

Luma glanced at the low position of the sun and realized she had been gone longer than she had anticipated. As she made her way carefully back across the boulders toward the beach, she couldn't help turning to take one last look at the strange waterfall, wondering what secret it was keeping hidden behind it.

****

That night, at the dwelling atop the cliff, Luma and Eldamarr Rinn shared a simple dinner on the narrow balcony that overlooked the beach while the setting sun painted the black sand with a wide brush of red and gold.

The mage watched Luma out of the corner of his eye. "What is on your mind, Luma? You may speak."

Luma took her eyes off the magnificent sunset and turned to face him. She hesitated at first, then sighed as if making up her mind.

"Are you a wizard?"

Eldamarr Rinn chuckled softly. "No, Luma, I am an elf."

Luma cocked her head at him, unconvinced. "You can be both, you know." She challenged, "Vell is. She told me."

Eldamarr Rinn nodded, a sad smile crinkling the corners of his eyes in the dim light. "What Vell told you is true. The wizards of Malicath are a race, but their power can also be learned by those who already possess a unique, natural affinity for wielding magic. All those born on the world of Malicath have magic naturally, and they also take from Malicath itself to further enhance their powers. The elven race here on Edira is not naturally magical, except in very rare circumstances. We could use the raw magic within our world to enhance ourselves, but such a thing is abhorrent to elven culture. Edira may be the most magical world in the cosmos, but elves believe that their role is to be stewards of magic, not consumers of it. The wizards, however, feel differently."

Luma watched Eldamarr Rinn as he spoke, the silvery white streak in his hair clearly visible in the fading light. He saw where she was looking and raised his hand, lightly running his fingertips through his hair. He smiled at her.

"The mark of a mage, my dear. Still fully elf."

Luma returned her gaze to the sunset. The waters of the Inland Sea undulated beneath a slowly rising half-moon.

"Vell said you trained her." In her periphery, Eldamarr Rinn nodded.

"Yes. Well, I tried to. At my home in the forests surrounding Aquea." He sighed sadly. "Back then, I had never seen such talent, such innate affinity for wielding magic. Such unbridled ambition." He looked over at Luma.

She returned his gaze, and the eyes that met hers were full of sadness as he continued.

"Vell had the makings of an unparalleled elf mage— my perfect protégé. But…" he paused and shook his head. "Elf mages are first and foremost stewards of Edira and its magic. It soon became clear to me that Vell had no desire to be a caretaker. She wanted only to use Edira's magic for herself, to enhance and expand her many natural gifts. I indulged her at first, thinking that she would soon have enough. But I was wrong. It only fueled her greed. It was never enough. When I tried to tell her that she must stop using Edira's magic for herself, she refused any more of my training."

Eldamarr Rinn shook his head again. "By this time, you had been born during the Alignment of The Four, and word of the Daughter of Starlight's power had reached the wizards on Malicath. Starlight is the most powerful of all magics—and it cannot be learned. It must be bestowed. The wizards had been trying to invade Edira and steal its magic for years, and, using her ambition as leverage, they convinced Vell to help them. Once they had Vell on their side, the wizards knew that you would be the only one capable of stopping them. With her powerful natural ability, combined with the training I had already given her, Vell was able to crack the Sacred Stones that protected this world. The result was catastrophic. There was so much death…" Regret brought a heaviness to Eldamarr Rinn's voice. He paused and took a steadying breath before continuing. "And it was my fault, Luma. I'm so sorry."

"Is that why you live here alone, in exile?" Luma's voice was small in the gathering darkness.

The mage shook his head. "I came here shortly after Vell refused to continue with her training, but I didn't know that she had succeeded in cracking the Sacred Stones until after the battle was already lost." He ran his hands through his hair once again. "I knew that Vell was ambitious, ruthless, even. But I truly never thought she would betray Edira."

Luma reached out and laid her hand on the mage's forearm. "It wasn't your fault."

Eldamarr Rinn smiled, but sorrow clung to the edges of the expression. He patted the top of Luma's hand. "The night grows late, my dear. You should get some rest, and we will continue your training tomorrow." He looked up at the sky, where high above, the Four Stars twinkled over them, their jagged line looking straighter by the day. "After all," he continued, "the alignment…"

"Waits for no one." Luma interrupted and finished the sentence for him. "So I've been told."

****

That night, as Luma lay in her bed, listening to the sound of waves against the beach, she realized that she had forgotten to ask Eldamarr Rinn about the strange waterfall she had discovered on the interior of the island. She made a mental note to bring it up with him tomorrow before her training began.

"Focus," she whispered to herself as a delicate tingle ran across the scars on her palms. "Don't fight it. Just focus." And when she closed her eyes, she could still see the Four Stars, dancing ever closer together, ever closer to the moment of truth.

Luma clenched her teeth and her fists. She couldn't let them all down. She wouldn't.

Chapter 16

Back on the mainland, the morning dawned misty and cool. Birds, whose voices normally heralded the early hours, hunkered down in their nests, their songs unsung. Heavy fog caressed the trunks of trees and swirled around the base of the rocky cliff that was the façade of Northhelm.

Aire turned from a slit in the rock that served as a window. "Wow, the fog is thick this morning."

From across the room, Figg looked up from her meal and shrugged. "It will be gone by midday, so it won't hinder us at the quarry. Don't worry."

Aire arched a single eyebrow in Figg's direction. "I'm not worried."

Figg met Aire's eyes evenly. "Good."

Figg's prediction turned out to be correct, and by midday, the fog was gone, replaced by high, puffy clouds and filtered sunshine. A soft breeze from the west tickled the forest's upper canopy.

****

The day progressed, and as the sun began to dip, Figg and the other elves from Northhelm took up unseen positions along the edge of the quarry, armed with bows and quivers of arrows whose tips had been carefully coated in Fireburn plant oil. Below them, Naro and the other wizards gathered, unaware that they were being watched.

Figg glanced at the soft glow along the western horizon and then back down to the quarry below. Her breath caught in her chest as she saw Vell stride gracefully toward the group of wizards. Figg glanced to her right and left, and the grim faces of the other elves told her that they had seen the wizard leader, too. A shiver of anticipation ran up Figg's spine, and the corners of her mouth lifted slightly. It was almost time.

Vell and the other wizards moved into a tight circle, standing shoulder-to-shoulder around the crystal canisters. The raw magic trapped inside swirled placidly, softly glowing.

At Vell's direction, the wizards shifted their staffs so that every other one was pointed either upward at the sky or downward facing the canisters. Their lips began to move, but they made no sound, the incantation silent but clearly powerful. The end of their staffs began to glow, softly at first, then brighter.

Figg watched through narrowed eyes as an orb of blue light began to form around the stolen magic from the staffs that pointed downward. At the same time, blue light gathered between the staffs pointing upward. It grew in intensity until, directly above them, a wide blue circle had formed. The threshold of a bridge to Malicath.

Out of the corner of her eye, Figg saw Haryk fidgeting, his hands straying toward the shaft of an arrow in his quiver. Figg caught his eye and gave her head a firm shake, mouthing quietly. *"Not yet. Wait for the link."*

Haryk set his jaw and nodded back. But he didn't have long to wait.

Vell stepped between two of the other wizards and positioned her staff so that the end of it was midway between the canisters on the ground and the portal above them. Then she, too, began a silent incantation, and a wide shaft of blue light began reaching down from the circle toward the orb surrounding the canisters. As the shaft made contact with the top of the orb, the canisters began to quiver.

Vell wrapped both her hands around her staff to hold it steady, intensely focused on the link between the threshold and the canisters, her eyes gleaming with impending success.

"*Now!*"

At Figg's yell, the elves surrounding the quarry arose in unison, and in an instant, the still evening air hummed with the sound of arrows zipping downward.

Four of the wizards that were creating the threshold bridge went down, elf arrows protruding from their chests. Another wizard was grazed in the upper arm, but the Fireburn plant oil on the arrowhead worked its way into what would have been a simple flesh wound, and the victim was soon writhing in agony as his skin began to blister.

The threshold bridge above the canisters flickered and faded as the wizards chaotically responded to the new threat. Naro threw himself to the ground behind a small boulder just as an elven arrow whistled past his head.

Vell vented her anger in a scream as she saw the threshold disappear. Eyes blazing, she skillfully dodged an arrow meant for her heart and pointed her staff at the quarry ledge. The powerful blast of the battle magic hit the ledge with a small explosion, and Vell smiled as the cries of injured elves quickly followed. Two more blasts at different areas around the quarry edge reaped similar results, and Vell's smile widened.

"Fight back, you fools!" Vell screamed to the wizards around her. "They are along the edges of the quarry!"

Having gotten over the initial shock of the surprise attack, the wizards began firing back, their battle magic wreaking havoc on the walls of the quarry and the elves that were positioned there.

Figg cursed through clenched teeth. The element of surprise was gone, as was their advantage.

Corr, Aire, and Emalet were pinned behind a large boulder directly above where the canisters were grouped. They worked together, taking turns firing their arrows and then ducking behind the boulder to reload. Aire watched Emalet out of the corner of her eye as the Plains Clan Elf stood bravely and loosed another shaft with deadly accuracy. She grudgingly admitted to herself that Elas had been right. Emalet was indeed a skilled archer. Still, Aire knew they couldn't keep this up for long: one well-aimed blast of battle magic would be all it took.

Figg ran up, keeping her head low and bleeding from a gash along her cheekbone, Elas and Haryk on her heels. They all crouched behind the boulder, and Figg nodded to Aire, Corr, and Emalet. "Time to go, elves. You all spread out and give the order to retreat."

Elas, Haryk, and Emalet nodded and, keeping low, hurried off in opposite directions around the rim of the quarry.

Corr and Aire lingered behind, and Aire cocked her head at Figg. "And what about you?"

Figg gave her a small smile. "Before I go, I'm going to release that stolen magic back where it belongs."

Corr and Aire exchanged glances. "We are with

you."

Figg nodded, and the three of them began a scrambling descent, while above, the rest of the elves kept the wizards pinned down by firing the last of the arrows to cover their retreat.

In the chaos of the fight, the canisters had been left unguarded. Figg dropped to her knees and began unfastening their tops as quickly as she could.

From his hiding place, Naro could see that the elves were withdrawing. He got up and moved quietly out of the quarry after them, taking great care to keep enough distance to remain unseen and out of arrow range.

Figg had gotten one of the canisters open. She upended it on the ground and smiled with satisfaction as the contents poured out. It spread like molasses over the ground and then began to seep into the rocks, still glowing softly.

"Hey! Wha…"

Aire fired at the wizard who had spotted them, and his shout of alarm reduced to a gurgle as her arrow buried itself in his chest.

Corr nocked a shaft to his bow, his face grim. "We're out of time."

Aire slung her bow over her shoulder and dropped down next to where Figg was feverishly working. She grabbed another canister from the pile. "Hold them off just another minute, Corr. We can do this."

Figg shot Aire a grateful glance as she released more of the stolen magic back into the ground.

There was a crash above them, and rock fragments rained down over their heads. Aire screamed and threw up her hands as shards of stone battered her and Figg. She looked up through watering eyes and saw Vell approaching, her beautiful face contorted with rage, and her staff leveled at Corr. Corr stood his ground and released his arrow, but Vell dodged easily to one side, and the shaft soared harmlessly past.

Vell smirked and aimed her staff, but before the deadly battle magic burst from its end, Figg launched herself forward. Vell grunted and stumbled backward as Figg's shoulder hit her in the side of the torso.

Figg tumbled to one side and rolled to a crouch on the sandy ground. Vell growled in rage and swung around to take aim once again at Corr, but Figg leaped up and threw a handful of sand into Vell's face just as the battle magic burst from the end of her staff. Vell's hand automatically jerked upward, and the blast from her staff flew off course. It missed Corr, but instead, the battle magic crashed directly into the group of opened canisters—and went off like a bomb.

Aire, Figg, Corr, and Vell were all within the blast zone.

Corr was tossed upward. He slammed halfway up the quarry wall and slid down into a limp heap. Aire and Figg were thrown far to the left, just past the entrance to the quarry, where they came to a rolling stop a short distance apart in the surrounding long grass, both unconscious.

Vell was knocked onto her back, the air forced from her lungs in a painful whoosh as she hit the stony ground. She lay there, gasping, her ears ringing and her eyes watering, trying desperately to convince her spasming lungs to refill. After a few harrowing moments, she finally managed to take small gulps of air, but it was another several minutes before she was able to move.

Reaching her arms out on either side of her body,

Vell searched until her fingertips felt the familiar smooth polished wood of her staff. With a sigh of relief, she slowly, painfully pushed herself up to sitting. Warmth trickled down the side of her neck, and Vell put a hand to her head, then pulled it back to find her fingers stained with a dark smear of blood. A deep pain throbbed from behind her eyes, and she closed them for a second while mustering her incredible willpower for the strength to stand.

Blinking several times to clear her vision, Vell took in the scene around her in a half-daze. Throughout the quarry, wizards leveled by the explosion lay strewn where they were thrown, all in varying states of injury and confusion. The spot where the canisters had been was now a small crater in the floor of the quarry. Its sides were blackened, and curls of blueish-gray smoke wafted upward like angry specters.

Rage churned in Vell's stomach, and she muttered several colorful wizard and elf curses as she scanned the devastated area, searching for those responsible for ruining her plan.

But there were no elves in sight. Wait. Vell took an unsteady step forward, stopped, then took another. Slowly, she skirted the small crater and approached a limp figure at the base of the quarry wall. A grim smile played on Vell's lips as she looked down at Corr's unconscious form. *Got one.*

Vell motioned to a pair of wizards who were sitting in a daze a short distance away. "Irdil, Aegrond! Get over here and help me with this elf. Bind him quickly before he regains consciousness. He's coming with us to the White Keep."

****

Several hours later, Figg stirred in the tall grass, and her eyes fluttered open. Groaning, she blinked a few times to make sure she was really awake—such was the complete darkness that surrounded her. Her entire body was stiff and sore, and her head throbbed. Figg wiped her eyes with the back of her hand, then, grunting with exertion, rolled onto one side and pushed herself up to sitting. Even from a seated position, Figg swayed as bursts of light flashed in her periphery, and waves of dizziness overwhelmed her senses.

A groan came from somewhere to her left, and Figg startled before suddenly, the memories of what had happened came flooding back.

"Aire? Aire?" Figg groped around next to her in the darkness until her hands finally came into contact with a figure lying a short distance away. "Aire! It's me, Figg. Are you hurt? Can you move?"

Out of the darkness, Aire's voice was weak and raspy. "Figg? Is that you? Where are we?" The sound of the rustling grass told Figg that Aire was also sitting up.

Figg's smile of relief sounded in her voice as she responded, "We are just outside the quarry, I think." Figg carefully got to her feet, then reached down toward where Aire was sitting. "We need to get back to Northhelm. Can you stand?"

Aire clasped Figg's forearm with her hand. "I think so...oww!" Aire let go and sat heavily back down with a grimace. "It's my ankle. I must have hurt it when I landed. That was some explosion!" She paused and gasped. "Corr! Where is Corr? Is he here, too?" Panic rose in her voice as she twisted and turned in the darkness, searching in vain. "Corr? Are you there?"

Figg crouched next to Aire. "Shh! Aire, we must be

quiet. I don't know if there are still wizards around. But Corr isn't here. I...I don't know where he is."

Figg gently slung Aire's arm across her narrow shoulders. She tried to sound both comforting and confident. "It's not safe here. We've got to get back to Northhelm before dawn. Maybe Corr already made it there and is waiting for us. And the others, too."

Aire gritted her teeth in pain as Figg hauled her upright, then did her best to limp forward, loathe to put too much weight on Figg's small frame. She swallowed hard, trying, and failing to keep the sob out of her voice as she spoke. "I hope so."

Chapter 17

The first thing Corr noticed was the pain in his head. The second was the pain in his ribs when he tried to move. The third was his location: the cells below the White Keep.

Corr's long groan of defeat was followed by immediate regret as pain coursed through his battered ribs. He put a hand up and felt a large, tender lump on the back of his head. His lips were cracked and parched.

"Here."

The voice came from the cell next to his. Corr peered through the dim light at the thick bars that separated his cell from the other. A hand holding a large canteen was thrust through the narrow space between the bars. Corr stared at it, and the hand jiggled the canteen, eliciting a soft sloshing noise.

"It's okay. It's just water."

The voice sounded familiar, but Corr couldn't place it until a face appeared on the other side of the bars.

Corr blinked, barely believing his eyes. "Ruvyn?"

The wizard smiled sadly. "I thought you looked familiar. I freed you and your friends from these very cells not long ago, and yet here you are again."

Corr took the offered canteen and gratefully drank, then handed it back between the bars. "Yeah. There was a…mishap at the quarry. Thanks for the water."

Ruvyn took the canteen, then slumped onto the floor

next to the bars and leaned against the stone wall at the back of his cell.

"So, it's true then. From the whispers I picked up on from down here, a group of some elves have been disrupting Vell's efforts to extract and transfer raw magic from Edira to Malicath." He shook his silver-haired head in frustration. "It doesn't have to be this way between our worlds."

Corr regarded Ruvyn through the bars. His clothes and hair were disheveled, and his face was thinner than Corr remembered. "What happened to you?" he asked cautiously.

Ruvyn snorted. "Vell suspected that someone helped the elf prisoners and Luma escape last time. I was the natural culprit, of course, given my previous oppositions, and in the end, I could not deny it."

Corr furrowed his brow. "Oppositions?"

Ruvyn glanced at Corr through the bars and arched an eyebrow, indignation creeping into his tone. "We wizards are not all the same, you know. There are some of us, a small number, to be sure, but some that didn't think it was right to invade Edira. To steal magic. We have enough magic on Malicath to support ourselves if we use it wisely. I have been leading the campaign for conservation and restraint for years, but those in power will not listen. They only want more. More magic for Malicath, more power for themselves. They've gotten so used to excess that they can't see beyond it. But all it does is bring conflict and war."

Corr took in this information with quiet surprise, his mind whirling. This was not what he had always been told about the wizards of Malicath. He was about to ask more questions when the door that led to the cells opened with a scrape and a groan.

Immediately, both Ruvyn and Corr shifted to opposite ends of their respective cells. Vell strode confidently down the hall toward them. Her beautiful face wore a look of pity, but her deep blue eyes burned with malice.

She stopped in front of Corr's cell. "Well. Hello again, elf. I thought you looked somewhat familiar when we dragged you back here. How in the name of Stars did you manage to survive that nasty fall into the River Aque?" Her voice rang with mock sincerity. "Oh well, no matter. Welcome back." She smirked at Corr through the bars, and he glared back at her with unreserved hatred.

Vell returned his gaze coolly, then shifted toward the other cell. She reached for a staff that Corr hadn't noticed at first leaning up against the wall opposite the cells. What he did notice immediately, however, was how Ruvyn flinched when she picked it up.

Corr moved away from the front of his cell, determined not to let on that he and Ruvyn knew each other, lest Vell try to use that against them. If Vell noticed Corr's movement, she didn't acknowledge it. She stared through the bars of Ruvyn's cell, the staff held lightly in her right hand.

"It is painful, isn't it? For a wizard to be separated from their staff." Her voice had regained its tone of mock sincerity. "But it is even more painful when this happens."

Vell closed her fingers tightly around the top end of the staff, her fingernails digging in. A sickly, bluish-green glow began to emanate from beneath her hand as she squeezed, her mouth curling in fiendish satisfaction.

In his cell, Ruvyn writhed as if in agony, gritting his teeth. From the far edge of his own cell, Corr watched in horrified fascination, unable to look away.

After a moment, Vell released her grip, revealing splintered wood and deep, half-moon indents left by her fingernails. Hairline cracks now marred the finely polished wood, running in chaotic lines down the length of the staff.

Ruvyn stumbled forward and collapsed onto all fours. Vell laughed, the soft gentleness of the sound misaligned with the situation and the tortured wizard in front of her. Tilting her head, she crouched and looked at Ruvyn with glittering blue eyes.

"This is what happens when you oppose me. And this is still much less than you deserve. How does it feel to be a traitor to your race, your world?"

Ruvyn lifted his head; his eyes were red-rimmed but flashing with defiance. "Everything I do is for my race, for my world! You will bring nothing but ruin to Malicath!" His voice shook slightly, and he collapsed fully onto the floor of the cell.

Vell sneered down at him. "You always have had such misplaced ambition. It's pathetic." She laughed coldly this time. "You are lucky that I don't just break your staff and be done with you." Vell paused, her gaze flicking from the staff in her hand then back over to Ruvyn's prone form. "Soon enough, traitor. Soon enough."

She leaned the staff back up against the wall opposite the cells and turned toward Corr once again. "And you, dear elf. You have a very special role to play in all this now that we have you here. You are going to tell me where that band of so-called 'resistance' fighters are hiding so I can deal with them at the source, once and for all."

Despite the ache it sent through his ribs, Corr charged forward, his fists clenched and his face flushed with anger. He glared at Vell through the bars as he spat out one word. "Never."

Vell rolled her eyes upward and let out a long sigh as if she were dealing with an overly dramatic child. "*Never,*" she mocked, giggling. "Oh, my dear. Never is a very long time, you know. So much longer than you are going to get." She smiled sweetly at him. "See you again soon." Then she turned away, her long, silvery hair shining even in the dim light. With a creak and a groan of the door, she was gone.

****

Corr rushed to the side of his cell and reached a hand through the bars. He prodded at Ruvyn's elbow with his fingertips. "Ruvyn? Hey. Are you all right? She's gone."

Ruvyn groaned, his arms trembling as he pushed himself up from the floor of the cell.

Corr stared at him with both relief and puzzlement. "What was that with your...staff?" The word felt odd in his mouth.

Ruvyn shakily picked up the canteen and took a small swig. He offered it again to Corr, who shook his head, still waiting for a reply.

Ruvyn swallowed and took a few deep breaths before explaining. "As soon as we come of age, all wizards on Malicath are physically bound to their staffs. The staff is a conduit for our magic, but it is also a connection—a bond of body, spirit, and magic woven together. Once the bond is made, all the life-force magic that resides naturally within the wizard flows to the staff.

We are dependent on them—not only for use in wielding our magic—but for our very lives. If a wizard is killed, their staff disappears, and if a wizard is physically separated from their staff, they are weakened and…uncomfortable."

Ruvyn paused and looked over at Corr with bloodshot eyes. Then he continued. "And if a staff is broken, the wizard that is bound to it dies."

Corr's eyebrows hit his hairline. He had never heard that before.

Ruvyn gave him a small smile as if hearing Corr's thoughts. "Yeah, we don't exactly advertise that fact to our enemies." He shrugged. "Plus, it is really hard to do. It takes someone with incredible power to be able to break a wizard's staff."

Corr lowered his head, his stomach churning. "Vell?"

"Yes." Ruvyn's answer through the bars was quiet, almost resigned. "Vell. And Luma."

****

Sunrises across the Inland Sea are spectacular. The undulating water shimmered, reflecting the shades of deep red and brilliant orange. Even the black sands of the beach sparkled as if made from billions of tiny diamonds.

Luma didn't see any of it.

She stood in the sand just above the waterline, hands spread in front of her, palms facing a long, flat rock that had been erected before her. A thick, charcoal line had been drawn down its center.

The mage stood to Luma's left, wand in hand. He nodded to her.

"Breathe, focus, begin."

Luma took a deep breath and exhaled slowly,

focusing her eyes on the charcoal line. The scars on her palms ached, and she clenched her jaw.

"Don't fight it." The mage's voice seemed to come from far away, even though Luma knew he was standing right beside her.

Don't fight it. The words echoed in her mind.

Luma took another deep breath. The scars that crisscrossed her palms began to glow. Another breath. White light shot forward from her palms, and Luma took an involuntary step backward but quickly recovered, digging her feet deeper into the fine, black sand. She moved her hands closer together so that the stream of light was focused on the charcoal line.

Another breath, shallower this time.

Luma moved her hands in unison, slowly drawing the light up the line, removing the charcoal as it went. The ache in her scars increased, and heat simmered through her body, burning as if her very blood was on fire. Barely halfway up the rock, sweat began to bead along her temples.

Another breath, which was more of a gasp. Drops of blood trickled from her ears.

Luma's hands began to shake uncontrollably, and suddenly, a wild blast of light pulsed outward. Luma was thrown back as the blast hit the rock and blew it apart. Then the light was gone. Luma lay on her back where she had landed for a second, then turned to one side and vomited into the shallows.

Eldamarr Rinn leaned over, his face a mask of concern. "Are you all right?"

Luma continued to dry-heave for several minutes, unable to stop herself. Finally, she took a shuddering breath and wiped her mouth, her face flushed with embarrassment. "I'm fine. Let's try again." Her voice cracked.

The mage shook his head. "No, Luma, let us rest. Here." He handed her a stone cup filled with tea. Luma took the cup gratefully with shaking hands, enjoying the soothing warmth it brought to her palms. Together, she and Eldamarr Rinn sat at the base of the cliff.

Luma scowled at the flat rock, which now lay in several broken pieces a short distance away. Her shoulders slumped. "Only halfway."

The mage nodded. "But that is better than yesterday. You are making progress, Luma."

Luma raised her eyes skyward to where the Four Stars twinkled overhead. "But not fast enough."

Eldamarr Rinn said nothing, and his silence confirmed to Luma that she was right. She hung her head.

The mage placed a comforting hand on her shoulder. "The chaos level in your starlight is becoming more potent as the alignment draws nearer. It would be a lot for anyone to handle. If we had had more time, I could have slowly prepared you for this, but time is running short, so we must do the best we can."

Luma turned and looked at him. "How can I expect to heal the huge cracks in each of the Sacred Stones during the alignment when I can't even control the starlight long enough for *that?*" She gestured angrily toward the broken pieces of rock.

The mage stood up. "You are making great strides but come with me. I just thought of something that may help you."

****

The structure on the top of the cliff overlooking the

Inland Sea was built entirely of rough-cut sandstone quarried from the west side of the island. Not quite a castle but larger and more fortified than a house, its builders and initial purpose had been lost in the misty shrouds of Edira's early history. The highest room in the building was the mage's library, accessible by a long flight of tightly winding spiral stairs.

To an outsider's eye, the library was a complete mess. Jumbles of books, scrolls, and parchments lay piled in the corners and across the floor. Stacks of loose paper, some adorned with drawings, others with scrawled text written in languages Luma didn't recognize, cluttered the top of a large desk in the center of the room.

A small fireplace was nestled on one wall, while the wall opposite the door had two large windows through which sunlight streamed in, lighting the dust motes in the air like minuscule jewels. While others would consider the room to be in a perpetual state of disarray, the mage moved about it with the certainty of someone who knew exactly where everything was, regardless of the mess.

Luma stood awkwardly in the doorway, but it didn't take long for Eldamarr Rinn's "A-Ha!" to let her know he had located whatever it was he had been looking for.

From the opposite end of the room, the mage waved her in, a smile lighting up his face. Curiosity burned in Luma's stomach as she walked forward to see what it was he had found.

The box was small and unremarkable, made from what looked to Luma like polished cherry wood. But the way the mage's eyes sparkled as he gazed at it gave Luma the impression that whatever the box held was something special. Eldamarr Rinn nodded as if hearing her unspoken thoughts.

"What is inside this box is very ancient and has been passed down in the keeping of elf mages for generations and generations, back to the time of the first elves on Edira. An especially powerful conduit, suitable for controlling chaos and channeling extremely high levels of magic."

Luma took a step closer, her curiosity rising. "A conduit? You mean, like your wand?"

Eldamarr Rinn nodded. "My wand is a conduit for my magic, yes, just as a wizard's staff is a conduit for theirs, although a wizard's staff is more than that as well. But this," he looked down at the box and then back up at Luma, "this is different...or should I say, *they* are different."

He opened the top of the box, and Luma peered into it. There, nestled in four separate carved slits, were four thin silver rings.

Luma stared down at them for a moment, then lifted her eyes back to the mage questioningly. "Rings?"

The mage set the box down atop the desk and carefully removed the rings from their individual holders. Like the box that held them, the rings themselves were simple, very thin, and unadorned with jewels or markings of any kind.

The mage motioned for Luma to step closer. "Give me your hands."

Luma cautiously stretched out both hands toward him. Smiling at her reassuringly, the mage slid a ring on the first and middle fingers of both her hands.

As the fourth ring slid into place, an audible gasp escaped Luma's mouth, and she immediately turned her hands over. The dark scars that crisscrossed each of her palms had begun to glow, and a soft tingle coursed up and down her forearms, but not in the scorching, unpleasant way that the starlight within her normally flexed its power. Luma spread her fingers wide and stared down at her palms in speechless astonishment.

The mage's smile widened, crinkling the corners of his eyes. "Good, Luma. Now, focus."

Luma took a deep breath, and as she exhaled, mentally focused a current of energy down her arms. The glowing increased until warm white light began to radiate up and outward from her palms. Luma held her hands flat in front of her, palms facing up, and the glow illuminated the awestruck look on her face.

Eldamarr Rinn nodded approvingly, excitement creeping into his voice. "It is as I suspected, Luma. The starlight inside you is so powerful but with so much chaos that it requires a conduit—and a simple wand will not do. The conduit itself must be strong enough to keep the chaos levels in check while allowing you to channel the starlight with true precision. It is written that in the beginning, a small particle of each of the Four Stars fell to Edira and, in doing so, seeded this world with its inherent raw magic. These four rings were forged from the metal found at the site of impact." He smiled at Luma and raised an eyebrow. "That is if the legends are to be believed."

Luma wiggled her fingers, and the glowing light undulated with her movement. She focused more energy on her palms, and the light responded by glowing with brighter intensity. And yet, she felt no nausea, and the painful fire that had once burned in her blood was replaced with a pleasant, pulsing warmth.

Luma tore her gaze from her palms and looked up at the mage, her eyes shining. "This changes everything."

Chapter 18

Exhausted and aching, Figg and Aire arrived at Northhelm just as dawn painted the eastern horizon with delicate shades of pink.

Elas, who had been pacing back and forth between windows throughout the night, dashed to meet them just in time to catch both Figg and his twin sister as they collapsed. Haryk also came rushing to them, with Emalet on his heels.

Elas immediately noted Aire's swollen and bruised ankle.

"She's hurt. Someone help!"

Emalet darted over, and together she and Elas hoisted Aire and carried her into the main entrance of Northhelm, while Haryk gave Figg some water and escorted her in as well, his arm protectively around her waist.

Once inside, Aire was brought to the small infirmary, where she was attended to by Tsarra, the Plains Clan healer. The elf, whose faded tattoos bore the only hint of her age, prodded and pressed at various spots on Aire's ankle, her thick eyebrows knit together in concentration. Aire clenched her jaw and grimaced but made no sound.

Finally, Tsarra dropped her hands and looked up.

"It's not broken," she said matter-of-factly. "But it's taken a beating, to be sure. I wouldn't advise putting weight on it for several days at least. You are lucky it wasn't worse."

Aire gave a small snort. "Yeah, lucky. That's how I feel."

Tsarra fixed Aire with a stern stare. "We lost a fair number of our own to those wizards at the quarry. And I've been caring for and treating far worse injuries than this throughout the night, most of which will not recover in just a few days...So yes, child, I hope you *do* feel lucky."

Aire lowered her eyes, shame bringing a deep flush to her cheeks. "It...was a joke. I...I'm sorry."

Tsarra's stern gaze softened, but only slightly. "Soaking your ankle in cold water will bring relief for both the swelling and the pain. And to help you get around, use this." She handed Aire a long, slender piece of wood that had been carved into a crutch. Aire took it and thanked her. Then, with the crutch under one arm, hobbled from the room.

Tsarra watched her go. She shook her head slowly and pursed her lips before muttering to herself, "Forest Clan Elves..."

****

A short time later, Aire, Elas, Emalet, Haryk, and Figg were all sitting along the banks of a small stream, an offshoot of the River Aque, which ran a short distance behind Northhelm.

The five of them shared a small meal while Aire submerged her injured ankle in the fast-moving water, a look of relief on her face.

"Aahh, that does feel better." Aire sighed. "Now, does anyone have any information about what may have happened to Corr?"

The left side of Figg's face bore a dark purple bruise that spread outward from the deep laceration across her cheekbone. She scratched absent-mindedly at the small bandage covering it.

Emalet reached out and batted Figg's hand away. "Leave it alone, Figg, or I'll tell Tsarra."

Figg dropped her hand and made a face at Emalet, who simply rolled her eyes in response. Then, as if looking for something else to do with her hands, Figg pulled up a long blade of grass and spun it back and forth between her index finger and thumb. She glanced at Aire. "All of our elves, dead and alive after yesterday, have been accounted for, except your friend Corr. My guess is that he has been captured."

Sitting beside Aire, Elas nodded grimly. "Which means that, most likely, Vell has got him in the cells below the White Keep. We should mount a rescue!"

Emalet shook her head. "The White Keep is like a fortress! How do you expect to do that without getting caught or killed? That place must be swarming with wizards now that the alignment is so close."

Aire pulled her ankle from the stream and placed it out in front of her on the bank, the water beading atop the black and blue skin. "We know there is a secret staircase leading to the river from the cells. We went down it to escape the last time—this time, we can go up it to get Corr!"

Figg looked at Aire and raised her eyebrows, sarcasm edging into her tone. "Yeah, I'm sure that after you escaped that way last time, Vell just left that *secret* passage wide open for possible later use. Come on, Aire, Vell's no fool. I'm sure the stairway you're talking about is either heavily guarded or sealed off by now. Maybe both."

Aire's jaw ticked, and she dipped her leg back into the fast-moving stream, gasping as the cold water hit her skin. "Well, we can't just leave him there!"

Haryk nodded his agreement. "Aire's right. We can't leave him there, especially since Vell knows he was fighting with us at the quarry. If Corr tells her where Northhelm is…" his voice trailed off.

Aire and Elas both glared at him.

"Corr would never do that," Elas said. His voice was quiet but had a hard edge to it.

Haryk looked back and forth between the siblings, meeting their combined glares coolly. "Look, I'm not saying he'd do it *voluntarily* if…if you know what I mean."

A heavy weight settled in the pit of Aire's stomach. She was about to say something when Figg piped up.

"So, it's settled then. We agree that we need to get Corr out of the White Keep for both his safety and all of ours. We will call a meeting with the others on the Council and put together a plan for his rescue. There is no time to waste."

****

Vell spun around as the wide doors to one of the inner chambers of the White Keep creaked open. The wizard Idril poked his head inside the room. Vell looked at him expectantly.

"Well?"

Idril stepped into the room and puffed out his chest. "We spotted Naro headed back this way through the forest. He should arrive here any minute."

"Excellent. Send him directly to me," Vell responded curtly.

Idril nodded. "Of course, Vell. I will send him up immediately."

It wasn't long before the door creaked open once again, and this time Naro entered.

Vell had a pot of tea and two cups on a table at one side of the small room. She motioned for Naro to join her, then poured a bit of tea into each cup. She blew delicately on hers and took a dainty sip while her fierce blue eyes scanned Naro up and down.

"Well now, where have you been, pray tell? And make it quick. I have an elf prisoner to interrogate."

Naro picked up his cup of tea and also blew on it softly. Steam rose from the top and billowed upward. "There will be no need for an interrogation."

Vell cocked her head to one side. "Is that so? Why?"

Naro took a sip of his tea and then set the cup back down on the table. "Because I already know where the rest of those trouble-making elves are hiding." He leaned forward, his face creasing into a joyless smile. "A place called Northhelm."

Chapter 19

Luma threw herself to one side, and black sand sprayed upward where she had been standing a moment before. She tucked and rolled, then sprang to her feet, hands outstretched, the four rings shining on her fingers. The streak of white light hit the next incoming blast from the mage's wand and knocked it sideways.

Triumphantly, Luma dropped her hands, but Eldamarr Rinn wasn't done yet. Two blasts from his wand shot toward her in rapid succession. Caught off guard, Luma didn't get her hands all the way up before channeling her starlight. White light burst from her palms while they faced the ground, and as she raised them, the light streamed out to create a shimmering veil in front of her. The blasts from the mage's wand smashed into it and were repulsed, but at the impact on the veil, Luma stumbled backward and fell hard on the sand, and the wall of shimmering light disappeared.

Eldamarr Rinn put up his wand in a show of defeat. He chuckled as he leaned forward with his hands on his knees, panting slightly. Luma stood up and walked over, a smile lighting up her face as she dusted herself off.

The mage looked up at her. "That was new. How do you feel?"

Luma's smile broadened. "Honestly, a little bit shaky in the arms, but other than that, I feel good."

The mage nodded approvingly. "Starlight is a very

versatile kind of magic. It can be used to protect as well as attack. You have made incredible progress in just a few days, Luma. I am pleased. But remember, simply defending against the wizards' battle magic is not your primary goal. The most important thing is that during the alignment, you channel your starlight into the cracks of the four Sacred Stones until they are completely filled. Only then will the bridge to our world be protected once again. As soon as the Sacred Stones are fully healed, the wizards will be banished back to Malicath, but," he cautioned, his voice dropping, "channeling that much starlight will be no easy task, even with the conduit rings, the chaos within the starlight will try to overrun your control." The mage's eyes searched Luma's, his face serious. "Wielding that much starlight magic for that long will be risky."

Luma nodded solemnly and then spent the rest of the afternoon working on maintaining her focus long enough to drag the starlight in a line across an array of flat stones that the mage had erected for her.

The smaller ones she could now do with relative ease, but the bigger stones, the ones that required a much longer focus, still made her hands shake violently. When Eldamarr Rinn finally convinced her to stop and rest, the two of them sat on the beach, drinking tea and watching as the sun dipped toward the western horizon.

Soon, Eldamarr Rinn finished his tea and left to return to the dwelling structure atop the cliff. Luma, however, decided to stay on the beach for a while, enjoying the tranquility of the warm evening after a busy day.

Sitting directly in the sand, with her back against the base of the rough stone cliff, Luma held her cup with both hands and felt the pleasant warmth from its sides radiate across her palms. The four silver rings clinked softly against the cup when she moved her fingers.

A sense of accomplishment and, with it, a sense of confidence swelled in her chest for the first time in a very long time, and Luma took a deep breath as she looked over the glistening waves caressing the island shoreline. It was just then that the strange waterfall she had come across during her exploration of the island's interior rose again to the surface of her memory. With all her training and the excitement about the conduit rings, she had nearly forgotten all about it.

Luma stood up and brushed the fine black sand from the back of her pants, determined to ask Eldamarr Rinn about the waterfall now. She was about to hike up the cliff when movement from above caught her eye.

Trill soared across a sky made red from the setting sun and landed, silently as usual, on the beach a short distance from Luma. Folding his wings, he hopped forward in the ungainly way that owls move on land. Luma smiled widely at him, happy to see a familiar face.

The words poured excitedly from her mouth as she crouched to greet him. "Hello, Trill! What a surprise! I know how you love to surprise people when you fly in, and you sure did get me there! I didn't expect to see you here at all! How are you doing? Have you been with Corr, Aire, and Elas all this time? How are they?"

Trill swiveled his head from side to side, his large eyes blinking. He ignored her questions and posed his own in a business-like manner. "Is Eldamarr Rinn here? Where is the mage?"

Luma, still smiling, pointed toward the cliff behind them. "He's up there. Probably in his library, if you ask me. He's always puttering around in there. Well, when we aren't training, of course. I've been doing so well with my training, Trill! Look!" She thrust her hands forward, wiggling her fingers so that the light from the setting sun glinted off the four silver rings. "Eldamarr Rinn found them in his library and gave them to me to use. They are conduits!" she said proudly. "They help…"

"No matter, no matter." Trill cut Luma off mid-sentence. "You are the one I am here to see anyway. As I believe it is important for you to know."

Luma instantly forgot her initial annoyance at Trill's interruption and dropped her hands. "Trill, what do you mean? What is important for me to know?"

The big owl paced back and forth in the sand for a second, then turned to face Luma. He fixed her with his wide, amber eyes and clacked his beak once before speaking, as owls often do.

"The location of Northhelm, the final stronghold of the elf resistance, has been discovered. It is under attack by Vell and her wizards as we speak. The elves there will not be able to hold out much longer."

****

Eldamarr Rinn jumped and dropped the bundle of scrolls he was holding when Luma burst through the door of the library moments later. The scrolls landed with a dusty thump and rolled haphazardly across the stone floor.

The mage put his hand to his heart, panting. "By the Four, Luma! Don't come storming in here like that! For Star's sake! You nearly scared me to death!"

Still panting, Eldamarr Rinn searched for the scattered scrolls, one of which had rolled beneath his desk. Muttering darkly under his breath, the mage dropped to all fours and groped around until his fingertips closed on the wayward scroll. Grunting, the mage pulled the scroll out, along with several dust bunnies. Then he sat back, only to come face-to-face with Trill, who had landed silently on the top of the desk.

"Gaaaahh!" The mage reeled backward, clutching the scroll defensively across his chest. "Trill! What are you doing here? My poor nerves! I didn't know you'd be visiting. What is going on? Luma? What is the matter?"

Luma's face was ashen, and at her sides, her hands were visibly trembling. Eldamarr Rinn got to his feet, the rest of the scattered scrolls forgotten.

He approached Luma, concern written on his face. "What is it?"

****

A short time later, having shared all the information he could about the recent events with both Luma and the mage, Trill departed the library to perch outside.

Luma, who had been sitting in a small wooden chair during Trill's recounting of the attack on Northhelm, now stood up. She took a deep breath and fixed the mage with a level stare.

"They need help. I'm going."

Eldamarr Rinn sighed and shook his head. "Luma, listen to me. It is important that you complete your training before the alignment, and this is the only place you can do that. You are safe here."

Luma threw up her hands in frustration. "Safe! Exactly! *I* am safe here, but no one else is! It doesn't matter how fortified this Northhelm place is—it cannot withstand a direct assault from battle magic for long. You and I both know that! The elves are out there fighting, they…they are *dying!*" Luma's voice was shrill with emotion, and her eyes burned with frustrated tears. She paused and wiped a shaking hand across her eyes, then continued. "I cannot stay here, *safe and sound*," she said bitterly, remembering Figg's previous barb, "knowing that my friends are under attack out there and that I have the power to help them."

The mage paced back and forth across the cluttered floor of the library, the emotional turmoil plain on his face. "Luma, the alignment is coming. You are the Daughter of Starlight—the only one who can defeat the wizards, the only one who can heal the Sacred Stones and stop this war once and for all."

Luma nodded. "Yes! Exactly!"

But the mage held up a hand for silence. "No, listen. This is just what Vell wants. Don't you see? She is trying to draw you out, Luma, away from the safety of this place so that she can kill you before the alignment. If that happens..." Eldamarr Rinn stepped forward and grasped both of Luma's still trembling hands in his own. He looked at her imploringly. "If that happens, all will be lost."

Luma's eyes searched the mage's face, pleading. "Why don't you come with me? We can go together. Between the two of us, we can surely drive the wizards back from Northhelm!"

But Eldamarr Rinn shook his head. He let go of Luma's hands and walked back toward the desk. Sitting down heavily in the wooden desk chair, he brought his forehead to his hands. When he spoke again, his voice was slightly muffled.

"I can't."

Luma shook her head. "What? No, no, it's okay. If we go together, we can keep each other safe. It will work!"

The mage sighed and raised his head to look at her while his hands fidgeted on the desk. "You don't understand, Luma. I cannot leave the borders of the Inland Sea."

Shock widened Luma's eyes. "What do you mean?"

Eldamarr Rinn took a deep breath. "When Vell cracked the Sacred Stones, it gave the wizards access to large parts of Edira, but not all of it. The Inland Sea and this island have long been a place for mages. Because of that, it is protected by its own kind of magic. Mages and elves with special gifts," he nodded toward Luma, "such as yourself, can access it, but the wizards cannot, which is why, when you were called back to Edira, Izarre knew how important it was to get you here."

Eldamarr Rinn looked at Luma, wanting to make sure she was following. She nodded, so he continued. "I was already here before Vell cracked the Sacred Stones, and once she did, the same magic that surrounds and protects this place now prevents me from leaving. I can travel to the outer edge of the Inland Sea, but until the Sacred Stones are healed, I can go no farther."

Luma stared at him in silence for a moment, and when she spoke, her voice shook slightly. "Can I?"

Eldamarr Rinn paused, then nodded reluctantly, so Luma posed another question. "And what if the alignment comes and the Sacred Stones are not healed?"

Eldamarr Rinn held her gaze, his voice somber. "If Vell succeeds in her plan to kill you, then, as you know, the Sacred Stones will crumble during the alignment, and the wizards will have full access to this world and all its magical resources. The magic I can channel from my wand is powerful but not powerful enough to withstand battle magic for long, especially Vell's battle magic." He shrugged. "I will die fighting them, like every other elf on Edira."

The resignation in the mage's tone felt like a vise on Luma's heart. She let out a long, frustrated sigh.

Turning, she strode to one of the library's tall windows and stood silently for a moment, gazing out over the placid water of the Inland Sea.

"Elves are out there fighting and dying right now." She spoke without turning around, and although there was still a slight tremor in her voice, a hard edge had crept into her tone.

From behind her, Eldamarr Rinn nodded sadly. "Yes."

Luma now turned to face him, her body silhouetted against the last rays of the setting sun. "I'm not going to stay here, hiding in safety while my friends need help. My help."

Still seated at his desk, Eldamarr Rinn looked at Luma. The red and orange light streaming through the tall window shone like a fiery halo around her curly brunette hair. At her sides, her hands had stopped shaking.

The mage stood and walked closer so that he could clearly see her face in the dim light. "Luma. Vell is dangerous."

Luma raised both her hands in front of her, palms facing up. From the tangled web of scars that covered them, shimmering starlight began to glow.

It rapidly grew in intensity, swirling and flashing upward.

The light from her palms cast Luma's cheeks in an alabaster sheen as she gazed back at the mage, fierce

determination snapping in her dark eyes.
"So am I."

Chapter 20

In his cell below the White Keep, Corr paced continuously, his shoes scraping on the rough stone of the floor with every turn.

"Can you reach it yet?" he asked anxiously.

"If I had ahold of it already, you'd know. And Corr, stop with the pacing. That sound is driving me crazy." Ruvyn's voice grunted back.

The wizard was lying on the floor of his cell, his arm stuck through the thick, iron bars up to his shoulder, his fingertips stretching forward.

****

That morning, in the predawn hours, a couple of wizard guards had been down in the cells, giving Corr and Ruvyn their daily ration of food and canteens of water, when someone had shouted from above.

"Hurry up down there! Vell wants all staffs for the attack on Northhelm! Let's go!"

The two wizards, not wanting to be viewed as delinquent in following Vell's commands, had rushed up the passageway, each trying to be the first back up the stairs. In their haste, one of them had knocked Ruvyn's staff, which had been leaning up against the wall opposite the cells, askew. It had teetered and then toppled to the ground and rolled, coming to a stop directly across from the front of Ruvyn's cell.

Ruvyn had thrown himself down and grabbed for it,

but his fingertips clawed at nothing but air. The staff was still too far away.

****

An hour later, Ruvyn was still trying, clenching his teeth as he pressed his shoulder painfully into the unyielding bars of his cell in a futile attempt to stretch just a little farther.

Finally, with an exasperated sigh, he pulled his arm back through the bars and rubbed his aching shoulder. "Ugh. If only it was a little closer." Ruvyn shook his head. "Vell doesn't even need to carry her staff with her, you know. Its essence is bonded so strongly to her now that she can manifest and call it to her hand." He cocked his head and looked up at Corr standing anxiously in the other cell. "I always thought she did it just to show off. Sure would come in handy now, though."

Corr clenched his fists, his upper body trembling with frustration. "We've got to get out of here, Ruvyn! You heard them. Northhelm is probably being attacked as we speak! We've got to help!"

Ruvyn sighed and nodded. "I know, Corr. I'm sorry. If I just had my staff, I could bust us out of here. Okay, I'll try again."

Ruvyn was about to reach his arm through the bars once again when Corr's voice stopped him.

"Wait. Let me try something."

Corr went to the back wall of his cell and, using the metal edge of his canteen lid, began working around the chunks of rough stone. It wasn't long until he was able to pry loose a piece from the wall, about the size of his palm.

Triumphantly, Corr tossed the chunk of stone in the air and caught it again, but Ruvyn rolled his eyes. "Nice work, elf. Maybe in about two hundred years, you will have the beginnings of a tunnel in the wall…going the wrong way."

Corr shot him a withering glance. He walked to the front of his cell, took careful aim through the bars, and gently tossed the stone toward the staff. The stone hit the end of it, and it shifted slightly—in the opposite direction. Ruvyn snorted.

Corr ignored him and began prying loose another chunk of rock from the back of his cell. "I can't believe I'm actually helping a wizard get his staff back," Corr muttered to himself, just loud enough for Ruvyn to hear.

"Oh, helping? Is that what you're doing?"

Pretending not to hear the wizard's retort, Corr returned to the front bars of his cell and narrowed his eyes, mentally gauging the distance. He tossed the rock again, a bit harder, and this time, it hit the opposite wall of the passage, bounced off, and struck the back side of the staff, rolling it toward the cells.

Corr's gasp of success was followed by Ruvyn throwing himself down and reaching through the bars once again, his fingertips falling a fraction from where the staff now lay.

Breathless with excitement, Ruvyn gestured to Corr. "Again! Once more, just like that, and I'll have it!"

Corr raced to the back wall of his cell and soon returned with another chunk of stone. "Okay. This is it."

With a soft *clack,* the stone ricocheted off the wall and hit the staff from behind again. It rolled over once, and Ruvyn's fingers closed around it.

"Got it!" Ruvyn's cry of relief mingled with Corr's shout of triumph.

Carefully, Ruvyn guided his staff through the bars

of the cell, then scrambled to his feet. Closing his eyes, he grasped the staff tightly in both hands, his whole body shaking with relief. Then, opening his eyes, he gently traced the multitude of hairline cracks in the polished wood, his fingertips hovering over the half-moon indents still visible from Vell's nails.

His jubilant expression darkened, and he looked over at Corr, his eyes shining with determination and vengeance. "Let's get out of here."

****

"Emalet, get down!"

Elas jumped forward and pulled Emalet back from one of the narrow windows at Northhelm a split-second before the blast of battle magic blew it apart.

Emalet stifled a cry of pain as shards of rock pummeled her head and shoulders before scrambling back to her feet. She jumped forward into the now wider hole where the window had been, an arrow in her bow. A split-second to aim, and she loosed the shaft before ducking down again, smiling at the resulting scream that told her the arrow had found its mark.

She nocked another shaft to her bow, shook rock dust from her long blonde hair, and winked at Elas. "That's another one down. How many to go?"

Elas ducked as another blast of battle magic caused a fresh shower of rock dust to swirl over their heads. He stood up and sent his own arrow whizzing through the hole. It, too, was answered with a scream, but Elas didn't smile.

His voice was hoarse as he answered Emalet. "Too many."

****

Deeper inside Northhelm, Tsarra cared for the

wounded elf fighters while explosions of battle magic pummeled the cliff's façade. She looked up as Aire, her crutch in one hand, stumbled into the small infirmary, supporting Haryk with her other arm.

Haryk was semi-conscious. His head lolled to one side, and his eyes were half open. He was bleeding from a deep laceration over his left eyebrow, and the right side of his torso, down across his right arm, bore the deep, burn-like wounds of battle magic. Aire wobbled under Haryk's weight but stayed upright, leaning on her crutch. She grimaced at the added pressure on her injured ankle.

Tsarra rushed forward and took Haryk's uninjured arm from across Aire's shoulders and onto her own. "All right, bring him over here."

Aire helped guide Haryk over to a small cot near the door, where he collapsed. Aire made sure he was still breathing before turning back to Tsarra, who was making up a salve to treat the battle magic wounds.

"I saw him slip out into the woods, so I followed. Fool tried to take on Vell by himself." Aire shook her head.

"I almost had her." Haryk's voice was raspy.

Aire took a canteen of water and held it to Haryk's lips while Tsarra began carefully applying the salve to his injured arm. Haryk raised his head and sucked down the offered water gratefully. He flinched as Tsarra moved down his arm with the salve.

"Hey. Easy on the tattoos."

Tsarra shook her head and smiled, looking over at Aire. "This one has fight in him yet. He'll be okay."

Aire turned to leave, but Tsarra called out to her. "Wait a moment, you're bleeding. I have bandages."

Aire looked down at the blood spattered across her

arms, then she met Tsarra's eyes again and flashed a mischievous smile. "That's not my blood. It's Vell's."

****

At the edge of the forest, Vell grimaced as she blotted at the slash across her upper torso made by the keen edge of Aire's dagger, mentally berating herself for letting that elf get close enough to wound her before she could finish the other one off. She awkwardly wrapped a piece of cloth around herself to stop the bleeding and made a mental note to find that elf and kill her personally.

From her position just behind the tree line of the forest, Vell watched as her army relentlessly battered the front of Northhelm with their battle magic. Vell had to admit that this was taking longer than she had anticipated. Northhelm was impressively fortified, and the elves defending it fought with unmitigated ferocity. But, of course, her victory was inevitable. No normal elf could withstand battle magic for very long, as history had already shown.

At first, the wizards were kept from storming into Northhelm by the barrage of arrows fired by the elves. But now, the arrows were becoming fewer, and the elves were getting more strategic with their targets. Vell knew that meant the arrows were running low, and soon, the wizards would be able to breach the front entrance. Then, if the remaining elves inside were dispatched before they could get close enough to use their daggers, this fight would be over.

The last elven stronghold, the final pocket of resistance, was on the verge of collapse, and still, there was no sign of their precious Daughter of Starlight. Vell smiled. It would have been nice to rid herself of Luma before the alignment, but no matter. Even with all her power, Luma needed allies if she was to get to and heal the Sacred Stones in time. And after today, the last of her allies would be gone.

Chapter 21

The metal gate in front of Ruvyn's cell crashed into the opposite wall with a loud clang.

Ruvyn froze, worried the noise would bring unwanted attention from any wizards left in the White Keep. But after several seconds of waiting, Ruvyn looked at Corr and shrugged.

"I guess Vell has taken the full force to this Northhelm place of yours. We'd better hurry if we want to get there in time to be of any help." He leveled his staff at the gate in front of Corr's cell. "Stand back."

Corr flattened himself against the right side of his cell, desperately hoping that when the gate went flying, it didn't hit him. He closed his eyes and waited.

Despite himself, Corr flinched as the gate blasted apart. He cracked one eye. Ruvyn was standing in front of him, a look of wizardly smugness on his face. Corr rolled his eyes and stepped out of the cell to join him.

"Okay, okay. Nice job," he said begrudgingly. Now, let's go."

Ruvyn went to the opposite end of the hallway and ran his hands along the area that had once concealed the secret door to the river. He shook his head. "It's been sealed. We will have to go up and out."

Corr nodded in agreement. "Once we leave the White Keep, we head immediately for Northhelm, but we can't go a direct route, or we will run into the wizard forces that are probably attacking the front. I know these woods by heart. I can take us another way, and we will come in from the west."

Ruvyn gripped his damaged staff in his right hand. "Okay. Follow me until we are clear of the White Keep. After that, you take the lead." He looked at Corr, his face grim. "Thank you for your help, Corr. I hope we can make it in time to aid your friends."

Corr put his hand on Ruvyn's shoulder. "Me too, Ruvyn."

****

The thundering of the waterfall illusion was still ringing in Luma's ears when the hull of the little ship ran aground at the edge of the Inland Sea.

Luma hopped over the side and splashed ankle-deep in the clear water, then waded ashore. Once on the beach, Luma turned back and raised a hand to shield her eyes from the glare of the sun off the water. Eldamarr Rinn strode to the side of the ship, his hands resting lightly on the railing.

Their eyes locked, and he nodded down at her. "This is as far as I go, Luma. The Four protect you. I will be waiting."

Luma nodded back, her eyes burning with unshed tears. She suddenly felt very small and weak, but she clenched her fists and lifted her chin, refusing to show it.

"Thank you for everything. I will return once my friends are safe." With that, Luma turned and crossed the beach to the base of the cliff and began ascending the staircase carved into the stone. Soon, she had reached the top.

Trill dipped his wing and soared over her left shoulder, swiveling his big head toward her as he spoke.

"Come, Luma, there is no time to waste. I will guide you on the shortest route to Northhelm."

****

Ruvyn and Corr pushed open the door that led to the cells and emerged onto the White Keep's main level. There, they paused, straining their ears for any sound, but were met with silence. Corr looked at Ruvyn and shrugged, and together they continued on.

Ruvyn led the way, his staff held defensively in front of him. They walked a short distance through the building unopposed, but neither one was willing to let down their guard. As they approached the main doors, Corr suddenly darted to the left and disappeared down a narrow hallway. Ruvyn saw him detour and followed quickly, muttering a wizard curse under his breath. He found Corr rummaging around in the corner of a small room just off the hallway.

Nervously, Ruvyn looked right and left, his shoulders tense. "Corr, what are you doing?" He hissed. "I thought we were in a hurry to get out of this place!"

Corr turned around, holding a dagger and a large shield, a triumphant smile on his face. "I heard that the wizards destroyed the elf armory when they took control of the White Keep, but I remembered that this had previously been used as a storeroom, so I thought it was worth checking out. And look what I found! This is my dagger! It was stolen when the wizards captured me with Aire, Elas, and Luma. Now, I'm taking it back, and this too!" He held up the shield a bit higher, grinning widely.

Ruvyn raised his eyebrows and sighed. "Yes, very nice, but you know that shield won't actually protect you, right? Elvish weapons can't withstand battle magic—especially from Vell."

Corr shrugged and slid the shield onto his left arm, hoisting it experimentally to get a sense of the weight. "Yeah, I know. But it's got to be better than nothing, and it may come in handy." He stuck the dagger in his belt. "Now, come on, let's go. We are in a hurry, remember?"

Ruvyn muttered another colorful wizard curse and glared at the back of Corr's head as he turned to leave. All was still quiet, and Ruvyn once again took the lead. He had just rounded the corner from the side hallway, mere steps from the main entrance doors, when a shout echoed from his left.

"Hey! Traitor!"

Ruvyn spun just in time to see the wizard Aegrond pointing an accusing finger at him. He was about to raise his staff when there was a blur to his right, and Corr rushed forward from around the corner of the hallway.

Aegrond had only been focused on Ruvyn and was caught off guard by Corr's sudden appearance. In one fluid movement, Corr pulled the shield off his arm and smacked it heavily into the side of the wizard's head. As Aegrond crumpled in an unconscious heap on the polished stone floor, Corr turned back toward Ruvyn. He slid the shield back on his arm as he sauntered past. "No need to call more attention to ourselves with some big, noisy battle magic when a little bump on the head will do." He winked at Ruvyn, who lowered his staff and cocked his head sarcastically at Corr.

"Are all elves this insufferable? Or is it just you?"

A deep chuckle from Corr was his only response, and a moment later, the two of them emerged from the main doors of the White Keep.

With Corr now leading the way, they quickly disappeared into the thick forest.

****

Following Trill, Luma was making good time. She was already well past the plains with their thick grasses and rolling hills and now entered the fringes of the forest. Stopping briefly for a few sips of water, Luma hurried on through the trees, relishing the leafy shade after the heat of the open plains.

The thickness of the trees and shrubs in this part of the forest made it more difficult to follow Trill as he flew, and Luma struggled to keep the big owl in her sights. Still, she pressed on, concern for her friends and the knowledge that every moment that passed meant more elf casualties fueling her onward.

A short time later, Trill swooped down and landed on the low branch of an oak tree in front of Luma's path. He clacked his beak.

"It is not much farther now. Not much. Straight ahead, there is a small stream. Follow the stream due east a short way, and you will see the back of a large sandstone cliff rising from the forest. That is Northhelm."

Luma stared at the owl, anxiety bringing a tightness to her chest. "Aren't you coming with me?"

Trill swiveled his head back and forth. "I have other matters, Daughter of Starlight. But do not worry, I will be seeing you again before long."

Then, before Luma could say another word, Trill launched himself silently from the tree limb and was quickly out of sight in the vastness of the green forest.

Luma watched him go incredulously for a second, then sighed and trudged onward, resolved to find the stream that she was supposed to follow. She had only taken a couple of steps when she heard a commotion nearby.

Then, she was running.

****

Ruvyn was on the forest floor, his staff wrenched from his grasp, and two wizards stood over him, sneering. Nearby, Corr struggled against a holding spell from another wizard, trying to reach the dagger in his belt.

"Let him go!"

Her face flushed from running. Luma stepped out from behind some trees, her fists clenched at her sides. The three wizards turned and stared at her in astonishment.

The one holding Corr was first to recover from the shock. He bashed Corr in the chest with an elbow. The blow sent Corr stumbling backward while the wizard swung his already glowing staff and aimed it at Luma's chest.

"No!" Corr's cry of dismay barely registered to Luma. The world around her narrowed as she focused on the wizard in front of her.

Breathe in and out.

She saw the battle magic burst from the end of the staff, almost as if it were happening in slow motion. Her hands came up, and the four silver rings around her fingers glinted in the dappled sunlight. The intensity of the light that burst from her palms threatened for a moment to push her backward, but Luma set her feet and stood strong.

The starlight met the blast from the wizard's staff and completely absorbed it. Gritting her teeth, Luma pushed her arms out farther, and the starlight responded, rushing toward the wizard and striking him square in the chest. The wizard flew backward like a ragdoll then came to an abrupt stop against the trunk of a huge maple tree. He crumpled at the base of it, and his staff hit the forest floor before quickly disappearing.

The two other wizards stared at Luma, then raised their own staffs. Ruvyn took advantage of their change in focus and leaped to his feet. He grabbed his staff from where it had been dropped nearby and sent a blast toward one of the wizards as he advanced on Luma. But Ruvyn's staff, badly damaged as it was, could no longer channel battle magic effectively, and the other wizard easily avoided the attack.

Luma raised her hands once again and sent white light arcing toward the two wizards, who both tried to dodge but were knocked off their feet.

Scrambling up, one of the wizards spun and sent a blast of battle magic toward Corr. Knowing he couldn't get out of the way in time, Corr threw up his shield and braced himself. At the same moment, Luma jumped forward and sent a stream of starlight to intercept the wizard's blast, but her aim was off, and the white light hit Corr's shield instead. Corr stumbled backward at the impact, and a split-second later, the wizard's battle magic crashed into the center of the shield.

Cold fear raced through Luma's veins, but instead of shattering, a shimmer ran across the surface of Corr's shield. The metal vibrated softly and remained intact, with Corr safe behind it.

Luma gasped in amazement and relief, but she quickly raised her hands again, preparing to defend Corr from another blast. It was unneeded. The two wizards had fled.

Luma dropped her hands. It was only then that she

realized how badly they were shaking. Corr ran toward her, and without a word, he dropped the shield and wrapped Luma in an embrace that pushed the air from her lungs. Luma gave a small, strangled gasp, and Corr released her and stepped backward, though his hands lingered on her shoulders.

Luma smiled up at him, her cheeks flushing red. "Nice to see you again, Corr."

Corr shook his head, concern and relief warring behind his moss-green eyes. "Luma, what are you doing here? The plan was for you to stay safe beyond the Inland Sea until the alignment!" His fingertips lightly caressed her upper arms before he pulled them back.

Luma's heart thudded, and she swallowed hard before replying. "Yes, that was the plan. But I…I couldn't. Trill showed up and told me that the elves at Northhelm were in trouble. I could not stay away knowing what was happening. Knowing I could help."

Ruvyn stepped forward, and Luma turned to him, recognition dawning on her. "Ruvyn? It is Ruvyn, right? I met you in the forest, and then, you were at the White Keep…with Vell!" Light began to swirl upward from her palms, and she took an angry step toward the wizard, but Corr caught her arm.

"It's okay, Luma. He's with me. With…us."

Luma raised an eyebrow skeptically, and Ruvyn took a nervous step backward. "I didn't give up your location after you helped me in the forest, Luma. I promise. The other wizards I was with abandoned me once I ran into those Fireburn plants. They must have come across signs of your whereabouts and reported to Vell before I made it back to the White Keep. I'm sorry."

Luma stared at Ruvyn for a moment longer, then

relaxed, and the glowing light faded. "Okay…if you say so."

Corr picked up the shield once more and studied it before placing it back on his arm. "This thing should have been blown apart by that close-range battle magic, but there's not a scratch on it. How did that happen?"

Luma shook her head. "I have no idea. But we can figure it out later. Right now, I need to get to Northhelm before it is too late. Are you coming with me?"

Corr and Ruvyn both nodded. "We're with you. Let's go."

Chapter 22

Northhelm was falling.

The elves fought on with the strength born of desperation, but their arrows were almost gone, and the wizards continued their relentless assault.

Vell was not interested in picking off individual elves. Instead, she instructed her forces to direct their powerful battle magic at the structure of Northhelm itself, reveling in the idea of bringing the once mighty fortress down and, with it, the group of would-be rebels.

Northhelm had only one small back exit on the far west side of the cliff, and it could only be accessed by a narrow, winding tunnel cut through the rock. It was in that tunnel that Aire hobbled along, once again, with Haryk on one side and her crutch on the other. The tunnel was dark, but from somewhere ahead of her, Tsarra's voice echoed through the gloom.

"Not too much farther now. Stay close. Once the wounded are safe, we can start evacuating the rest of the fighters out this way."

Aire only grunted in response, and she paused briefly to shift Haryk's weight over her right shoulder. On her left side, the wooden crutch dug painfully into the underside of her upper arm. Aire gritted her teeth and started moving again, trying her best to keep her voice light and casual as she talked to Haryk, who was still semi-conscious.

"Hear that? Not much farther now. And don't you worry, once we get you out of here, I'm going back to get Elas, Emalet, and yes, even Figg. So don't worry, it'll be okay."

That last sentence was more for herself than Haryk, and with that, Aire fell silent and focused on moving forward one slow step at a time. Suddenly, a thundering sound boomed from above, followed by a loud crunching. Aire flinched as rock dust floated down from the tunnel ceiling, coating the top of her head and shoulders. She squeezed her eyes closed and wiped a hand over her face.

When she opened her eyes again, Tsarra's face loomed in front of her out of the darkness. She, too, had rock dust covering her hair. She shook her head at Aire. "Turn back."

Aire rubbed her eyes again and blinked, not sure she had heard correctly. "Wait…turn back? What do you mean? I thought we were almost there."

Tsarra shook her head again as she helped Aire and Haryk turn around in the narrow space. Then she prodded Aire along, back the way they had come.

Another boom reverberated above them, and Tsarra raised her voice to be heard over the sound. "The back exit just caved in; it's completely packed with rocks. Stars have mercy. There will be no escaping for us or anyone else. Not anymore." The resignation in the healer's voice sent a shiver down Aire's spine.

****

At the main entrance of Northhelm, Emalet had traded her bow for a short sword, which she now swung in a deadly arc, and the enterprising wizard who had tried to rush the main door of the fortress fell back, lifeless.

Elas descended from the upper portions of the crumbling fortress and was joined by Figg, both of their quivers empty. The remaining resistance fighters also clustered on the main level. Faces grim, they shielded themselves as best they could from the barrage of battle magic behind the shuddering stone, armed now with daggers and short swords, ready to fight to the last elf.

****

Vell paced as she watched the fortress being relentlessly battered beyond repair. A satisfied smile spread across her pretty features. This was real power. No one could stand against her for long.

"Keep it up!" she called to the wizards as she turned and paced in the other direction. "Focus on the supporting stone! Bring that cliff down!" Her smile broadened. *We've got them now.*

Vell was about to pace back when she caught movement in her periphery, and she stopped, her keen gaze scanning the edge of the forest. Then, her mouth hung open in shock. Three elves had just skirted around the corner of Northhelm from the edge of the woods on the western side. No, not three elves, two elves, and…Vell gasped. A wizard! It was that traitor, Ruvyn, and he was with the elf that she had captured at the quarry.

Vell's eyes narrowed as she watched the traitor wizard and her recent prisoner. Then her gaze moved to the other elf with them, and realization crashed into her like an ocean wave. The other elf was Luma. *Yes. Finally.*

The rest of the wizards were focused on the front of Northhelm and hadn't yet noticed the three that had recently arrived. A malicious smile creased Vell's face as she began making her way toward them from just behind the tree line.

****

Luma's stomach dropped at the scene unfolding before her. She could tell that Northhelm had once been a mighty fortress that was now in its death throes. Huge chunks of stone were crumbling away under the onslaught of the wizards' battle magic. Slain elves, as well as quite a few wizards with arrows protruding from their bodies, littered the area in front of the cliff. The elves had fought fiercely, but the tide had clearly turned against them.

Rage coursed through Luma's veins, and heat crackled and burned beneath her skin. Without waiting to consult Corr or Ruvyn, she sprinted toward the closest group of wizards firing on Northhelm, her hands raised.

White light, so intense that Corr and Ruvyn threw up their arms to shield their eyes, burst from Luma's palms as she ran. The blast hit the group of wizards and scattered their bodies like leaves in a gale. Fueled by her rage and heedless to any danger, Luma charged forward, and another group of wizards was leveled by the starlight streaming from her hands.

She was almost directly in front of Northhelm now, and Luma could see elf faces crowded around the front entrance. One of them, she recognized. Figg's mouth was moving. Luma skidded to a stop but couldn't hear the words Figg was saying. Shaking her head, Luma took a step closer. Figg continued to shout something, and this time, her hand went up, pointing. Realization dawned on her, and Luma spun around a split-second too late.

The blast from Vell's staff caught Luma high on the left shoulder, and she screamed in pain as she was thrown off her feet.

Agony coursed through Luma's body from the deep, burn-like wound on her shoulder as she pushed herself up from the ground. Looking up, Luma saw Vell stalking closer, a smug smile on her beautiful face. Eyes watering, Luma scrambled backward. She had just thrown up a trembling hand when a blast of blue battle magic hit the ground at Vell's feet. Halting, Vell looked over as Ruvyn leveled his staff and fired again, this blast harmlessly hitting the ground slightly to her right.

Vell sneered at him. "Looks like someone damaged your staff," she called mockingly. "You'll never be able to kill me with that."

Ruvyn faced her, his damaged staff still glowing slightly. "I don't need to."

While Vell was distracted, Corr ran up to Luma, his shield still fixed on his arm as he gently pulled her up. Luma gritted her teeth and swayed on her feet. She glanced at the elves trapped inside Northhelm, then back at Corr, her voice an urgent whisper. "You and Ruvyn get all those elves out of there. I'll hold Vell off."

Corr shook his head, his voice pleading. "No, Luma, you can't do it alone."

Luma glared at him, her eyes flashing. "I am the *only one* who can, and you know it. Go. Now!"

Vell spun away from Ruvyn just as Luma pushed Corr behind her and threw up her hands. Vell's battle magic met the stream of Luma's starlight in midair.

Quickly realizing that this magic was too powerful to absorb as she had with the other wizard, Luma threw her hands to one side and deflected the blast, then set her feet and sent another stream of starlight toward Vell.

Unable to send off a blast of her own as quickly, Vell

dodged to one side, then spun back and returned fire with her staff.

Luma, pushing down the pain that screamed through her wounded shoulder, deflected the attack again. All the while, the other wizards continued their assault on Northhelm, their battle magic hammering relentlessly on the trapped elves and their once great fortress.

Grimly, the elves fought on with whatever weapons they had left, refusing to accept defeat, even in the face of certain death.

As Luma focused on Vell in front of her, one wizard crept up from behind. Smiling, he lowered his staff at Luma's unprotected back as she used her starlight to deflect another blast of battle magic from Vell.

Luma had just sent the blast from Vell careening to the side when she heard a grunt directly behind her. She spun just as the wizard, who had been sneaking up, fell forward, a small dagger protruding from the side of his neck. Stunned, Luma looked over and saw Figg standing just inside the entrance to Northhelm. She grinned in dark satisfaction, another dagger held lightly in her right hand.

Luma gave Figg a quick nod of thanks before leaping aside to avoid another blast from Vell. Sweat beading at her temples, Luma let out a wild yell of rage and raised both hands. Vell was just barely able to deflect the intense white light with her staff, but in doing so, she was pushed backward and slammed into the trunk of a large tree at the edge of the forest.

Gasping at the temporary respite, Luma spun back around and faced Northhelm. Corr and Ruvyn had made it to the main entrance, but the wizard forces were keeping them pinned down so no one could escape.

Her heart galloping in her chest, Luma stared wild-eyed at the crumbling cliff fortress, then at the unrelenting wizard forces and their battle magic, and at Vell, who was now beginning to stir again at the base of the tree.

Luma's breathing came fast and shallow, and cold fear rippled through her body. Screams of wounded and dying elves filled her ears. They were dying because of her, and she couldn't help them.

Gritting her teeth, Luma sent a stream of starlight into a group of wizards who were about to breach the entrance of Northhelm, but more were still advancing. Luma threw herself to one side a moment too late, and the blast from another wizard's staff clipped her in the side of the torso. Her scream of pain rang out above the sounds of crumbling stone.

Vell had recovered and gotten up. Grunting and holding her side, Luma threw up her hands just in time to deflect an attack from Vell, but the intensity of the blast made her stumble awkwardly backward, tripping on her own feet. Vell continued to advance, smiling.

Hot tears filled with rage and grief burned in Luma's eyes. She couldn't do it. She couldn't stop the other wizards and hold off Vell's more powerful battle magic at the same time. She was failing—and they were dying.

Luma swallowed hard and tried desperately to control her breathing. Her hands trembled, and the scars on her palms throbbed painfully. The thin, silver rings felt hot around her fingers.

Her panicked mind raced. In a matter of minutes, Northhelm would be destroyed. If only there was a way to protect the remaining elves just long enough for them to escape. Then, something from her training flashed in

Luma's memory. A tiny bit of hope rose to the surface, and Luma clung to it, a life raft in a churning sea of despair.

It might work. It had to work.

Standing directly in front of Northhelm's entrance, Luma took a wide stance and put her arms straight down at her sides, fingers spread wide.

Breathe in and out.

The familiar pulse of energy rolled through her, and white light streamed from her palms down toward the ground. Moving her hands slowly on either side of her, Luma pulled the light upward, so instead of coming out in blasts, the starlight from her palms created a smooth, shimmering curtain from the ground up. Luma took another deep breath and focused all her energy, carefully spreading the curtain of light above her head and outward, until a translucent wall shimmered in front of the entire cliff face.

Luma then brought her hands to cross in front of her chest, wrapping the light up and around while simultaneously keeping it streaming to the right and left in front of Northhelm. The wound on her shoulder protested, but Luma clenched her jaw and pushed the agony away.

The wizards stumbled backward as the wall of light rose in front of them, but at a screech from Vell, they began attacking once more.

The first blast of battle magic ripped a hole through the shimmering wall and exploded on the ground not far from Luma's leg. Luma flinched but held her ground and sent more starlight rushing outward to fill the tear. Gasping for air, Luma refocused all her energy on keeping the starlight flowing continuously in either direction in front of Northhelm. It was working! Subsequent blasts from the wizards couldn't get through to the elves on the other side.

Luma's breath was ragged, and sweat from her forehead trickled down the sides of her face to mingle with the droplets of bright red blood that dripped from her ears.

Breathe. Just stay strong until everyone can get out.

Behind her, Luma heard the sounds of Northhelm being evacuated and Corr's voice urging everyone on. Was that Aire's voice as well? Someone was telling them to retreat to the banks of the Inland Sea.

Good. That is good. They should be safe there. If I can just hold on a little longer…

Crossed in front of her, Luma's arms began to shake. Sweat dripped into her eyes and stung. She blinked rapidly, trying to clear her vision. That's when she saw Vell's face looming in front of her.

The shimmering wall of light contorted Vell's pretty features, but Luma could clearly see her malicious smile as Vell took a step backward and pointed her staff directly across from where she was standing. Luma squeezed her eyes shut as the first blast from Vell's staff made the wall of starlight quiver violently and caused shockwaves to reverberate across Luma's chest.

Luma's eyes flew open in panic at the sheer strength of Vell's battle magic, but to her relief, the wall of starlight remained intact. Panting, Luma braced herself again, knowing that Vell wouldn't stop. She kept her arms crossed in front of her, palms pointing right and left, pushing all the energy she had into maintaining the flow of starlight outward.

Two more blasts from Vell's staff in rapid

succession, and Luma took a small step backward before resetting her feet.

The wall of starlight flickered, and more blood oozed from Luma's ears and trickled down the sides of her neck. Luma's eyes were watering, but she could see through the shimmering wall that Vell's smile had grown wider. Any minute now, she would break through.

Luma strained her ears for sounds behind her—any indication that Corr had taken the last of the elves and escaped. Was it enough? Had she given them all enough time? Luma couldn't hear anything, and she dared not turn her head to look and make sure.

Another blast, and this time, Luma felt the heat from it scorching across her face. Was Vell's magic getting stronger, or was she getting weaker?

Luma's arms now shook violently, and the wall of starlight flickered several times. Luma's knees threatened to buckle at any moment, and dizziness clawed at her mind. The wounds to her shoulder and side burned. Through a haze, she saw Vell raise her staff once again.

Luma held her breath. *I'm sorry. I hope everyone got away. I'm so sorry.*

Luma braced herself for what would surely be the final blast, but suddenly, there was a flurry of motion on her right. Corr, shield raised, threw himself in front of her just as Vell blasted a hole in Luma's shimmering wall. The battle magic hit Corr's shield dead center, and though they were thrown backward from the force, the shield once again absorbed the battle magic, leaving Luma and Corr unscathed behind it.

Vell's cry of frustration mingled with Luma's gasp of surprise. Mustering a surge of strength she didn't realize she had left, Luma scrambled to her feet and stepped defensively in front of Corr. A wild yell ripped from her throat as she uncrossed her arms and swung them in a wide, sweeping motion in front of her.

Blinding white light poured from Luma's palms and exploded outward in every direction. Vell, along with the remaining group of wizards, were thrown violently backward toward the edge of the forest, all of them knocked unconscious by the concussive force.

****

Corr rushed to Luma, who was, through sheer force of will, still standing, though she swayed wildly on her feet. Corr's gaze roved worriedly from Luma's ghostly pale face to the fresh blood coating the sides of her neck to her hands that trembled uncontrollably.

Luma turned her head to look at him with red-rimmed eyes. Her voice grated hoarsely in her throat. "Did it work? Did everyone get away?"

Corr nodded wordlessly and was about to speak when a rumble and a crash came from behind them. The huge limestone slabs that had made up Northhelm's façade were irreparably damaged and still crumbling. The ground beneath Corr and Luma's feet shook as a huge chunk of stone broke off and crashed downward.

Corr jumped forward, his arm protectively encircling Luma's waist. "Everyone got out. I made sure of it. Now, we need to get out of here too!"

Luma nodded, took a step forward, and stumbled, her head swimming. Corr steadied her and offered a small smile, his dimple showing briefly. "Ruvyn is waiting for us at the border of the plains. Then we will meet the others by the edge of the Inland Sea. I've got you, Luma. Let's move."

****

The sun was beginning to set over the western horizon when Corr, supporting a semi-conscious Luma, emerged from the fringe of the forest where the plains began. Corr paused for a moment and looked around, then breathed a sigh of relief when he saw Ruvyn step out of the shadows and hurry toward them.

"I was about to give up hope for you two. Is she all right?" Ruvyn looked worriedly at Luma.

Corr nodded and shifted slightly under Luma's weight. "She's okay but moving slowly. That fight took a lot out of her."

Ruvyn shook his head in awe. "I've never seen anyone, wizard or elf, be able to take on as much battle magic as she did for as long as she did."

Corr looked over at Ruvyn, his face reflecting a mix of pride and concern. "She's a lot stronger than most know. I don't even think she knows."

Ruvyn glanced back at Luma. "She doesn't look so good right now. Do you think we should stay here and rest until morning?"

Corr shook his head. "No, we are too exposed out here. We can't risk it while Luma is so weak. We must press on and join the others at the edge of the Inland Sea."

****

It was almost fully dark when Corr and Ruvyn, now both helping to support Luma between them, made it to the cliff above the shore of the Inland Sea. They were making their way toward the carved stone steps when a harsh voice rang out in the darkness.

"Stop! Who goes there?"

Corr recognized Figg's voice immediately and

smiled as she materialized out of the darkness at the top of the stairs. "Heya, Figg. I'm glad someone has the sense to keep watch."

Figg strode up to them, a small torch glowing softly in one hand, her dagger in the other. She stuck the dagger back into its sheath and held up her torch toward them, speaking to Corr while glaring at Ruvyn in the flickering light. "So. You believe this one really is with us?" She arched an eyebrow. "What's in it for him?"

Ruvyn gripped his damaged staff in one hand and met Figg's hostile gaze calmly. "Not being killed by Vell, I suppose. Same as you."

Figg took a step forward, and her eyes flashed dangerously in the soft light from the torch. "You helped us escape back at Northhelm, which is the only reason why I haven't killed you where you stand." Her fingers toyed with the hilt of the dagger hanging at her side. "But let's get one thing straight right now, wizard. You and I are *not* the same."

Corr stepped forward and put his free hand on Figg's arm, gently easing it away from the dagger hilt. "Easy there, Figg. Let's focus. Luma needs to recover her strength, and quickly."

Figg glanced at Luma and nodded. "Right. At the base of the stairs, there is a little cave where she can rest in safety tonight. The other survivors are camping a short way down the beach. In the morning, we can see where we stand. Follow me."

The cave entrance was partially covered by hanging vines and tucked discreetly just behind where the stone stairs ended at the narrow beach. It was very small, only big enough for one person to lie down comfortably. Figg gathered some blankets, then went back out to keep watch while Corr and Ruvyn laid Luma down and covered her with the blankets. She was instantly asleep.

Corr watched Luma for a moment in the semi-darkness, noting that her face was still very pale, but now, in sleep, her breathing was deep and steady. With a small sigh, Corr stepped outside the cave entrance and sat down in the pebbly sand. Then he raised his eyes skyward to the Four Stars, now forming a nearly perfect line, and hoped desperately that Luma would be much better by morning.

Chapter 23

The sun rose the next day bright and clear, and Luma slept on. Outside the little cave, the crystalline waters of the Inland Sea lapped softly against the shoreline.

Since before dawn, Corr had busied himself gathering kindling and driftwood for a small fire. As he walked back up the beach, he noticed Ruvyn. The wizard was sitting with his back against the cliff wall, his staff across his lap, and his head cradled in his hands.

Corr put down his small pile of kindling and approached slowly, concern written on his face. "Ruvyn? What's the matter? Are you all right?"

Ruvyn slowly lifted his head at the sound of Corr's voice. His face was pale, and there was a sheen of sweat along his brow.

He sniffed and gave Corr a weak smile. "Hey, Corr. Yeah, I'm...I'm okay. It's just," he paused as if searching for the right way to explain. "It's something about this place. It makes me feel...off. It started when I was waiting at the edge of the plains for you and Luma. But it's gotten much worse since we arrived at this beach. Mainly these terrible headaches."

He sniffed again, and Corr noticed a thin trickle of red from beneath Ruvyn's nostrils. Ruvyn twitched his nose and dabbed at it with a small kerchief. He looked down at the blotch of red left behind and shrugged, raising his eyes again to Corr. "Oh yeah, and the nose bleeds started this morning."

Corr was about to say something when an angry shout rang out from farther down the beach. A small group of Plains Clan Elves approached. The one in the front, a tall, burly elf, stopped a few feet from Corr and Ruvyn. He crossed heavily tattooed arms in front of his wide chest and glared with open hostility at Ruvyn.

"You shouldn't be here, *wizard,*" he growled through clenched teeth.

Corr stepped forward and regarded the other elf calmly. "Hello, friend. This is Ruvyn, and he's with us now. He and I escaped the cells of the White Keep together."

The burly elf let out a short, barking laugh and sneered at Corr. "I am no friend of yours, forest dweller. You two are working together to help the wizards destroy us!"

Corr's face flushed a deep crimson, and at his sides, his hands clenched into fists. The elf took a step forward and thrust an accusing finger at Corr. He raised his voice so that the others behind him could hear.

"The location of Northhelm has been a closely kept secret of the Plains Clan for generations!" He turned, now addressing the crowd of survivors that was beginning to gather. He pointed again at Corr. "Then, we started bringing in *outsiders!* Forest Elves who don't belong in our territory! Then, one of those Forest Elves," he shot a cold glance at Corr, "gets himself captured by the wizards, and shortly after, Northhelm is attacked!" He raised his voice louder. "This elf is a traitor!" He turned and glared back and forth between Corr and Ruvyn. "An elf traitor and a wizard spy!"

The comment pushed Corr past the limits of his

normally even temper. With a yell, he launched himself at the other elf, bringing them both to the ground in a spray of sand. Over and over, they rolled, evenly matched, each one fighting to maintain the upper hand. Ruvyn scrambled to his feet and clutched his damaged staff, unsure of what, if anything, he could do to help.

From farther down the beach, Aire heard the commotion. She cried out in dismay and began hobbling as fast as her injured ankle would allow toward the two combatants, cursing as her crutch sank awkwardly into the sand. Elas and Figg also ran forward.

"Enough!"

The unmistakable voice of Eldamarr Rinn boomed above the sounds of the scuffle. Corr and the other elf broke apart, panting slightly. Corr brushed away the sand that clung to the side of his pants and looked over to see the mage walking toward them, his ship bobbing gently in the shallows a short way down the beach.

The group that had gathered around the fighters parted deferentially to allow the mage to pass through. He stopped a short distance from the two elves, his wand held lightly in his left hand. He nodded to Corr and then turned his attention to the other elf.

"What is your name?"

The other elf stared at Eldamarr Rinn for a second, almost as if not truly believing his eyes. Then he found his voice. "I am Taene." He raised his chin. "Of Plains Clan."

The mage nodded. "Well, Taene. Do you speak for all Plains Clan in your accusations against these two?" He gestured to Corr and Ruvyn.

"No. He does not." All eyes turned toward Haryk as he stepped confidently forward, flanked by Figg and

Emalet. Haryk rolled his shoulders, stretching the bandages that covered his battle magic wounds. He fixed Taene with a hard stare as he repeated himself slowly, punctuating each word. "He. Does. Not."

Taene returned Haryk's stare for a moment, then looked away. Corr stepped forward toward Haryk and the others. He looked earnestly into their faces, his hands held wide. "I swear, I didn't tell them Northhelm's location. I would never do that."

Haryk met Corr's gaze and held it. "I know."

Ruvyn, still looking very pale, sat back down. He leaned his back against the wall of the cliff and wiped his nose again with his kerchief. Another smear of blood stained the cloth as he pulled it away.

Eldamarr Rinn raised his voice to address the whole group of elves on the beach. "Mistrust in one another makes us all weak. The alignment is nearly upon us, and there is no time for weakness. Infighting is the quickest way to ensure Vell's ultimate victory." He looked over at Corr. "I can sense Luma's starlight power, but it is very faint. I am here to bring her back to the island where she can quickly recover the strength she will surely need not long from now."

Corr nodded. "I will bring you to her."

Eldamarr Rinn started to follow Corr but then turned and walked back toward Ruvyn as the crowd of gathered elves dispersed. He crouched in front of the wizard and looked him over appraisingly.

"You are Ruvyn. I remember you from many years ago when you were allowed special access across our bridge from Malicath. You came to the Elders Council with a proposal for establishing trade between our two worlds. You spoke passionately about the need for magical moderation. Quite unusual for a wizard."

Ruvyn looked up at the mage and nodded slowly. "Yeah. And a lot of good it did me."

Eldamarr Rinn shrugged. "For what it's worth, I thought it was a good proposal, and I told King Tarak and the elders as much. But at that time, the river of mistrust ran too deep to ford."

The mage's eyes slid from Ruvyn's pale face to the blood-smeared kerchief in his hand. "It must be quite uncomfortable for you to be here by the Inland Sea. The deep magic surrounding this place is not gentle on your kind."

He glanced at Ruvyn's battered staff. "Incidentally, it is only because your staff is so damaged that you can tolerate being here at all. Still, the lingering effects are quite unpleasant, I am sure."

Ruvyn's thumb traced over the deep half-moon marks left in the polished wood from Vell's fingernails. A subtle nod was his only answer. He sniffed again.

Corr looked down at Ruvyn, then back up at Eldamarr Rinn. "He can't leave here. Vell would kill him immediately. Isn't there anything we can do to help?"

The mage thought for a moment, then nodded. "Just a minute."

He returned to his ship and, a short time later, walked back across the beach and crouched once again in front of Ruvyn. He held out a medium-sized leather pouch, closed at the top with a drawstring.

"Dried seaweed harvested from the shallows around the island. Good for a number of magical ailments. Rather bitter in flavor, I must say, but chewing some pieces a few times a day should ease the symptoms you feel."

Ruvyn reached out and took the pouch gratefully. He opened it, pulled out a small piece, and popped it into his mouth. "Thank you."

The mage nodded to him and stood back up, looking at Corr. "Now, take me to see the Daughter of Starlight."

Chapter 24

Izarre raised a hand to shield her eyes and squinted upward. The sky was a cloudless deep blue, and the forest surrounding the small cottage hummed with the gentle sounds of late summer. Izarre scanned the sky once more, then lowered her hand with a sigh. Where *was* he?

"Beautiful day, is it not?"

At the sound of the voice behind her, Izarre jumped and spun, her right hand reaching for the handle of the dagger sheathed at her hip. But her surprise quickly turned to relief, then just as quickly, to annoyance. She put her hands on her hips and glared down at the speaker.

"Trill! My poor nerves."

The big owl stretched out one wing, then crossed it in front of his chest and began preening his flight feathers.

"I'm sure I don't know what you mean, Izarre. I can't help it if you are unobservant to changes in your surroundings."

Izarre pursed her lips and decided to change the subject, knowing it was folly to get into an argument with an owl.

"Well. Now that you are here, *finally*." She arched an eyebrow at Trill.

He continued preening and pretended not to notice her tone.

Izarre continued, gesturing toward the door of the cottage. "Come in and tell me how it went."

Once inside, Trill perched on the back of a stout wooden chair across from the small fireplace. Izarre made a cup of tea, sat down across from him, and took a sip. Her stomach churned with anticipation, but she did not want to rush Trill about sharing his news. Owls could be so snobbish about that sort of thing.

Finally, Trill clacked his beak once and began. "With the help of my other six, we flew far and wide. You were right, Izarre. More elves survived the initial wizard invasion than previously believed. They were scattered, disorganized, and in hiding, but we found them." There was pride in his voice.

Despite herself, Izarre leaned forward, urging Trill on. "And?" she pressed, her normally quiet voice becoming shrill with excitement. "And, what of it?"

Trill blinked his huge eyes several times and clacked his beak once again. Izarre leaned back and fell silent.

"And…" Trill continued. 'Once they were assured that the Daughter of Starlight had indeed returned, they agreed to come to the banks of the Inland Sea and ready themselves for war."

Izarre leaped to her feet in jubilation, her tea sloshing over the edge of her cup and onto the stone floor of the cabin. Trill watched her with haughty censure. Izarre put her cup down sheepishly and wiped up the spill with a small towel.

Trill shifted from foot to foot, his huge talons digging into the back of the chair. "There is something else. Vell and many of the wizards have regrouped since the attack on Northhelm. They are back at the White Keep."

Izarre nodded. "I understand. Thank you, Trill."

A short time later, Trill had once again launched himself silently into the blue sky, and Izarre stepped out of the cottage, closing the door tightly behind her. She shouldered a small pack of supplies and a canteen of water and checked to make sure her dagger was secured at her hip.

Pausing, Izarre took a deep breath, exhaling as she looked up the small path that led up the mountain and into the cave. Then, with quick, purposeful steps, she started walking, bound for the shores of the Inland Sea.

In less than a week, Izarre knew she would be back in the mountains, and she wouldn't be alone. Luma would enter the cave, get to the Cavern of the Four, and use her starlight to heal the Sacred Stones.

And Izarre would protect her. They all would. Or they would die trying.

****

The little ship skimmed easily over the gently rolling waves of the Inland Sea, bound once again for the island.

Eldamarr Rinn turned away from the water and entered the ship's small cabin, where Luma lay on a narrow cot. Tsarra had treated and bandaged her battle magic injuries as best she could, but it wasn't the physical wounds that the mage was concerned with. Gently, he reached out his hand and placed it on Luma's forehead. She twitched in her sleep but did not wake. Her forehead felt slightly warmer than normal, but her breathing was steady, and a healthy flush had returned to her formerly pallid cheeks.

Before they had left the beach, Corr had told Eldamarr Rinn about what happened at Northhelm. The mage looked down at Luma with a mixture of pride and concern. The amount of energy and focus it must have taken for Luma to channel enough starlight to hold a wall against Vell's battle magic for that long was a testament to her extraordinary power.

But he knew Luma's ultimate test was yet to come.

****

Eldamarr Rinn got back up and went to stand at the bow of the ship. In the distance, he could hear the rumble of the waterfall illusion. They would arrive back on the island soon.

Alone in the cabin, Luma shifted on the narrow cot and murmured something in her sleep. Behind her closed eyelids, her eyes moved back and forth as she sank deeper into her dream.

Flashes of light and images danced before her, abstract and blurred at first, then becoming sharper and more focused. The Cavern of the Four. And the Sacred Stones themselves, their cracks like deep, festering wounds. Stoic and still, they loomed before her, and she could hear their cries echoing through her bones. They were dying. Hot tears of anguish burned behind Luma's eyes. She tried to reach out to the Stones, to help them, heal them, but her arms felt as if they were made of lead and refused to move.

Lying on the cot in the ship's cabin, a single tear trickled from beneath Luma's closed eyelid and ran a wet path down the side of her cheek.

I'm not strong enough.

In her dream, Luma tore her gaze from the Sacred Stones and looked up to find that the cavern roof had vanished to reveal an inky night sky. And then, there they were. In a near-perfect line, the Four Stars twinkled against the black velvet backdrop. Outshining all others, they called to her in voices both familiar and foreign.

And then, they, too, were gone, along with the cavern and the Sacred Stones.

Now, Luma was on the island, standing where the black sand beach gave way to thick, coarse grasses, and a little stream trickled over rocks to meet the Inland Sea. Slowly, Luma's gaze followed the stream backward to where it ended in a small pool underneath a waterfall. A waterfall that looked like bars.

In the depths of her dreaming, Luma stared at the waterfall, and suddenly, a thought rose in her mind. Not a waterfall—a prison. A prison with a prisoner.

The scars on Luma's palms began to ache and throb. She took a step closer, then another step, and another until she was standing directly in front of it. Leaning forward, she tilted her head and squinted her eyes, straining to see past the bars of falling water and into the darkness beyond them.

Who are you?

Luma felt a weight on her shoulder. It was shaking her gently, slowly pulling her away. Without turning her head from the waterfall, Luma tried to shrug it off, but the weight remained. The area around her was becoming unfocused, the rocks and the stream blurring together as the weight tugged again at her shoulder. Luma blinked, and someone, something, just behind the bars of water, moved in the darkness. Luma's scars ached, and the four rings encircling her fingers started to feel warm. The something moved again—it was hovering just behind the bars of water. Any moment, it would step forward just a bit, and she would be able to see it. Just a tiny bit more…

"Luma!"

Luma's eyes flew open, and she surged upright, throwing her hands in front of her, her scars glowing in the dim light of the ship's cabin.

Eldamarr Rinn, who had been leaning over and gently shaking Luma's shoulder, jumped back. "It's okay, Luma! It's okay. It's just me. I was worried when you didn't wake at first."

Breathing heavily, Luma dropped her hands and stared around in confusion. "Are we on the ship?"

The mage nodded. "Yes, the elves that you helped escape from Northhelm are safe for now on the banks of the Inland Sea. The alignment will begin in one week's time, and it will demand all of your strength. The deep magic that surrounds this island will help you recover more quickly."

Luma's eyes, which had been roaming the cabin while the mage talked, snapped up. "Are we there now? At the island?"

Eldamarr Rinn nodded again. "We just arrived. Can you walk?"

Without answering, Luma swung her legs over the side of the narrow cot and stood up. She faltered slightly for a moment, then, squaring her shoulders, she walked to the door of the cabin and pulled it open, calling over her shoulder as she did.

"There's no time to lose. I have some questions for you, but I can ask them on the way. Come on."

Eldamarr Rinn followed behind Luma. "What do you mean? What questions? Where are you going?"

Luma had already hopped over the edge of the ship and was splashing her way through the shallows toward the black sand beach. Once there, she turned and waited impatiently until the mage joined her.

"We are going to the waterfall, and you will tell me what is imprisoned there and what it has to do with starlight magic."

****

Along the banks of the Inland Sea, things had begun to settle into a routine. Humble dwelling shelters were constructed, and kindling for small cooking fires was gathered and stacked. Foraging and hunting parties were sent out, and Aire organized groups for fishing off the shore.

With Luma gone and the alignment fast approaching, the small group of elves that had survived the attack at Northhelm were keenly aware that their position was tenuous, and they were constantly on their guard.

Early one morning, Figg was sitting at the base of the stone stairs, inspecting the group's meager supply of remaining weapons. She sensed movement on the stairs and looked up to see Haryk, now almost fully recovered from his battle magic wounds, descending from the top of the cliff.

Figg rolled her eyes. She turned toward him as he approached and threw her hands up in exasperation. "Oh, come on. My last shift at the watch lasted most of the night! You've barely been up there ten minutes!"

Haryk pursed his lips but couldn't hide the excitement dancing behind his eyes. He took Figg's arm. "I'm not asking you to relieve my watch already, Figg. But I promise you'll want to see this. Come on! Hurry!"

Confused and intrigued, Figg twisted her arm out of Haryk's grasp. "All right, all right. I'm coming. You don't need to pull me around."

Figg was still grumbling as she neared the top of the

stairs, but when she stepped over the lip of the cliff, she fell silent, her eyes wide.

A large group of elves, nearly one hundred by her quick estimate, approached from across the plain. Figg's mouth hung open as she stared at them.

The majority of the newly arrived elves looked strong and capable, and from among them, weapons bristled: swords, shields, bows, and arrows. Figg tore her gaze away from the incoming group long enough to glance at Haryk, who raised a single eyebrow at her, a smirk curling the corners of his mouth.

"I told you you'd want to see this."

Figg turned back to the approaching group just in time to see Trill soaring down from over their heads. He landed a short distance to her left and folding his wings judiciously behind his back, hopped over to stand beside her. Figg smiled down at the big owl, and he swiveled his huge eyes up to meet hers.

"It was Izarre's idea, though executed flawlessly by myself and the other six. The time has come for elves to unite fully once again. The alignment requires it."

Figg nodded gratefully to Trill and then looked over at Haryk, her eyes shining. "Can you believe it? All these years, I never even knew there were that many left in hiding."

Haryk, who now seemed to find himself at a loss for words, nodded silently in agreement. Upon hearing Figg's remark, Trill hopped closer. "These are but the first. There will be more arriving over the next day or so."

Figg stared down at Trill in disbelief. "More? How many more? Do they also have weapons?" Her voice brimmed with excitement.

Trill stared at her with cool passivity. Owls never got overly excited. Figg coughed awkwardly and fell silent.

"More. Yes. As I said," Trill answered snobbishly. He blinked slowly and turned his head away, indicating that that was all the information Figg was going to get from him.

As Trill took to the sky once again, the incoming group of elves stopped a short distance from where Figg and Haryk stood at the cliff edge. One elf stepped forward. She had a large shield fixed on her arm and a sword at her hip. Together, Haryk and Figg approached her.

Figg was the first to speak. "You are welcome here. My name is Figg. This is Haryk. We have a small group of others on the beach below."

The other elf removed the shield on her arm and spread her hands wide in a symbol of peace. "My name is Nuela. I have been appointed to speak for this group. We joined together to journey from the far south, where we have spent many long years in hiding, always under threat of being hunted down by the wizards. But now, we are told that the Daughter of Starlight has returned, that now, there is hope. We have come to fight."

Figg smiled broadly. "Then I will say again, Nuela. You are welcome here."

Chapter 25

That night, the banks of the Inland Sea hummed with excitement and a palpable sense of relief.

Aire's ankle had finally healed so that she no longer needed her crutch, and her group of fisherelves had had a bountiful catch. Along the shore, cooking fires blazed while elves from all over Edira met, mingled, and shared stories of triumph and tragedy, but mostly of survival.

****

Trill had spoken true; more groups of elves, some comprising of only a handful, others as large as Nuela's group, had continued to arrive throughout the day. Ruvyn, whose nosebleeds had stopped but was still looking rather pale, was initially met with fear and suspicion by the incoming elves. But with the constant advocacy of Corr and Haryk, he was grudgingly accepted in their midst, though most elves continued to give him a wide berth.

Figg could barely contain her giddy excitement when she saw the variety of weapons these newly arrived elves had managed to keep hidden from the wizards over the years. Elas, Corr, and Ruvyn walked up as she was eyeing one of the newcomers' longbows covetously.

Elas looked at it too and nodded approvingly. "It's a beauty. And arrows can kill wizards, but their battle magic can still do far more damage to us than any weapon we have. The odds are always against us."

Figg responded without taking her gaze off the longbow. "Yeah, but now we have Luma."

Elas shrugged. "True, but she isn't going to be taking on Vell and the whole wizard army singlehandedly. During the alignment, Luma will need to be in the Cavern of the Four, using that starlight of hers to heal the Sacred Stones. That's going to take all her strength as it is."

Figg finally pulled her gaze off the longbow and looked over at Elas. "So…we get her to the cavern, and we protect her as best we can with the weapons we have." She crossed her thin, battle-magic scarred arms over her chest and cocked her head at Elas. "And hopefully, she will get it done before we are all dead. You got a better idea?"

Elas was about to retort when Corr gasped. "That reminds me of something, Elas. My shield, the one I found at the White Keep!"

Elas looked at Corr, annoyed. "Yes, Corr. It's a very nice shield. Good job."

Corr raised his eyebrows at Elas. "Um, yes, it is. But that's not my point. That shield stopped battle magic during the fight for Northhelm—it even took a direct blast from Vell, and it didn't shatter."

Figg chimed in. "I remember you mentioned that it helped you and Luma escape. But that shield actually withstood battle magic from *Vell* herself? How is that possible? No elf weapon has ever been able to do that."

The four of them stared at each other in silence for a moment before Ruvyn piped up. "I think it was Luma."

Corr fixed him with a skeptical expression. "Luma? What do you mean?"

Ruvyn shook his head as if trying to clear it. He

popped another small piece of the seaweed that Eldamarr Rinn had given him into his mouth and grimaced at the bitter taste, then explained.

"Well, not Luma herself, but her power...her starlight. When we were fighting near Northhelm, some of her starlight hit that shield, remember? I don't think she did it on purpose. But after that, the battle magic wasn't effective on it anymore. Almost as if the shield had some kind of protective barrier on it or something."

Corr's mouth hung open as realization dawned on his face. "Ruvyn, you're right! It was just after the shield was hit by Luma's starlight that it was able to withstand the battle magic. I never realized the two were connected!"

Figg looked back and forth between Corr and Ruvyn, her eyes dancing with excitement. "Do you think that Luma could do that again? Transfer starlight protection onto more shields?"

Ruvyn shook his head. "I don't know. But if she can, it could help even the odds."

****

Although Luma's excitement drove her onward, she was still physically weak, and the trek to the waterfall was arduous.

Eldamarr Rinn followed a short distance behind and implored her to slow down, stop, and rest, but Luma just shook her head and stumbled resolutely onward.

Finally, she reached the far edge of the beach, where the black sand gave way to a jumble of small boulders and coarse grass. Her legs trembling, Luma put a hand on one of the boulders to steady herself. After a second, she started forward again, but the mage caught her arm and held her back.

"Wait, Luma."

Luma turned to face him. "Come on. We are almost there."

She tried to pull her arm away, but the mage held firmly. "Just wait a moment. Please. There is something I must tell you before we approach that waterfall."

Luma nodded slowly, and the mage let go of her arm. She stood there, watching him intently. He knew something. At her sides, her hands opened and closed into loose fists.

Eldamarr Rinn glanced down at them and then back up at Luma's face. "Are your scars bothering you?"

Luma, who hadn't noticed what her hands had been doing, blinked in surprise and then brought them up in front of her, inspecting the dark scars that crisscrossed her palms. She looked back at Eldamarr Rinn.

"Well…yeah, I guess. They don't hurt, exactly. It's just sort of a really deep ache. And it gets worse as I get closer to the waterfall. Why is that?"

Eldamarr Rinn nodded. "I thought so."

He motioned for Luma to sit with him on the rocks. Luma, impatient to get to the waterfall, shook her head at first but then sighed and sat down next to him.

The mage took a breath. "I told you before that there is deep magic on this island. I also told you that this island has long been a place for elf mages. And that is true—but it was not always so."

Luma eyed him skeptically. "I don't understand."

The mage nodded. "Let me try and explain. In Edira's earliest days, it was this island that rose from the churning, primitive seas that covered our world to become the first land. And then, from the depths of those seas, came the first creatures up onto this new land."

Luma leaned forward, her eyes wide. "What creatures?"

The mage returned her gaze, his voice barely above a whisper. "The dragons."

The sound of Luma's laughter filled the still air, and she nearly tumbled off the side of the rock she had been sitting on. Eldamarr Rinn looked at her incredulously, not sure what to do about this unexpected bout of mirth. He shifted awkwardly.

Luma finally got control of herself. She snorted and giggled a few times, wiped her eyes, and then smiled over at the mage. "Dragons. Yeah. Okay." She winked at him. "Elves, wizards, talking owls, fighting for my life, and yet, everyone forgot to mention before that there are also *dragons* to deal with." She rolled her eyes.

The mage pursed his lips and shook his head. He looked into Luma's face, his voice low and sincere. "Not dragons, plural, not anymore. Dragon. Singular. And the reason that you haven't heard about this before is because most elves don't even know that there is one that still lives. It is the last of its kind, as far as I am aware, and has been imprisoned behind that waterfall for generations."

Luma stared back at the mage, still trying to determine if he was serious or playing a trick on her.

The mage held her gaze and nodded. "According to the ancient writings, dragons were once plentiful when the world of Edira was young. They adapted incredibly quickly to life on this island, aided by the deep magic here. Time passed, and they continued to adapt and soon took to the skies. By this time, the water around the island had become ringed with land, making it the Inland Sea we know today. And that land had become populated by elves." Eldamarr Rinn took a breath and let it out in a long sigh, then continued. "The dragons wreaked havoc on those early elven settlements. But it wasn't long before the elves adapted as well. They invented new weapons—longbows and spears, and soon prey had become predator. Early elf kings used dragon heads and hides as trophies, symbols of their status. According to what is written, in the face of the onslaught, the dragons retreated once more to this island, but they were no longer safe, even here. Eventually, they were hunted to extinction, all save one. The last dragon was magically imprisoned behind that waterfall by one of the first elf mages to take up residence here.

Luma shook her head, still in disbelief at what she had been told. "But what does this all have to do with my starlight? Why does it make my scars ache when I am near the waterfall?"

Eldamarr Rinn explained. "Remember the metal I told you that was used to make your conduit rings?"

Luma nodded, looking down at the thin, silver bands that encircled the first and middle fingers on each of her hands.

"As I mentioned before," the mage continued, "bits of each of the Four Stars fell to Edira in those early days, seeding this world with its magic. They fell on this island when the dragons were first emerging from the sea. Much later, when one of the elf mages mined the site of the impact, he wrote that he believed the dragon population shared a strong connection to the Four Stars. I believe the starlight within you is picking up on a familiar energy signature from behind the waterfall."

Luma had heard enough. She leaped to her feet and began scrambling over the boulders toward the waterfall.

The mage followed her, calling as he went.

"Luma! Hold on! You must be cautious! No elf has been in contact with a dragon in generations, and there's a good reason for that! Plus, I…I don't even know if it is still alive!"

Luma spun around, her hands clenched into tight fists, the rings on her fingers glinting in the sunlight. "Oh, it's alive, all right."

Chapter 26

It was midday, and Vell stood in the meeting hall of the White Keep, watching the River Aque as it twisted a wide silver line through the forest below. She didn't turn when the door banged open, and heavy footsteps approached.

"Hello, Naro."

Naro bowed slightly at the back of Vell's head. "I have a report."

Vell spun to face him, her long, silvery hair swishing over her shoulder. Casually, she flicked her left wrist, and her staff materialized out of the air. She wrapped her fingers around it delicately. "Yes?"

Naro squared his shoulders. "It appears that the elves are mobilizing. They are coming out of hiding from all over Edira and have amassed at the edge of the Inland Sea."

Vell raised her eyebrows. "Is that so? And is Luma with them?"

Naro shook his head. "I don't believe so. I believe she went back to the island. The rest of the elves seem to be waiting for her."

Vell nodded, a cruel smile playing on her lips. She turned back toward the window, and when she spoke, it was almost to herself. "Interesting. If she went back to the island with the mage, then that little stunt she pulled at Northhelm must have weakened her significantly.

Even more than I thought." Her smile broadened, and she turned back to Naro. "Gather a traveling party of a dozen wizards and ready two raptera as well. We leave for the shore of the Inland Sea before first light tomorrow."

"But, but Vell…" Naro faltered, "we can't go in the Inland Sea. The deep magic…"

Vell rolled her eyes, cutting him off. "I know that, fool. I'm not saying we take a swim in the waters—I am saying we get close, just close enough to send a message."

****

Luma didn't slow her pace until she arrived at the small pool beneath the waterfall. Then, she stood still, her chest heaving as she studied the cascading bars of water. The deep ache in her scars pulsed from her palms up to her wrists, and a small shiver ran along her spine. Eldamarr Rinn approached and stopped a few paces behind her.

Luma glanced back over her shoulder. "Can you open it?"

The mage shook his head. "I…I don't think so. There is nothing written in the ancient scrolls about releasing the dragon, and probably for good reason!"

Luma sighed and turned back to face the waterfall. "Fine. I'll do it."

The mage opened his mouth to protest, but Luma had already raised her hands. Instead, he closed his mouth and held his breath.

Luma didn't know exactly what she should do, only that she must do something, so she closed her eyes and turned her attention inward as she held her hands out directly in front of her. With slow, careful breaths, she focused on the sensation, the pulses of energy running like a current through the crisscrossed maze of scars that covered her palms.

Don't fight it.

Across Luma's palms, the dark scars began to glow with soft, white light, and across the small pool, the center bars of the waterfall began to quiver. From behind her, the mage's eyes widened, but Luma's remained tightly closed. She took a deep breath and slowly, keeping her palms facing forward, moved her arms out to the right and left as if drawing open a curtain.

In response, the center bars of water trembled, and then they began to split. Elbows locked and eyes still closed, Luma continued to move her arms slowly out to either side while Eldamarr Rinn watched in stunned fascination as the bars of water pulled apart.

Once Luma had moved her arms all the way out on either side of her, she stood in stillness for a moment. Eyes still squeezed shut, she took a deep breath and dropped her arms. Silence pervaded the area until suddenly, somewhere in front of her, the sound of a splash.

Luma's eyes flew open, and she found herself staring into twin orbs of deep, obsidian black. A small noise, somewhere between a scream and a sigh, escaped Luma's mouth, and she took an involuntary step backward. The black gaze followed her movement unblinkingly.

Luma swallowed hard as she stared into those eyes, and somewhere in the back of her mind, a nagging question arose as to whether this was going to be the last moment of her life.

The eyes were so deeply black that she could see her own reflection in them. How very small and fragile she appeared. But as she continued to stare into the obsidian depths, Luma realized that the emotion she was feeling wasn't fear, as she had first thought. It was something else: curiosity, perhaps? Yes, but also a mix of other things: kinship and grief.

Cautiously, Luma brought her hands forward, palms facing up. Her scars throbbed painfully. The creature shifted backward, and Luma's breath caught in her throat as she saw it fully for the first time.

She recognized that what was standing before her was indeed a dragon, but it was not the hulking, demon-like creature from the fairy tales she had heard as a child. Though distinctly reptilian in appearance, it was similar in size to a very large horse. Its chest was broad, and just behind the wide shoulders were folded bat-like wings, each with a large, hooked claw at its top point.

The muscular torso was supported by four thick legs, and behind it, a long, well-muscled tail swished back and forth, churning the water of the pool into small waves. In single file, beginning at the tip of the tail, ran a line of sharp-looking spines that stopped at the center of its back. Two more larger spines protruded from where the back of the neck met the shoulder. Its neck was about half the length of its body, and under its chin, a double line of shorter spikes bristled from one side of the jaw to the other.

But it was the dragon's face that most captured Luma's attention, for starting halfway up the wide muzzle and ending between the two large obsidian eyes were four distinctly star-like markings. The markings, each one identical to the others and spaced evenly apart, were a pale creamy white, which stood in stark contrast to the dark, blue-gray coloring of the rest of the dragon's scaly body.

Luma stood in silent awe, her hands still palms up, raised slightly in front of her.

Inching forward to the very edge of the pool, Luma lifted her right hand and reached out toward the dragon. At her movement, a low hiss formed at the base of the dragon's throat, and the area under its chin swelled, pushing the double row of spikes menacingly outward. The shining black eyes watched her with suspicion, and the thickly scaled corners of its mouth pulled upward to reveal an impressive set of teeth, shockingly white and razor sharp.

That nagging question once again rose in her mind, and Luma's stomach churned with fear, but she didn't lower her hand. The scars along her palm began to glow faintly.

The dragon prowled forward, and it took all Luma's considerable willpower to remain where she was, hand outstretched, when every fiber of her being was screaming for her to run. She glanced up as the dragon moved closer until it was staring down, directly over her. Luma reached up her hand farther, while at the same time, the dragon lowered its head slightly.

A second later, Luma's hand made contact with the front of the dragon's face, her palm covering the four white star-like markings.

A small gasp escaped Luma's lips, and she closed her eyes as a warm current of energy pulsed through her, simmering beneath her skin. A moment later, her eyes fluttered open, and she pulled her hand away.

The dragon crouched in the shallow pool, spread its wings, and launched itself into the air, scattering droplets of water over the heads of Luma and a very stunned-looking Eldamarr Rinn.

Luma glanced at the mage. An awed smile spread across her face, and the fingers of her right hand, the one that had touched the dragon's face, trembled visibly.

The mage stepped cautiously forward and stared at Luma with concern. "Luma? Are you all right?" He took Luma's hand in his and squeezed it gently. "By the power of the Four, I cannot believe it!"

Luma raised her chin skyward, her gaze following the swooping circles of the dragon high above them. Then she looked back down at Eldamarr Rinn, her smile broadening.

"His name is Ketu. And he's going to help us."

Chapter 27

It was Corr's turn to take the overnight watch, and as he paced the cliff edge in the darkness, his mind churned with questions. Was Luma all right? Was she recovering her strength, and would she be ready in time? Corr stopped walking and raised his eyes skyward. The Four Stars twinkled brilliantly against the velvety black sky, and very low on the horizon, bands of pink and gold shimmered, whispering of a new day to come. Corr sighed into the still night air. The time of the alignment was almost upon them.

Just then, movement from across the plain caught Corr's attention. He squinted in the dim light and watched cautiously as a single figure approached through the grass.

"Who goes there?" Corr called out gruffly. He hoisted his shield on one arm while the fingers on his other hand strayed to the hilt of the dagger in his belt.

"Corr? Is that you?"

Corr's eyes widened. He dropped his shield and dashed forward, a smile lighting up his face. "Izarre! You're here!"

Izarre reached out, and the two of them gripped each other's forearms in the greeting of elves. She was also smiling, but there was worry behind her large, dark eyes. Corr motioned for her to follow, and together, they walked to the top of the cliff stairs. There, they paused, and Corr turned to her.

"It is good to see you, Izarre. Many others have come to join us as well. The clans are uniting as never before, but you are troubled. What's wrong?"

Izarre nodded. "I'm glad to know that Trill was successful in gathering our scattered brethren, and I'm happy to be here, but I'm afraid I come with bad news to share. On the journey, I saw from a distance a group of wizards headed this way, led by Vell."

Corr sucked in his breath. "Wizards—coming here? To the shore of the Inland Sea? How is that possible? Does she mean to attack?"

Izarre shook her head. "I don't think so. She is traveling with a smaller group, only about a dozen wizards, by my estimate. And the deep magic surrounding the Inland Sea should still offer us protection while on the beach. I don't know what her plan is, but I know it can't be good."

Corr clenched his teeth, his face grim. "We must warn the others."

Corr ushered Izarre down the stone stairs ahead of him and cast a worried glance over his shoulder at the plains stretching behind him to the edge of the darkened forest. Then he hurried to follow her to the beach.

An agitated murmur ran through the gathering of elves at Corr and Izarre's news. Figg immediately began gathering arrows for her new longbow that she had managed to sweet-talk away from its previous owner.

Seeing this, Emalet put a steadying hand on Figg's shoulder. "Easy there, Figg. We can't fight them. Not like this. We aren't ready."

Figg shrugged off Emalet's hand and resumed what she was doing. "Speak for yourself, Emalet. I'm always ready."

****

To both Luma and Eldamarr Rinn's surprise, Ketu was an excellent fisher.

The two elves sat on the black sand beach, watching the dragon circle offshore. Then, like a great bird of prey, he folded his wings and dove, striking the surface of the water with barely a ripple. Soon, he emerged from the depths with a triumphant splash, a large fish clenched in his formidable jaws. Then, aided by the swishing of his powerful tail and semi-webbed feet, he swam easily to shore, gulping down his meal as he went.

Luma's gaze moved with the dragon as he stepped out of the sea and onto the beach, his huge black claws leaving deep indents in the wet sand along the tide line. The water beaded as it slid off his scaly body and glistened across the four creamy white markings on his face.

The dragon swung his head, his black gaze roving suspiciously across Eldamarr Rinn before coming to land on Luma. Luma held his gaze for a moment, then the dragon turned and walked with reptilian grace farther down the beach, where he eventually curled up in the shade of the cliff.

Eldamarr Rinn watched the now-napping dragon for a moment, then cocked his head at Luma. "He doesn't seem to like me much."

Luma smiled. "Well, you said it was an elf mage that imprisoned him all those years ago, and I have heard that dragons are prone to holding grudges." She paused for a moment, thinking. "How did he survive all those years trapped behind the waterfall anyway?"

The mage shrugged. "Most likely, he went into a

state of deep hibernation. I've heard it is not uncommon for dragons to sleep for decades, waiting for the right conditions. Probably the combination of the coming alignment and your starlight energy on the island finally roused him." He looked over at Luma. "Can you communicate with him?"

Luma tilted her head. "Yes and no...it's hard to explain. It's something to do with the starlight energy that we both share. When I touched the markings on his face, I could sort of...sense things about him. And I'm sure he can do the same with me. His starlight is different, though. It is more peaceful, quieter, less...chaotic than mine." She shrugged, almost apologetically. "I know it doesn't make a lot of sense, but that's the only way I can think to describe it."

Eldamarr Rinn smiled and patted Luma's arm reassuringly. "It makes enough sense for me, Luma. I can't wait to add all this information into the chronicles in my library."

Luma gave the mage a playful shove. "With you, everything comes back to your library."

Eldamarr Rinn chuckled, then raised his chin and sniffed haughtily. "Indeed. Just as it should be. And you are welcome for it."

****

The two of them then lapsed into silence for several moments, watching the waves of the Inland Sea reach up to caress the black sand that sparkled under the clear water like so many diamonds.

Luma finally raised her eyes from the water and looked back at the mage, her face serious. "Being on this island and something about Ketu's presence has reenergized my starlight, and the alignment fast approaches. I must go back to the mainland."

Eldamarr Rinn looked back at her but gave no response, only a small nod. Luma nodded back, then turned away and hung her head.

The mage put a hand on her shoulder and felt it tremble. He leaned closer, trying to get her to look at him. "Luma, what is it?"

In her lap, Luma wrung her hands together. When she finally looked up, her chin quivered, and her eyes were bright with unshed tears. Her voice wavered slightly as she spoke. "At the battle for Northhelm, the elves were fighting, they…they were dying. I couldn't save them all. I tried, but I failed. What…what if the alignment comes, and I fail again? They are all counting on me! But what if, in the end, I am just not strong enough?"

Luma hung her head once again, and her cheeks flushed with shame as her words made real the depth of her innermost fears.

Eldamarr Rinn was quiet for a moment, and when he finally spoke, his voice was soft. "Luma, as I have said, strength comes in many forms. As a mere babe, you were chosen worthy to wield the most powerful force in the cosmos. You are the Daughter of Starlight—you have always been, even during those years spent on the world of Earth, even when your mind forgot. Your body, your blood, remembered. All you must do now is simply step into it. Embrace your power without question and without apology. It is your gift, your birthright—it is who you were always meant to be."

With that, the mage stood up, and Luma did the same. Farther down the beach, Ketu had awakened from his nap and came padding over, his heavy footfalls making no noise in the sand. He stopped a short distance from Luma's left, facing the sea.

Eldamarr Rinn glanced at Ketu, then back at Luma. He nodded toward the dragon. "The alignment may wait for no one, but he has been waiting for you. We all have."

Luma took a deep breath. She wiped her eyes and squared her shoulders. "I leave at first light."

BOOK THREE

The Answer

Chapter 28

Vell and her group of wizards arrived at the edge of the forest just before sunrise. She ordered two wizards to stay back behind the tree line with the two tethered raptera, and then she stepped boldly out onto the plain, the tall, thick grass swishing around her as she walked.

They were about halfway to the edge of the cliff when the other wizards in her party started feeling distinctly unwell. They continued to push forward with their leader, but soon, many began to falter.

Leaning heavily on their staffs, the wizards clutched their heads in agony and wiped blood from their noses. Then some collapsed. Callously ignoring the pain of her fellows, Vell strode purposefully forward toward the lip of the cliff, though she, too, was starting to feel a painful ache in her head. Naro made it farther than the rest of the group of wizards until, finally, he, too, was forced to stop.

Clutching his staff, Naro called to Vell, his voice grating in his throat. "We can go no farther!"

Without turning around, Vell made a dismissive motion with her hand. "Fine. Stay back. I don't need you for this anyway. Just be ready to respond when I give the order."

Naro nodded and made a hasty, stumbling retreat.

He started to feel slightly better once he had put some distance between himself and the edge of the cliff, so he stopped and turned, waiting for Vell's command.

The sun had just crested the eastern horizon when Vell made it to the edge of the cliff. Before her, the shimmering waters of the Inland Sea stretched as far as she could see. Directly below her, crowding the narrow, pebbly beach, was a large gathering of elves, all staring up at her in grim silence. Weapons bristled in their midst.

Vell seethed inwardly as she surveyed the crowd below. If only she could use her battle magic right now. A few well-aimed blasts into these insolent rebels would give her the greatest pleasure, and those weapons of theirs would be useless to protect them. But she knew it was pointless. The deep magic that surrounded this place made using her staff impossible. *Pity.*

The ache in Vell's head intensified. She blinked several times as her vision blurred around the edges. Shoving aside the pain, she raised both hands above her head and called in a loud voice.

"Attention, elves! Very soon, the alignment will be upon us all! There is no stopping it, and there is no stopping me! Before the alignment is over, the Sacred Stones *will* crumble. You must by now realize that there is no fighting this inevitable truth!"

A rumble of anger went up from the group below, and then an answering shout came from somewhere among them.

"We fight for Edira! We fight for the Daughter of Starlight!"

Vell dropped her hands and prowled along the edge of the cliff. She moved with the confidence of someone who knew she couldn't be beaten, of someone who had already won.

Pausing, she smirked down at the group on the beach below. "Oh yes. The Daughter of Starlight, upon whose shoulders all your hopes lie." Her voice dripped with sarcasm, and she spread her hands wide, questioningly. "But…where is your beloved Daughter of Starlight now? Oh! I hear she is gone…again. Run away, back to the island with that useless mage? You fools! Don't you see? Luma couldn't stop me when I destroyed your little hideout, and she will not stop me now."

Vell scanned the crowd below, her deep blue eyes glittering. "But! I am prepared to be merciful in my victory. Give the traitor wizard, Ruvyn, to me now, and when the Sacred Stones fall, I will spare…some of your lives."

"I'll give you something!"

Vell leaped to one side as a longbow arrow whistled upward from the beach and buried itself in the rocky soil where she had been standing a split-second before.

Figg cursed under her breath and immediately began nocking another arrow to her bow when Aire put a hand on her forearm.

"Save your arrows, Figg," she whispered.

Figg glared at Aire but relaxed her arm and grudgingly slid the arrow back into her quiver. Vell bent and ripped the arrow that Figg had fired out of the ground, then held it aloft and contemptuously snapped the thick shaft in two.

Dropping the broken pieces at her feet, Vell glared down once more at the gathering of elves, a malicious smile curling her mouth. "So be it."

Vell spun on her heel and began walking back, away from the edge of the cliff, discreetly wiping a droplet of blood from her nose as she went. When she approached Naro, she called out, "Release the raptera. Send them to the beach. Leave no survivors."

Naro nodded, then rushed toward the tree line where the other wizards and their monstrous charges were waiting.

A few minutes later, two raptera, free of their restraints, launched themselves into the air in a flurry of black feathers. The grass on the plain below flattened under the beating of the enormous wings as the huge predators soared toward the cliff on their deadly mission.

Vell watched them for a moment, holding up a hand to shield her eyes from the rising sun. Wizards may not be able to get close to the Inland Sea, but raptera had no such limitations.

Vell drummed her fingers on the smooth polished wood of her staff, smiling.

Battle magic may not have been an option this time, but there is more than one way to kill an elf.

Vell's head was still throbbing, and when she looked around, she could tell that the other wizards in her party were also still feeling the lingering effects of the Inland Sea's protections.

Still smiling, she motioned for them to follow her. "Come. Let us leave the raptera to their important work. We have an impending victory to prepare for."

As Vell led the group of wizards back through the forest toward the White Keep, the first hunting calls of the raptera mingled with elven screams, and Vell's smile grew wider.

Chapter 29

Two deep shadows fell across the narrow beach, and before Figg could fit another arrow to her longbow, several elves were dead, slain by the merciless ripping claws and snapping hooked beaks of the raptera.

Rage coursing through her veins, Figg charged forward and took aim, her arrow striking one of the massive birds in the upper right wing. With an ear-splitting screech, the raptera wheeled upward, then reached over and yanked the arrow out with its beak before snapping the shaft like a twig. Dark blood spattered the pebbly sand below, but the raptera continued its relentless attack, heedless to the wound.

Corr and several other elves who also had shields scrambled to form a barricade to protect those who were currently unarmed.

Corr dove in front of a young Plains Clan Elf as she dashed toward the cliff for cover. Pain coursing through his shoulder, he gritted his teeth as the massive talons of the raptera raked across his shield, driving him hard into the sand.

Ruvyn, unable to use any battle magic from his staff, had armed himself with a bow and an elven short sword. He rushed forward and sliced at the huge bird's leg as it hovered over Corr's raised shield, its talons ravenously seeking flesh. Under attack from Ruvyn's blade, the raptera launched itself back into the air just as the strength in Corr's arm gave out. He collapsed in the sand, panting.

Another screech split the air, and Ruvyn spun just in time to see the other raptera barreling down on him from above.

Before he could get an arrow to his bow, a spear flew up toward the descending bird, forcing it to wheel off course at the last moment. Ruvyn looked to where the spear had come from and saw Taene, the Plains Clan Elf who had accused him of spying. Ruvyn nodded gratefully to the elf, and Taene nodded back in unspoken solidarity.

Most of the elves on the beach had now found something with which to arm themselves, but the raptera were more than living up to their fearsome reputation. They attacked with untiring savagery, utterly impervious to numerous wounds. The exhausted elves could only hope to repel them from one brief moment to the next, with no hope for lasting victory in sight.

Figg went down with a deep talon wound from shoulder to elbow, blood spattering across the sand as she fell. The raptera who had attacked her landed a few feet away and stalked menacingly closer, snapping its huge beak.

Figg scrambled backward, but just before the creature made the killing lunge, Ruvyn charged forward and fired two shots from his bow in rapid succession. The raptera screeched and reeled backward, beating its enormous black wings upon the sand before once again taking to the air.

Gasping in pain, Figg's arms shook violently as she tried to push herself up from the sand. She looked up at Ruvyn in surprise and then reached toward the longbow that she had dropped. "Um, thanks, wizard. I'll get the next one." She tried to smile, but there was nothing she could do to mask the agony in her voice.

Ruvyn's gaze ran worriedly from Figg's badly injured arm to the amount of blood that soaked the sand where she had fallen. All around them, cries of the wounded filled the air as the elves battled courageously on, pushing past the point of exhaustion, refusing to accept the futility of their situation. Somewhere high above, the blood-curdling hunting cries of the two raptera cut the air.

****

Then, another sound. It boomed out from across the water and reverberated off the stone of the cliff. It was a roar unlike any of them had heard before, and across the beach, elven eyes raised upward, searching for the source of this terrifying new sound.

The two raptera circled directly over the beach, still focused solely on their prey below. One of them zeroed in on an elf and prepared to attack. But just as the huge bird tucked its wings to dive, there was a blur of motion followed by a surprised screech.

Another creature, its wide, bat-like wings beating the air, had struck the raptera hard from the side. The raptera was tossed like a ragdoll and sent careening, wings over tail, through the air until it landed with a mighty splash in the deep water offshore.

Screams and gasps went up from the beleaguered elves on the beach as they stared in wide-eyed terror at this new creature circling above them, scarcely believing their eyes.

It was a dragon.

The dragon flapped leathery wings slowly and

swung around to swoop low over the beach, causing the terrified elves to duck and many to grab for their weapons once again. Just then, a voice rang out from the crowd. Corr jumped forward and waved both his hands over his head, yelling to get the attention of the rest of the elves.

"Don't fire at it! Hold your fire!"

The dragon circled low once again, and a collective gasp of shock went up from the group on the beach. Seated upon the dragon's back, tucked securely between the wings, was Luma. Her face was pale but determined, and her dark hair blew across her shoulders as she gripped the two large spines at the base of the dragon's neck.

The dragon circled back over the water. From her seat between his wings, Luma peered down at the raptera as it flailed in the deep water, unable to take off. Then, another movement caught her eye—movement from beneath the surface.

An enormous something was gliding just under the waves, and it was heading straight for the struggling raptera. Luma's mind flashed back to her first journey across the Inland Sea and the behemoth she had seen swimming alongside the ship. A shiver ran up her spine as she watched from above, unable to tear her eyes away. A moment later, the water around the raptera bubbled and churned, and an enormous mouth rose from the depths to swallow the struggling bird whole. Then, with barely a ripple, it was gone, vanished entirely beneath the sparkling waves.

Luma's jaw fell open as she stared at the spot in the water where the huge bird had been just a moment ago while Ketu beat his wings and rose higher. A split-second later, the remaining raptera circled around from behind and attacked.

Catching its target in an awkward position, the monstrous bird's talons raked three bloody lines in the dragon's scales. Ketu roared and banked left as the raptera banked right, and the two creatures swung back to come face-to-face, high above the beach. The raptera beat the air furiously with its massive wings, trying to get higher so it could dive down and strike the dragon again with its talons.

Ketu, his wings smaller and more agile, banked sharply left. As the dragon soared past the raptera, Luma gripped his scaly body hard between her knees, then let go of the two spines she had been holding onto. Her hands rose in unison. Power fueled by rage simmered through her veins, and a blinding streak of light burst outward from her palms.

The raptera flared its wings and banked right to avoid the blast, but not fast enough. The starlight hit the huge bird on the upper wing, knocking it off course. The raptera spun backward and flapped awkwardly in the air for a moment before quickly righting itself.

Fierce, beady black eyes flashing, the raptera let out an ear-splitting screech, then dove at the dragon and its passenger.

Luma screamed and grabbed onto the spines once more, trying to make herself as small as possible as dragon and raptera locked together in midair. Talons and claws raked each other savagely, hooked beak and snapping jaws, each sought purchase in the other's flesh. From high in the sky, the combatants started to fall, tumbling together toward the water below. The dragon was using the long claws at the tip of his wings to stab at the raptera, while the raptera's deadly beak madly sought the dragon's eyes.

Cold terror gripped her heart, and Luma screamed again as the water rushed toward them. She had to do something, or they would crash. Gripping with her legs once again, she pushed aside the nagging doubt in the back of her mind and let go of the spines. Bringing both her hands up, she leveled her palms toward the raptera's chest.

Breathe in and out.

The crowd of elves on the beach collectively threw up their arms to shield their eyes against the intensity of the white light that shot from Luma's hands.

The light hit the raptera at the base of the neck and blew it backward. It careened wildly through the air and then hit the water below with a splash before sinking beneath the waves.

Luma grabbed onto the spines again, her heart galloping in her chest while sweat dripped from her brow. The elves on the beach dropped their hands and stared in wide-eyed disbelief as the dragon flared his wings at the last second and skimmed toward them over the water, the waves splashing across his wide, scaly chest. As he glided toward the beach, the elves retreated backward into a semi-circle.

Ketu landed with a soft thud on the beach and swung his huge head back and forth, taking in the new surroundings. A deep hush fell over the group of elves, and they shifted back nervously. Luma slid from between the dragon's wings and landed shakily on the sand.

After so long of riding and gripping with her knees, Luma's legs felt weak and wobbly on solid ground. She took a few small steps up toward the dragon's head, dragging one hand along his thick, scaly neck to steady herself. She reached Ketu's head and could immediately sense his uncertainty amongst all these elves. Reaching up, she placed her palm gently on his forehead, across the four white, star-like markings.

After a few seconds, his tension eased somewhat, and Luma removed her hand. She turned back to see Izarre step forward from the crowd. She approached Luma slowly, arms open wide and smiling through tears.

"Luma! Oh, thank the Four!"

Luma clasped Izarre's outstretched arms, smiling broadly. "Izarre! I didn't know if I would see you again! I'm so happy you are here."

By this time, Corr, Aire, and Elas, along with Haryk, Figg, and Emalet, had all rushed to the front of the crowd. Tears of relief flooded Luma's eyes, and emotion tightened her chest as she greeted them. She looked around in amazement at the large gathering of elves, then stepped forward and addressed the crowd. "Hello...everyone."

Her voice shook slightly, and Luma paused, embarrassed. She had never been much for public speaking, and she didn't even know exactly what she was supposed to say. Nervously, she looked over at Corr. He smiled at her and nodded encouragingly. Luma took a steadying breath and turned slightly to put her hand up high on Ketu's shoulder. She felt his energy pulsing through her palm.

Again, she faced the group and spoke, her hand still resting gently on the dragon's shoulder.

"This is Ketu. I released him from his long imprisonment. Do not be afraid—he is connected to the

Four, and he is here to help." Luma paused again and looked from face to face in the crowd in front of her, all of them staring back at her and the dragon in wide-eyed silence. She cleared her throat. "I don't know all of you, but I thank you for gathering here. My...my name is Luma," she faltered, feeling incredibly awkward. Still, she pressed on. "And, along with your help, I am going to heal the Sacred Stones during the alignment."

A ragged cheer went up from the group of elves, and Luma took a small step backward, embarrassment flushing her cheeks a deep crimson. The crowd was now alive with chatter as elves turned to each other, relief at having survived their recent ordeal flooding through them.

Through the commotion, Figg approached Luma. She had wrapped a piece of cloth around her injured arm, though Luma noticed with worry that a lot of blood had already seeped through the makeshift bandage.

Figg jerked her chin at Luma in greeting. "Hey there, Daughter of Starlight. Nice to see you again, and welcome back. Although I must admit, I had my doubts."

Luma smiled at her. "Hi, Figg. Good to be back. Are you okay?" She nodded toward Figg's arm.

Figg scratched at the blood-soaked bandage. "Oh, this? It's nothing. Tsarra will get me patched up, and I'll be back to fighting form in no time. Which is good because we have very little time." She looked to the Four Stars high above them. Three of them had already formed a perfect line, and the last and fourth one was just barely out of place.

Luma also glanced skyward, then looked back at Figg. "We must prepare to travel to the Cavern of the Four."

Figg nodded. "Yes. Tomorrow, we prepare. But today, we must attend to our wounded." She raised her chin, but her voice cracked despite herself. "And our dead."

Luma hung her head in sorrow, her stomach churning. "I'm sorry I didn't get here sooner."

Figg shook her head and fixed Luma with a hard stare. "We lost good elves in that fight, but those raptera would not have stopped until every last one of us on this beach was dead. You saved us today, Luma, make no mistake. And now, it's time for you to save the world. We are all here to fight for you, for Edira, our home. More elves will surely die in the battle to come, so don't let their deaths be for nothing. Don't be sorry—be ready."

Luma took a deep breath as she felt her sorrow shift, transforming into resolve. At her sides, the scars crisscrossing her palms began to emit a subtle glow. She clenched her hands into loose fists and felt the starlight power tingle up and down her forearms. From beside her, Ketu shifted his weight and tossed his head. He could feel it, too.

Luma returned Figg's stare and nodded. "I am ready."

****

That evening, the elves who had been killed in the fight with the raptera were carefully carried up the stairs from the beach and buried on the plain overlooking the Inland Sea.

Despite their many cultural differences, Forest Clan and Plains Clan elves observed similar funeral rights. And now, for the first time in generations, they worked together to complete their solemn task, united in their

255

grief as they laid their fallen side by side.

The setting sun painted the tall, swaying grasses of the plain with a brush of purple and gold while ancient elven songs honoring the slain sprang from the lips of every elf of both clans.

As their combined voices filled the air, Luma stood silently off to one side, her hands clasped in front of her, her head bowed. Corr approached, and when Luma raised her eyes to look at him, they were shining with tears.

Luma's face bore the deep flush of shame, and her voice trembled when she spoke. "Corr, I'm sorry. I…I don't know the words to these songs. I mean, maybe I did know them once. But now…I don't. I…don't remember."

Luma's voice caught with a sob in her throat, and she swallowed hard, once again lowering her head. Hot tears traced a shining path down her cheeks and dripped onto her clasped hands. Corr also had tears in his eyes as he looked at her. Then, wordlessly, he stepped forward and wrapped his arms around Luma, pulling her toward him. He felt Luma's shoulders shudder with the strain of emotion, and he held her all the tighter.

Hesitantly, Luma allowed her arms to encircle Corr's waist. She waited for him to speak, but he remained silent. He offered her no platitudes, only the quiet comfort of his embrace. Luma took a halting breath and dropped her head, bringing her cheek to rest on his broad shoulder. Her shoulders finally started to relax while her tears dampened the front of Corr's shirt.

And Corr stood strong and steady, holding Luma tight while the songs of loss, of bravery, and of hope echoed around them in the still night air.

Chapter 30

Later, as the sun continued to dip, the elves descended to the beach once again. Small fires were lit, and food was shared.

Apart from the rest, Luma slowly circled Ketu's body as the dragon lay near the edge of the water. Her fingertips bumped gently along his scaly hide as she walked, her shoulders tight with worry as she noted the several deep wounds left from the raptera's talons.

From across the beach, Tsarra approached. "The wizards didn't apply their poison this time and thank the Four for that."

Luma turned at the sound of the voice, and Tsarra nodded toward the dragon's wounds.

"I read once that dragons heal quite quickly. Still, I have a bit of salve that might be of help." She shrugged. "Though I must tell you, I've never had the opportunity to try it on a dragon before."

Luma smiled despite her worry. "You are Tsarra, the healer. Aire and Haryk told me about you. Welcome. A salve would be most appreciated."

Tsarra nodded and walked off to get the salve while Luma turned back to Ketu. Outwardly, the dragon didn't look as if he were in any pain, but Luma noticed that his flanks quivered when she touched near the wounds.

Luma dropped her hand and looked impatiently around for Tsarra, wishing she would hurry up. Then, to her relief, Luma noticed the healer approaching once again through the dim light, holding a small jar. When she arrived, Tsarra stepped forward with the jar in hand, but before she got close enough to administer it, Ketu swung his head around and fixed her with a hostile, obsidian stare. His lips curled back to expose massive teeth, and a low hiss formed deep in the dragon's throat while his thick, spiked tail swished agitatedly behind him.

Tsarra froze, her fingers sticking halfway into the jar of salve. She glanced at Luma, her eyebrows raised. "I think, Daughter of Starlight, that perhaps it would be better if *you* applied the treatment to the large, hissing dragon. After all, he is your beast, is he not?"

Luma cocked her head at the healer. "Ketu isn't mine. He is his own and belongs to no elf. But," she reached out and took the jar, "I will happily apply the salve."

Tsarra retreated several steps, and Ketu stopped hissing, though he continued to glare at the elf healer, unease radiating from his big body. Tsarra nodded curtly at Luma. "Just a thin layer down the length of each wound. Go ahead."

Luma stepped forward and gently spread the salve along each of the dragon's wounds where the raptera's claws had split open the scales. When she was done, she carefully wiped any excess back into the jar and exhaled the long breath she hadn't realized she had been holding. Ketu's tail had stopped thrashing, and he shifted into a more relaxed position on the sand.

Luma handed the jar back to Tsarra with a grateful smile. "Thank you." Then the jar reminded her, and she asked quickly before the healer took her leave. "Hey.

How is Figg?"

Tsarra sniffed haughtily. "We Plains Clan Elves are known to be driven and extremely tough. But that one," she shook her head, "that one has a grit unlike any I have seen. But she is also far too stubborn for her own good. Just a few minutes ago, I caught her with that Forest Clan friend of hers, already doing target practice with her longbow. This, of course, goes directly against my orders for her recovery. The action had reopened the wound on her arm, and she was bleeding badly. I had to redo her entire dressing." Tsarra let out a frustrated sigh and shook her head. "I gave her an earful, so I did. Doubt it will change anything, though. I fear that Figg doesn't know the meaning of the word 'rest.'"

Luma tried to suppress a smile. That sounded like Figg, all right. She thanked Tsarra again for the use of the salve, and then the healer bustled off to attend to her many other charges.

Luma walked slowly back over to stand next to Ketu's shoulder. The dragon raised his head to stare up at the bright line of the Four Stars, burning high above them in the twilight sky. Then he swung his head down and looked at Luma. She put her hand up to the dragon's face and felt through her palm a strong pulse of energy: a sense of anticipation and, along with it, hints of dread.

Luma nodded, and when she spoke, her voice was a hoarse whisper. "I know."

****

The sun had set, and the fires along the beach burned low. Some of the elves in the group had repaired what they could of their makeshift dwellings and slept there. Others, by preference or necessity, slept out in the open, under the stars. Luma had refused an offer to sleep in one of the repaired dwellings, preferring to remain at Ketu's side throughout the night.

The dragon scooped himself a little nest along the water's edge and began circling to pack down the sand. Still awake and seated on a small pile of blankets nearby, Luma smiled as she watched him, then leaned over toward Aire, who had come to sit beside her.

She poked Aire in the ribs with her elbow and nodded toward Ketu. "Look at that, Aire. He's just like a dog getting comfortable." Luma giggled.

Aire watched as the dragon finished his third circle and finally settled down with a small, reptilian grunt. Then she looked over at Luma. "A what?"

Luma giggled again. "A dog."

"What's a dog? Is that another type of dragon? Are you saying there are more of them?"

Aire swiveled her head as if expecting to see dragons burst from the encroaching shadows at any moment.

Luma laughed louder and prodded Aire again with her elbow. "What? No, of course not! A dog…you know…a canine?" She stared incredulously back at Aire's blank expression. "You actually don't know what a dog is, do you?" Her voice still had a trace of giggle in it.

Aire raised her eyebrows. "So, you're saying it's *not* another type of dragon?"

Luma sighed, shaking her head. "No. It's not another type of dragon, Aire. Dogs are animals! Four legs, fur, a tail, and they come in all kinds of colors and sizes. Do you really not have dogs in this world? What a pity. Dogs are wonderful creatures."

Aire looked at her, her face skeptical. "Are they as

big as a dragon?"

Luma shook her head. "No."

"Can they fly?"

"No."

"Talk?"

"No."

"Do they have magic?"

"No!" Luma threw up her hands, exasperated. "But dogs are very brave and loyal and can be trained to do all sorts of helpful things! Historically, dogs have even been used to aid humans in battle. They are often referred to as 'man's best friend.' So…" Luma's voice trailed off. Aire glanced over at Ketu as he slumbered in his shallow nest. The leathery wings were folded across his shoulders, and his forefeet stretched out in front of him with the huge, black claws half-buried in the sand.

Then Aire cocked her head to the side and looked down her nose at Luma with a superior expression. "Well, Luma, dogs sound fine, I guess. But I am a female elf, not a man, and for this battle, I'd prefer the aid of a dragon."

****

While Luma and Aire debated the benefits of dragons to dogs, farther down the beach Izarre shared her small fire with Corr, Elas, Emalet, and Ruvyn. The topic of their conversation was carried out in hushed tones. Ruvyn had run out of the seaweed that Eldamarr Rinn had given him and was once again looking distinctly pallid. Still, he leaned forward and spoke emphatically.

"We need to figure out if Luma can indeed transfer some of her starlight onto more shields and if doing so really can stop battle magic." He looked down at the damaged staff that lay across his lap, then back up at the elves around the fire. "My battle magic is severely weakened, and it's nowhere near as strong as Vell's, but I could use it to test the protection. Although, I don't think I could do it here."

Elas nodded. "That's right, Ruvyn. The deep magic of this place won't allow you to use any battle magic, but we will be leaving here soon. We can test it then."

At the words 'leaving here soon,' Ruvyn perked up. "Good. That's good."

Corr chimed in. "We have more shields now, thanks to the elves who have come to join us. Tomorrow, we will ask Luma to try transferring a bit of her starlight onto them." He smiled, his eyes shining with excitement. "This could be it. If just a few shields were able to withstand battle magic long enough, we could form a guard to protect Luma while she focuses her power to heal the Sacred Stones. She would be safe!"

Izarre smiled back at Corr from across the fire, but her eyes were sad. Corr cocked his head at her, confused. "What's the matter, Izarre?"

Izarre took a deep breath and let it out in a sigh. She looked back at Corr, shaking her head slowly. "Just because she has a guard around her doesn't necessarily mean that Luma will be safe when all is said and done."

Corr nodded. "Of course, I know Vell is strong, but we will stand stronger. We will not let anything happen to her. *I* will not!"

Izarre shook her head again. "Corr, you don't understand. I'm not questioning your bravery, nor am I questioning the determination of any elf here to protect Luma. But it is not only the wizards that pose a threat to the Daughter of Starlight during the alignment."

"Izarre, what do you mean?" Emalet asked, concern

edging into her tone.

Izarre leaned forward, her voice barely above a whisper. "What I mean is that the alignment will greatly enhance the levels of chaos in Luma's starlight. Wielding that power long enough to fully heal all four of the Sacred Stones will take an unprecedented amount of strength…quite possibly *all* of her strength."

Corr's stomach dropped, and it felt as though a cold hand was squeezing his heart within his chest. He shook his head, refusing to believe what Izarre was implying. "You're saying that Luma's act of healing the Sacred Stones may end up killing her?"

Izarre looked around at all of them as the flickering embers from the fire made light and shadow dance across her solemn face. Then she found Corr's gaze again and held it.

"Yes."

****

The morning sun was inching over the eastern horizon when Luma's eyes fluttered open and landed on the nest of sand that Ketu had made the night before. It was empty.

Luma was immediately wide awake. Sitting bolt upright, she frantically turned right and left, searching for the dragon. Then she heard a splash and looked seaward just in time to see Ketu's spiked tail disappear beneath the surface of the water. A moment later, his head reappeared, and he began swimming powerfully toward the shore, a large fish clenched in his teeth.

Luma breathed a sigh of relief and suddenly felt rather silly at her concern. Ketu swam to the beach and emerged onto the sandy shore, water running in smooth rivulets down his scales, which gleamed like diamonds.

Still giving him a wide berth, elves gathered nearby, staring in both fascination and fear at the dragon as he tore hungrily into the side of the fish. Luma watched Ketu closely as he ate and was relieved to see that the raptera wounds along his sides had already healed nicely. It appeared that Tsarra was right about dragons' ability to recover quickly. From down the beach, Aire trudged over. She was lugging a small fishing net, a sour expression on her face.

She stopped in front of Luma, dropped the net, and put her hands on her hips. "Hey, Daughter of Starlight, that dragon of yours is scaring away all the fish."

Luma gave a small laugh and smiled apologetically up at Aire. "Um…sorry." She shrugged and glanced at Ketu. "Maybe he'll share his?"

At the sound of Luma's voice, the dragon looked up from his meal with the final, large hunk of fish meat hanging halfway out of his mouth. His huge black eyes fixed on Aire, then he tossed back his head and swallowed the rest of the fish whole.

Aire raised her eyebrows incredulously at Luma. She pointed an accusing finger at Ketu. "Did you see that? He's *mocking* me. I am being mocked by a dragon."

Luma put her hands to her mouth and pretended to cough to hide her giggles. She was about to say something when Corr and Ruvyn walked over. In a huff, Aire gathered the empty fishing net and turned toward them.

"You two better not be coming to ask where the fish breakfast is because there won't be any." She glared sideways at Ketu. "And the dragon is mocking me."

Corr and Ruvyn looked at each other, then at Luma. Luma shook her head, indicating that it would be better if they didn't ask. Corr cleared his throat awkwardly.

"Sorry to interrupt whatever this is…but we need to talk to Luma about something important before we leave here." He patted Aire on the shoulder. "Sorry about the fish. I believe Elas and Emalet took a foraging party out before dawn. Why don't you go see what they have to share for breakfast."

Aire pursed her lips and heaved her net over her shoulder. With one more sideways glance at Ketu, who had now eaten his fill, she stomped off down the beach, muttering darkly about disrespectful dragons.

Corr watched Aire for a moment, then looked over at Luma. "Can you come with us? There is something that we'd like to have you try."

Chapter 31

A short time later, Luma was kneeling in the sand at the base of the cliff, flanked by Corr, Ruvyn, and a small group of curious elves. Five large shields, including the one that Corr had taken from the White Keep, were laid out in front of her.

Luma's hands rested on the tops of her thighs. She looked up at Ruvyn skeptically. "So, I'm supposed to, um, shoot starlight at these…and that will protect them from battle magic?" She fiddled nervously with the four conduit rings on her fingers.

Ruvyn shrugged. "Well, all we know is that after your starlight hit Corr's shield at Northhelm, it was able to withstand battle magic, even a direct attack from Vell, so I'm told. We figured it would be worth a try."

Luma lowered her eyes back to the shields in front of her. "Yes, you're right. Okay, I'll try. You all may want to stand back."

Ruvyn and the rest of the elves took a big step backward, and Luma focused her attention on the shield closest to her. Taking a deep breath, she reached out both hands, fingers spread wide. Hovering her palms just over the surface of the shield, Luma exhaled slowly. The scars along her palms glowed softly, and white light reflected off the metal of the shield. The observing elves took another step backward, murmuring to each other in awe.

Luma felt the familiar energy rising in her blood.

Pushing all distractions from her mind, she concentrated on her breathing as Eldamarr Rinn had taught her and slowly focused soft pulses of power downward across the surface of the shield. The shield vibrated slightly, and then Luma dropped her hands and looked up.

The elves watching stood silent, staring at her with wide eyes. Luma cleared her throat. "Um, shall I do the next one?"

This seemed to break the surrounding elves out of their stupor, and there was a rush of movement as they all tried to look helpful. Corr took charge and placed another shield in the sand directly in front of Luma. She looked up at him.

"I hope that worked."

Corr gave her an encouraging smile. "We will know soon enough, but I think that was perfect. Do that for all of these if you can."

Luma nodded and reached her hands toward the second shield. "I can."

****

As the sun began to dip in the west, Luma raised her eyes skyward. The Four Stars were now in a nearly straight line, and she could feel a radiant energy pulsing through her that had not been there before. A deep shiver ran up Luma's spine and down her arms.

Across the narrow beach, the gathered elves were busy arranging supplies and sorting weapons for the battle to come. At first light, they would all leave the safety of the beach and journey to the mountains. At midnight, the Four Stars would come once again into perfect alignment, and the fate of their world would be determined.

Luma stared at the Four Stars twinkling high above

her, but her reverie was soon disrupted by commotion farther down the beach.

"If you think for one *second* that I'm going to hide in the back for this fight, then by the Four, you've got another thing coming!" Figg's voice was shrill with anger.

Luma turned in the direction of the sound and saw a small group of elves had gathered near the base of the stone staircase. Worried, she walked over to see what was going on.

When Luma arrived, she found Figg, Tsarra, Corr, Aire, Elas, Emalet, and several other elves. Figg's cheeks were flushed, and her small hands were clenched at her sides as she glared at Tsarra. Tsarra had her arms crossed over her chest and glared back unflinchingly. Luma noticed that Figg had another fresh bandage on her arm covering the wound she had suffered from the raptera attack.

Corr, ever the peacemaker, stepped forward toward Figg. "No one said you needed to hide in the back, Figg, but..." Figg cut him off, thrusting her finger accusingly at Tsarra.

"She did!"

Tsarra shook her head. "All I said was, because of your injury, you can't be with the archers. That raptera sliced you nearly to the bone. Firing that longbow of yours reopens the wound and may cause permanent damage to your arm!"

Figg fired back through clenched teeth. "And I told you. I am one of the best archers of the Plains Clan, and I'll be fine. Haryk was also wounded, and he's leading with the archers!"

Tsarra sighed. "Yes, but his injury happened at

Northhelm, so he has had longer to heal, and his wounds were battle magic, not a laceration to his firing arm, Figg! Be sensible!"

Figg narrowed her eyes at Tsarra and was about to retort when Corr raised his arms, asking for calm.

He glanced at Luma and then placed himself between Figg and Tsarra and looked back and forth between them as he spoke. "Let me discuss everything with Luma. We must all be in agreement about the strategy; our victory depends on it, and we will not get another chance." He looked over at Figg. "We will figure something out, okay? Just give me a little while to get Luma up to speed on the plan."

A small derisive snort was Figg's only response, and with one more withering glance at Tsarra, she turned and stalked off down the beach.

Tsarra shook her head. "That one's pride is going to get her killed," she said to no one in particular.

****

A short time later, while Ketu wheeled and dove over the Inland Sea against a backdrop of red and gold, a large fire was constructed near the base of the cliff. Luma sat with her back to the cliff wall, flanked by Aire, Elas, and Ruvyn. She listened intently as Corr laid out their plan.

"The most important thing," Corr was saying, "is that Luma gets into the Cavern of the Four and that she is protected while she concentrates on healing each of the Sacred Stones. Once she starts that, she cannot be interrupted, whatever the cost."

Luma's stomach churned at that last part, and she looked at Corr, her face pale. He returned her gaze with a small smile and a confident nod.

"Don't worry, Luma, I…we will protect you."

With a shake of her head, Luma dropped her gaze. "It wasn't *that* that I was worried about," she said softly.

Corr didn't seem to hear her. He turned back to Aire, Elas, and Ruvyn. "The entryway to the Cavern of the Four is narrow, and at close quarters, it is difficult for the wizards to use their staffs effectively. Nuela has a small group of skilled sword fighters. Once Luma is inside, they will hold the entrance."

Aire and Elas nodded. Ruvyn's face was grim in the flickering light. "With my staff damaged, my battle magic can do little to help, and once Vell sees that Luma has entered the Cavern of the Four, she will throw everything she has at her."

Corr nodded. "That's where the shields come in. We think that the shields Luma has infused with starlight can withstand battle magic. This guard will form a protective barrier between Luma and any wizard threat so she can focus all her power on healing the Sacred Stones."

Luma raised her eyes. "Who will be the guard?"

Corr looked around at those present, nodding to each one in turn. "Aire, Elas, Ruvyn, and myself."

"That's only four," Luma protested, "I put starlight onto five shields."

Corr nodded. "We haven't decided on the fifth yet."

****

A few minutes later, Luma walked over to where Figg sat alone at the base of the stairs. Sullenly, she scratched at the bandage around her arm, her coveted longbow across her lap, and a full quiver of arrows at her feet. Luma gave Figg a small smile that Figg did not return.

Still, Luma came and sat down next to her, nodding

to the bow. "That is a beautiful weapon."

Figg snorted. "Yeah. I know." She flexed her bandaged arm and grimaced.

Luma turned on the stairs so that she was facing Figg. "I know you want to be with Haryk, Emalet, and the other archers, Figg. And they would be lucky to have you. But there is something else you can do—if you're up for it." Luma cocked her head. "And it doesn't involve hiding in the back."

Soon, Luma returned to Corr, Ruvyn, Elas, and Aire, with Figg following closely behind. Luma stepped aside to let Figg into the circle and smiled around at the others.

"Five shields, five elves. Welcome to the Starlight Guard, Figg."

****

As the night wore on and the fire burned low, Luma excused herself from the group to check on Ketu. Elas watched her go and then looked over at Corr, whose face was now half cast in shadow from the dying flames.

Elas kept his voice low so as not to have Luma overhear. "It's a good plan, Corr. I believe that Luma has the strength to heal the Sacred Stones, but Vell's power is unlike any we have seen before, even from the wizards. What happens if the shields cannot hold?"

Corr gazed up at the sky for a moment before answering. "We will each also have a short sword with us. If the shields fail, that is what we will use to buy Luma more time. And when we fall, we will take as many wizards with us as we can—and pray to the Four that it will be enough."

Chapter 32

From his library window in the high tower, Eldamarr Rinn looked out across the dark waters of the Inland Sea. The night was still, with not a breath of wind to stir the depths, and under the light of a nearly full moon, the water below shone like mirrored glass.

He could feel it, too, the coming alignment. It brought a deep ache in his bones, almost to match the ache in his heart. He ached for Edira, for his home, and for the loss of elven life that had happened since the start of the wizard invasion. And he ached with worry for Luma. How unfair it all was! That such a heavy burden, too heavy for just one to be expected to bear, should fall upon her young shoulders.

The light of the moon traced a glittering path across the water below him, but that was not the only thing reflecting on the calm sea. Four spots of white, dazzling in their brightness, also shimmered on the dark water. The mage stared at them and whispered a prayer for the girl who would soon go into battle and those who would fight at her side.

Power of the Four, please protect her. Protect them all.

The Four did not answer, and the mage lapsed back into solitary silence, with only the ache for company.

****

That same night, along the shore of the Inland Sea,

a feeling of palpable tension hung in the air, and there was little sleep to be had among the gathered elves.

Ketu was also restless, and when Luma put her hand up to his face, she could feel the strong current of agitated energy pulsing from his star-like markings before she even touched him. She ran her hand along the side of his neck in what she hoped was a comforting motion.

How does one attempt to comfort a dragon?

The scales were cool to the touch and felt nice as they bumped under her fingers.

Finally, the dragon circled in his shallow nest of sand, flexed his wings once, and settled down, closing his eyes. Luma, too, sat among the small pile of blankets that served as her bed, but her eyes remained open. With her hands in her lap, Luma used her thumbs to twist each of the thin silver rings that encircled her first and middle fingers on each hand, feeling a deep tingle of energy through her forearms as she did.

Then slowly, Luma turned her hands over and raised her palms closer to her face, staring at the web of dark scars that covered them. As if in response to her gaze, the scars began to glow, the white light increasing in intensity until it bathed Luma's face in brilliance. Luma wiggled her fingers and watched the light react to her movements while little waves of warm power coursed down her arms.

Starlight, Eldamarr Rinn had said—the most powerful force in the cosmos. Luma took a deep breath and raised her eyes to the water of the Inland Sea as if somehow knowing that far beyond the dark horizon, the mage was there, staring back.

****

The morning sun still hid its face beyond the eastern horizon when the elves filed up the stairs and onto the plain above. Luma was the last to leave the beach, but with one final glance across the water, she, too, climbed the stairs up to the plain.

Then, with Izarre and Corr leading the way, the large group of elves, weapons bristling and faces grim, headed on the most direct route toward their former capital city of Aquea.

Luma walked with Ketu until the edge of the forest; then, the dragon crouched and launched himself into the air and circled low, his bat-like wings skimming the treetops. Luma caught up with Corr and Izarre and walked on with them while keeping the dragon in her sights through the canopy.

The group moved silently through the forest, every one of them on high alert in case of a wizard ambush, but by midday, they had arrived on the outskirts of Aquea unchallenged. Ketu landed in a large open space in front of some burned-out buildings, and Corr posted sentries around the area while the group took some time to rest.

Ruvyn's face had lost its pallid color, and he looked much happier now that he had put some distance between himself and the effects of the Inland Sea's deep magic. With a spring in his step, he walked over to where Luma, Corr, Figg, Elas, and Aire were seated among the ruins of a stone building, sharing a water canteen between them.

He cocked his head at their shields and held up his staff with a grin. "Shall we test?"

Figg leaped to her feet. "Yeah, let's do it!"

Luma paced while the four elves picked up their shields and assembled themselves in a line. Figg was the smallest by far, and her shield was almost as big as she was.

Doing her best not to move her injured right arm too much, Figg grunted as she hefted the shield onto her left arm.

Elas, his shield already in position, reached over to help her, but Figg twisted away, her light eyes flashing. "Don't. I'm fine."

Elas raised his eyebrows and silently backed off while Figg got her shield ready and took her place in the line. Ruvyn walked back and forth in front of them, inspecting. He nodded in approval.

"In the Cavern of the Four, Luma will be behind you. All her focus must be on healing the Sacred Stones, so if Vell gets into the cavern and attacks, Luma won't be able to help you with her starlight. Keep the sides of your shields as close together as possible and hold that line." He stopped walking and turned to face them. "In the cavern, I'll be there with a shield too, but the battle magic from other wizards and from Vell will be stronger," Ruvyn looked ruefully down at his damaged staff, "but this test should give you an idea of what you will be up against. Ready?"

The elves behind the line of shields set their feet. "Ready!"

Ruvyn leveled his staff at them, and a blast of blue shot forward. It hit the middle shield just off center, and Aire grunted at the impact but held firm. The metal of the shield vibrated and shimmered as it absorbed the attack but showed no sign of cracking.

Ruvyn then fired several blasts in rapid succession at all the shields, probing for weakness. Figg gritted her teeth when a blast hit hers, and her feet slid back, but she quickly recovered and managed to keep her shield flush with the others.

A satisfied smile spread over Corr's face as all the shields successfully absorbed the battle magic, keeping the elves safe and untouched behind them.

Ruvyn put up his staff and nodded approvingly. He glanced at Luma, who had been anxiously watching the test. He smiled at her. "Nicely done. Your starlight offers great protection for these shields."

Luma gave a small smile back, but her forehead remained creased with worry. "Thanks, Ruvyn, but will the shields really be strong enough to protect against Vell's battle magic, if necessary? Her power will also be at its peak during the alignment." Luma gnawed on the edge of her lip, her face pale. Ruvyn put a comforting hand on her shoulder.

"They will be enough. I am sure of it."

Luma nodded slowly. "Okay."

Corr's gaze followed Luma as she turned and walked toward where Ketu had curled himself in the shadow of one of the buildings. The other elves in the group still cautiously kept their distance from the dragon. Ketu, in turn, watched them with his large black eyes and hissed threateningly if any elf ventured too close, his spiked tail twitching.

Corr put his shield down and clapped Ruvyn on the back. "It was a successful test."

Ruvyn nodded. "It was." His gaze flicked to Luma, then back to Corr. "I didn't want to worry her, but she's right. Vell's battle magic is considerably stronger than my own." He sighed. "Luma's concern is not misplaced. I hope this will work."

Corr raised his eyebrows at Ruvyn. "It will work

because it must. We must rid Edira of wizards once and for all!"

Ruvyn smiled and nodded, but his face was sad, and Corr immediately regretted his fervor. Clearing his throat, he put his hand on Ruvyn's forearm.

"I'm sorry, my friend. What I meant was...I mean, yes, you're a wizard, but you're not like them...well, what I'm trying to say is..." Corr lapsed into awkward silence, and Ruvyn chuckled.

"It's fine, Corr. No need to explain. Yes, I am a wizard. I love my home world, but I understand that the wizards who have invaded Edira need to be stopped. I want to see Malicath thrive, but as long as Vell and her supporters are in power, that will never happen." Ruvyn shook his head sadly. He looked down at his damaged staff and grimaced. "Vell's hunger for power is insatiable. Perhaps someday our two worlds can live in peace and cooperation, but whether I will live to see that day is unknown."

Corr dropped his hand, and a thought occurred to him, followed by embarrassment that he hadn't considered it sooner. "Ruvyn, when Luma succeeds in healing the Sacred Stones, the wizard army will be banished back to Malicath, and the protective barrier between our worlds will be restored. So...what will happen to you?" Corr asked the question hesitatingly, almost unwilling to hear the answer.

Ruvyn shrugged. "I'm not sure, Corr. But I have a feeling we will find out soon enough, my friend."

Just then, Luma and Izarre walked over, with Ketu lumbering behind. Luma nodded to Corr and Ruvyn. "The sun is starting to set. It's time."

Soon, the area was alive with movement. The elves

gathered their weapons and prepared for the final part of their journey to the Cavern of the Four. Luma was talking to Haryk and Emalet about the plan for the archers when Corr came over and pulled her aside.

"I need to talk to you for a moment." His voice was thick with emotion.

Concern brought a tightness to Luma's chest. "What is it, Corr? What's the matter?"

When Corr looked at her, there was deep pain in his moss-green eyes. He reached out and took both of her hands in his, gazing down at the four rings that encircled her fingers. He ran his thumbs over them gently. "The mage gave you these?"

Luma nodded. "Yes. He found them in his library. They're conduits. They help me control the chaos in my starlight, so I can use it without…adverse effects." She flushed slightly as the movement of Corr's thumbs over her fingers caused a small shiver to run up her spine.

Corr nodded, his eyes still downcast. "Will it be enough?"

Luma pulled her hands away from him, her temper flaring. "I will do everything I can to heal the Sacred Stones, Corr. I won't stop until it is done."

Corr shook his head. "No, no. Of course, I know you will. But that's…that's not what I meant!"

Luma stared at Corr, unused to seeing him flustered.

Corr took a steadying breath, then continued. "What I mean is, will those rings be enough to protect *you*, Luma, when the chaos in your starlight is at its peak during the alignment? I mean, the amount of energy it will take to heal all four of the Sacred Stones…Izarre said…"

Luma put up her hand, cutting him off. "I can do it,

Corr. Don't worry." Exasperated, she was about to turn away, but Corr grabbed her hands once more.

"Luma, it could kill you!"

Luma stared at Corr, and he stared back, his eyes shining, his voice quieter this time. "Izarre said that during the alignment, the process of healing the Sacred Stones could drain so much of your starlight power that…that…" Corr's voice trailed off. He paused for a moment and hung his head. When he spoke again, his voice shook. "I don't…I can't lose you again."

"Again?" Luma stared at him, confused. Then suddenly, part of the strange dream she had had after escaping the White Keep flashed in her mind.

In the Cavern of the Four, the young boy, his right arm broken and hanging limp at his side.

He had looked only a few years older than the girl covered in light from the Sacred Stones, and the sword he held was far too big for him. Still, he had charged recklessly forward. *"Leave her alone!"*

In Corr's, Luma's hands began to tremble, and tears sprang unbidden to her eyes.

"Twelve years ago…You were there that night."

Corr nodded and raised his eyes to meet hers, his broad shoulders slumping.

"Yes."

Luma opened her mouth, but no sound came out. She closed it again and shook her head, her heart pounding in her chest. Corr's plea echoed in her mind.

I can't lose you again.

Luma took a deep breath and gave Corr's hands a gentle squeeze. She tried to sound confident, but the tremor in her voice betrayed her. "It will be okay as long as I'm wearing the rings. If I have the rings on, they will keep me safe."

Corr arched an eyebrow, clearly unconvinced.

Luma smiled up at him, and a sudden stillness came over her. When she spoke again, her voice was strong and steady. "All my life, I have been living in a cage. A cage whose bars I could not see, but a cage, nonetheless. Now, whatever happens, I will be free." Luma squared her shoulders. "I was afraid. But I am not anymore. And I am not going anywhere."

Corr took a step closer, and Luma raised her chin, her breath catching in her throat. Corr's moss green eyes were overbright as they roved across her face as if trying to memorize each detail. When he spoke, his voice was a hoarse whisper. "Luma. I…"

"Luma! Corr!" Haryk and Emalet ran up, accompanied by several other archers, and Corr stepped back, dropping Luma's hands.

Haryk's voice was breathless with urgency. "Our scouts spotted wizards lurking in the woods just north of here. We'd better get moving, or we'll be outflanked." He looked toward Luma. "I suggest you not travel on foot for the remainder of the journey, Luma, if you know what I mean."

Luma tore her eyes from Corr. She took a breath to steady her pounding heart, then nodded at Haryk. "Yes. I understand."

****

Haryk and Emalet selected a small party of archers to move ahead and assess any potential threats. Corr grabbed his shield and short sword, and Luma walked to where Ketu was waiting in the clearing. She paused in front of the dragon and raised her hand to briefly touch the four star-like markings on his forehead. Then she climbed up and settled herself between his wings.

From her perch, she looked down at her Starlight Guard, their shields glinting in the late afternoon sunlight. She smiled at Ruvyn, Aire, Elas, and Figg, and then her gaze came to rest on Corr. "Don't worry. I will see you soon."

Corr nodded wordlessly, and then Ketu flexed his wings and launched into the air.

And with that, the last of the elf resistance moved toward the mountains, bound for the Cavern of the Four, ready to make their final stand.

Chapter 33

Led by Naro, the small band of twelve wizards had been ordered by Vell to track the movements of the elves and, as Haryk had predicted, try to outflank them if possible.

Luckily, the elven scouts had seen them in time to alert the others. Arrows nocked to strings; the archers moved through the tall, stately trees and undergrowth of the forest with the silent skill befitting their race.

But Naro was no fool, and he motioned for the wizard group to split, six and six, one to stay the course and the other to swing farther to the side.

Aegrond took charge of the second group, and it wasn't long before he noticed a cluster of elf archers moving through the trees. Darting behind a huge oak, he motioned for the other five in his party to likewise conceal themselves.

From his hiding place, Aegrond smiled cruelly to himself. In an ambush, he could easily pick the elves off with battle magic before they ever got the chance to loose an arrow.

****

In front of the group of archers, Emalet side-stepped a bramble of thorn bushes, unaware that she was being watched from behind the large oak tree a few paces to her left. Her gaze scanned the trees in front and to the right, where Naro's group was last seen. She took another step and silently motioned for the rest of the group to follow her.

A smirk curled his thin lips, and Aegrond leveled his staff at the side of Emalet's head.

Whomp!

Just before Aegrond let loose the deadly blast of battle magic, something smashed into him from behind and sent him careening face-first onto the ground. A split-second later, razor talons raked across the arm that held his staff. The wizard screamed in pain and dropped his staff, blood spattering across the forest floor.

All around him, screams of surprise and then of pain rang out from the other wizards in his party. Heavy, feathered wings beat the air above him, and Aegrond raised his arms to shield his face, only to have more of his skin laid open beneath the flailing talons. Gritting his teeth, Aegrond rolled over on the ground and groped wildly, desperate to get ahold of his staff.

"Looking for this?"

Still lying on the ground, Aegrond wiped dirt from his eyes and squinted in the direction of the voice, only to find himself staring into the circular, amber eyes of a large owl.

Trill shifted his weight back and forth along the length of the staff as it lay in the dirt a short distance from Aegrond.

The wizard flinched as the big owl's curved talons dug into the polished wood. Around him, chaos reigned as other owls dove at the wizards from above, wreaking havoc on the unprepared group.

Trill clacked his beak once, then beat his powerful wings and took to the air, Aegrond's staff clutched in his talons.

"No!" Aegrond scrambled forward and made a wild grab for his staff.

Lunging, he managed to grab ahold of one end just before Trill could get it out of reach. The owl flapped his huge wings rapidly, but Aegrond, eyes flashing with malice, clung to the end of the staff.

"Stupid owl, I'm going to kill you!" he growled through gritted teeth.

The words had no sooner passed his lips when Aegrond shuddered, a look of pure surprise flitting across his face. He took one halting step and fell forward, an arrow shaft protruding from the center of his back.

"No. You're not."

Emalet stepped over Aegrond's lifeless body, a new arrow already in her bow. She took quick aim and fired a deadly shot at a different wizard who had managed to get out from underneath another owl. Aegrond's staff disappeared from Trill's clutches, and the owl landed once more, blinking around as Haryk and the rest of the archers rushed in to aid the other owls.

It was over quickly, and one by one, all the wizard's staffs dropped to the forest floor and disappeared.

Haryk looked around in disgust. "An ambush. This group must have split off from the other group we had been tracking. And that plan would have worked too, I'm afraid, if it hadn't been for you owls." He stepped forward and bowed respectfully to Trill. "Thank you. My name is Haryk, and this is Emalet."

Trill gazed coolly around at the rest of the group.

"Plains Clan and Forest Clan archers, working together. It is good. Very good. I am Trill."

He spread one of his wings wide to indicate the other owls. "My six owl warriors and I will deal with the other wizard group lurking in the forest before they give you more trouble. We will also be there for aid in the mountains. The alignment requires it."

Emalet smiled at the stoic owl. "Thank you, Trill, truly. We are most grateful for your help." She looked disdainfully at the lifeless wizards on the forest floor. "Those wizards thought they were sneaky, but they never even heard you coming!"

Trill preened his flight feathers and then blinked his enormous eyes at Emalet haughtily. "No...of course they didn't."

****

The sun had set, and the mountain loomed in front of her.

From atop Ketu's back, Luma looked down, squinting as cool evening air blew into her face. In the light of the full moon, she saw the cottage at the base of the trail leading to the cave. The cottage where Corr brought her after the Sacred Stones had called her back, where she had first met Izarre. A tingle ran through her, and Luma shivered involuntarily. High above, the Four Stars shone brighter than ever.

****

The elves had taken the high ground while the wizards amassed along the mountainside leading to the cave, its entrance black and gaping. Ketu banked left and circled toward the craggy cliffs where the elven archers had positioned themselves.

Suddenly, an intense blast of blue shot upward. Ketu swerved hard to avoid it, and Luma screamed as she slid sideways across the dragon's back, grabbing one of his spines just in time to avoid tumbling off. Ketu righted himself and swung back around. Her heart pounding,

Luma looked down and saw Vell standing atop a large boulder halfway up the trail, her staff aimed at the dragon.

"Last chance, Luma!" Vell's voice echoed up through the still, moonlit night. "Join me now and live. We destroy the Sacred Stones and rule together with power such as the cosmos has never seen! Or choose to fight, and watch, powerless, as I burn this world and everyone who opposes me!"

Luma didn't answer, but Vell was forced to make an undignified leap to one side as a stream of starlight crashed into the top of the boulder where she had been standing a moment before.

Luma brought her hands back to grip Ketu's spines as a grim smile tugged at the corners of her mouth. *I am anything but powerless.* The chaotic, starlight energy pulsed deep in her bones, and even with the conduit rings encircling her fingers, the scars on her palms ached and throbbed more than ever before. Ketu tossed his scaly head, beat his wings, and rose higher into the night. Luma tore her eyes away from Vell and looked up. The Four Stars were shining so brightly now that it almost hurt her eyes to look at them.

Ketu banked right and swooped low over the cliffs where the elf archers were in position. He landed on a small incline just behind them, and in the light of the moon, Luma nodded to Haryk and Emalet. Faces grim, the two elves nodded back.

"Archers, now!"

The hiss of elven arrows filled the night air, whizzing like a mass of angry wasps into the ranks of the wizards below. Luma slid down from Ketu's back just as the first blasts of battle magic struck the mountain slope as the wizards returned fire with a vengeance.

Haryk and Emalet took evasive measures, shouting orders and encouragement to their ranks of archers.

"Hold your ground, elves!" Haryk bellowed as he took his place in the center of the first line of archers.

Emalet moved with calm efficiency along the line and up the slope, calling as she did.

"Two lines in front. First line, stand, fire, drop, and reload. Second line: stand, fire, and drop. Don't give them any easy targets. We have the high ground, and we will keep it that way! Use the boulders for cover!"

From around the side of the slope, Aire, Elas, Corr, Figg, and Ruvyn, each carrying their shields, ran toward Luma. Corr stepped forward, raising his voice to be heard. "We can approach the cave from around the far side of the mountain. Nuela and her fighters will meet us there."

Luma glanced at Emalet. The elf caught Luma's eye as she nocked another arrow to her bow and fired with ruthless accuracy. "Go, Daughter of Starlight. We will keep them busy." Then, her gaze shifted to Elas. Stepping forward, Emalet reached out and clasped his hand. "Be careful."

Elas looked back at Emalet, his voice thick with emotion. "You too."

Just then, the telltale screech of a raptera split the air. Ketu threw back his head and let out a deep answering roar. Then, the dragon spread his leathery wings and launched like a reptilian missile into the night.

Heart racing and palms throbbing painfully, Luma cried out to Corr, her voice breathless. "The Sacred Stones. They are calling me. We must go now."

As Luma and her guard made their way back and

around, Haryk took aim and dispatched a wizard who had attempted to climb closer.

Haryk threw back his head and shouted into the starlit sky, his cry soon joined by dozens of other elven voices along the mountainside, all saying the same thing.

"Eddiiirrraa!"

The final battle had begun.

Chapter 34

The full moon, coupled with the brilliance of the Four Stars, lit the landscape below with an ethereal light as the battle raged.

Standing well out of the range of arrows, Vell's silvery white hair practically glowed in the light of the moon. She could feel the imminent alignment, and she knew that the elven archers were trying to keep the wizards below pinned down for a reason. It was a distraction. A ploy to buy time. Fingernails drumming lightly on the smooth polished wood of her staff, Vell's beautiful, deep blue gaze roamed the mountainside.

I know you are there, Luma.

Vell wondered briefly where Naro and Aegrond were, then dismissed the thought. If that group had foolishly gotten themselves killed, it was no concern of hers. She had plenty of fighters. Walking briskly and still keeping well out of range, she pointed at three wizards.

"You, you, and you, gather some others and follow me. Leave the rest to keep the elven archers distracted. We go to the Cavern of the Four."

****

Izarre had joined Nuela and the small group of swordselves. They had met up with Luma and her five guards on the far side of the mountain. Swords drawn and faces grim, they moved silently, guarding Luma's back.

In front, Corr led the way on the narrow, curving trail, his shield gleaming on his arm. After a short distance, he stopped. Behind him, Luma and the others stopped as well. The sounds of battle echoed up the trail, and Corr turned, his face bathed in pale moonlight. He looked back and forth between Luma and the other four guards.

"Just ahead is where the main trail to the cave meets this one. Then it's a short distance to the entrance. We go in, and we get Luma to the Cavern of the Four. Nuela, the passageway at the back of the cave is narrow, and it curves just before the cavern. If any wizards make it that far, they won't be able to use their staffs as effectively in the tight space. That's where your swords come in. You must hold the entrance for as long as you can."

From behind Luma, Nuela nodded. "We will."

Just then, a blast crashed into the mountainside directly above Corr's head. He threw himself toward Luma, shielding her with his body as rocks pelted over them.

Figg's voice cut the air. "They've found us! Get to the cave! Now!"

Corr took Luma's arm and gently guided her behind him before edging forward to the main path. Shield raised, he squinted into the moonlit night. "I can't see them," he hissed.

Figg's answer came from behind his right shoulder. "Neither can I, but we know they're there."

As if in response to Figg's statement, a blast of battle magic shot upward from the scrub bushes just down the path and hit Corr's shield dead center. Luma caught Corr as he stumbled backward from the unexpected blow.

Blood pounding in her ears, Luma screamed in rage

and lunged forward. Throwing her hands out straight in front of her, she sent a powerful stream of starlight arcing into the scrub bushes.

A smile of morbid satisfaction spread across her face as she saw the two wizards who had been hiding there jump aside and retreat. Then she felt a hand on her arm. It was Izarre.

"Save your strength, Luma. Get to the cavern."

Luma turned and motioned to Corr, her voice tight with urgency. "Now! Before they regroup!"

Together, she, Corr, Figg, Aire, Elas, and Ruvyn made a mad dash up the main path toward the gaping mouth of the cave. Izarre, Nuela, and the group of swordselves followed closely behind.

Luma darted inside, then threw herself flat to the ground as more battle magic blasted around the entrance, causing rock dust to fill the air. Coughing, Luma scrambled on all fours to one side of the cave, pressing her back against the cold stone. Hidden from the moon and starlight, the cave was much darker than the outside, and Luma blinked several times, urging her eyes to adjust.

Nuela, Izarre, and their group came dashing in under a barrage of battle magic and quickly flattened themselves against both sides of the wide cave entrance.

Her chest heaving, Nuela gripped her sword and called to Corr. "Keep moving! Get to the cavern. We will hold the entrance!"

Her eyes finally adjusting to the low light, Luma saw Corr, Ruvyn, and Aire across the cave against the opposite wall. Elas was on her side, slightly to her left. Luma glanced nervously at Nuela's fighters, then a stabbing pain jolted through the scars on her palms, and she sucked in her breath. Time was running out.

More blasts of battle magic made small shards of rock pelt down over her head. Flinching, Luma glanced toward the narrow passageway that she knew led to the Cavern of the Four. Then her gaze collided with Corr's, and he gave her a quick nod. Luma was about to dash for the passageway when a strangled sound echoed from behind her.

Spinning back, a horrified gasp escaped Luma's mouth as she saw Nuela and Izarre caught in the middle of the cave entrance, their bodies rigid and suspended slightly off the ground. Vell stood just outside the entrance to the cave, bathed in silvery moonlight, her staff in one hand and her other hand held out in front of her, fist clenched, channeling a holding spell.

Luma's mind whirled back to the White Keep when she had watched helplessly as Corr struggled in vain against Vell's holding spell, only to then be tossed from the high window. Luma's breathing quickened, and she clenched her fists, fingernails biting the flesh of her palms.

One of Nuela's fighters charged forward, sword gleaming, but before he got close enough to strike, a blast from Vell's staff hit him in the chest. He smashed into the opposite wall of the cave and crumpled to the ground. Nuela gave a small cry of grief, her voice muffled from the spell.

Eyes flashing, Luma took two running steps forward and threw up her hands.

Vell's staff also went up, and the starlight and battle magic crashed together in midair. Gritting her teeth, Luma bent her elbows to cushion the impact and then, screaming with fury, pushed her arms straight. A blaze of white light pulsed from her hands, so intense that Vell was forced to stumble backward in retreat, dropping her other hand as she did so. Nuela and Izarre's feet hit the cave floor and they lurched backward, free of the holding spell.

"Take cover!" Luma yelled as she jumped forward and deflected a blast of battle magic shot at the two elves.

Nuela and Izarre dashed to one side of the entrance while Luma rushed to the other. She risked a glance around the edge, then pulled her head back just in time, and the battle magic meant for her hit the rock face instead. All around the cave entrance, wizards began firing battle magic at any elf they could see.

Ruvyn's staff, damaged as it was, was still effective at close range, which he demonstrated on a wizard who was trying to sneak farther into the cave entrance. Ducking back down, he bellowed at Corr. "There isn't time. We've got to get Luma to the Sacred Stones!"

Corr nodded his understanding and rushed forward, pulling Luma back and behind his shield. "Luma! We've got to go!"

Wild-eyed, Luma stared at him as the cave entrance echoed with the sounds of battle magic and the screams of elves. Barely able to breathe, she saw Izarre and the others pinned down under the onslaught. "I can't just leave them; they'll never make it!"

Corr grabbed Luma's wrists and pulled her close. His voice was strained with grief as he stared into her eyes. "None of us will make it unless you heal those stones."

Tears, hot with anger, filled Luma's eyes. She opened her mouth to protest when abruptly, the barrage of battle magic into the cave entrance stopped. Then, cries of surprise and pain began echoing from outside.

Luma stepped out from behind Corr's shield and darted to the entrance, once again peeking around the edge. With a sudden gasp of relief, she spun back to Corr. "It's the owls!"

Once again, Trill and his owl warriors had arrived on silent wings to wreak surprise havoc on the wizards from above.

It was the chance that Luma needed. "Let's go!"

Luma made a mad dash to the passageway at the back of the cave, flanked by Corr, Elas, Aire, Figg, and Ruvyn. Izarre, along with Nuela and her fighters, rushed after them, blocking the entrance to the narrow passage just behind where it curved, swords at the ready.

At the front, Luma charged into the Cavern of the Four and then skidded to a stop. High above, from the hole in the ceiling, the Four Stars filled the entire space with soft, shimmering light. And there before her, the Sacred Stones loomed. A small cry fell from Luma's lips, and she stumbled back, her hands on either side of her head.

Corr was immediately at her side. "Luma, what is it? Are you all right?"

Luma took a breath and slowly dropped her hands. She knew the Sacred Stones weren't actually making a sound, and yet, she could hear them, like an echo in her bones. They were crying out in pain.

A deep pulse of energy coursed through Luma's body, and at her sides, the scars on her palms began to glow, and so too did the markings at the base of each monolith. Luma looked up, where through the hole in the cavern roof the Four Stars shone down, creating four brilliant white marks on the sandy floor of the cavern.

Perfect alignment.

Luma's eyes traced the line of reflections, and then she looked over at Corr, her face pale but determined, her voice a strained whisper.

"It's time."

From outside the passageway, the sound of battle magic hitting the cave wall echoed into the cavern.

"Starlight Guard! In position!" Corr shouted.

Luma stepped forward and placed herself in front of the first stone in the line of four, while behind her, five gleaming shields went up, protecting her back.

With a deep, steadying breath, Luma stretched her arms out, palms hovering just over the deep crack that split the mighty stone halfway down. It was now or never.

Breathe in and out. Don't fight it.

Brilliant light shot forward in a steady line from the dark scars on Luma's palms and into the crack in the first stone. Slowly, slowly, Luma began to move her hands upward, leaving behind a glowing trail that filled the crack completely.

From behind her, Corr pulled his gaze from the entrance of the cavern and glanced over his shoulder at Luma. He could see the tips of her fingers trembling slightly, but she was slowly making progress toward the top of the first stone.

Corr's heart raced in his chest. It was working. Luma was doing it.

Shouts and the sound of clashing steel caused Corr to whip his head back around. The wizards had made it to the passageway.

Corr didn't know how many wizards had survived the attack from the owls, but he was willing to bet that

Vell was one of them. From his position in the center, he looked right and left at Ruvyn, Elas, Aire, and Figg.

His face grim, Corr addressed them in a whisper. "Stand strong. We protect the Daughter of Starlight, whatever happens."

****

The first wizards to round the curve in the narrow passageway were struck down by Nuela's sword just as the shouts of alarm escaped their lips.

Two others tried to rush Izarre and quickly met the same fate. Staffs clattered against the rock walls of the passageway and disappeared.

Nuela looked at Izarre, the light of battle in her eyes as she resumed a fighting stance.

"For Edira."

Izarre kept her eyes trained forward but nodded once in agreement. "For the Daughter of Starlight."

Vell prowled into the passageway to find the few remaining wizards of the group hanging back. She was breathing heavily, and several deep owl talon scratches along the side of her neck oozed bright red blood, but the end of her staff glowed a dark, menacing blue. She could feel that the alignment had started and knew Luma had begun healing the first Sacred Stone.

Vell gritted her teeth. Luma could not be allowed to succeed. She pushed the other wizards roughly aside and stopped just behind where the passageway curved. Then, she looked disdainfully back.

"We are not about to let these elves and their pitiful swords keep us from our victory, are we?" With a soft grunt, Vell swung out her staff arm in a wide half-circle, so when the battle magic blasted from the end, it ricocheted off the wall and around the corner. Elven screams quickly followed.

Vell smiled coldly as she turned back to the other wizards. "Kill them all."

Chapter 35

Corr, Aire, Elas, Figg, and Ruvyn stood side by side in the Cavern of the Four, each silently praying to the Four Stars for strength, not only for themselves but for their fellow elves. From the passageway, the sounds of battle raged.

Elas shifted his weight. He wanted desperately to aid the elves fighting in the passageway, to offer what defense he could. He glanced to his left, and Aire caught his eye. One look at his twin sister's face told him that she felt the same. Elas took a deep breath and faced forward once more, his jaw clenched. He knew that to break the line now would jeopardize Luma's success in healing all four of the Sacred Stones. He wouldn't do that—and neither would Aire.

And so, the five remained, standing strong, shields raised and hearts breaking.

Luma couldn't hear the battle raging just outside the cavern; her world had shrunk, the surrounding area blurring and fading away. Luma's hands trembled, but she was now so close!

With a final deep breath, Luma pushed the starlight streaming from her hands up to the very top of the crack in the first Sacred Stone, sealing it completely.

****

Corr jumped at the sound of Luma's cry from behind him. Without moving from his position next to the other guards, he strained to look over his shoulder at her.

"Luma? Are you okay?"

"I did it," came Luma's soft answer. She sounded happy, but Corr could also hear the deep fatigue clinging to her tone.

The world around Luma snapped back into sharper focus. She turned and looked nervously at the passageway where it entered the cavern. Flashes of battle magic reflected in her eyes and sounds of desperate fighting filled her ears.

Corr called to her again. "Luma? Great job. Do you need to rest?"

"No." With one more glance toward the passageway, Luma stepped in front of the next Sacred Stone and raised her hands. "I will rest when it is done."

Once again, white light streamed from Luma's palms, but immediately, she noticed that this Sacred Stone was different. Her starlight didn't fill the crack as easily—there was resistance. Not a lot, but some.

Luma set her feet on the sandy ground and focused harder, pushing the flow of starlight outward. Beads of sweat sprang up along her brow and dampened the thick, wavy hair around her temples. The trembling in Luma's fingers increased as she dragged the starlight slowly, painfully, upward.

Several minutes later, Luma's gasp of relief at successfully filling the second crack was offset by an intense blast of battle magic from the passageway, followed by screams. Rock dust drifted downward and into the cavern.

Luma spun around, but Corr called over his shoulder. "It's okay, Luma! It's okay. Are you all right? Are you able to keep going?"

Panting, her eyes wide with worry and her face pale, Luma nodded. "Yes. I'm all right."

She faced the third stone and raised her hands as Corr tried his best to keep his voice calm and confident. "Don't worry, Luma, we can handle whatever comes."

And he hoped desperately that he was right because a second later, through the cloud of rock dust, Vell stepped triumphantly into the Cavern of the Four.

****

Behind their shields, Luma's guard set their feet. Silence prevailed now as Vell stalked closer, her deep blue eyes radiating malice as they slid across the line of shields that stood between her and Luma.

A knot rose in Corr's throat, and he swallowed hard. He and the other four guards just needed to hold Vell off until Luma healed the last stone—they could do it. They had to.

Vell cocked her head to one side as she surveyed the five standing before her.

"Oh. Hello, Ruvyn." Vell's voice was soft, almost friendly. "I was hoping I'd run into you again. I would have preferred to kill you earlier, of course, but now will have to do." A small, mirthless laugh bubbled up from her throat. "I suppose it is rather fitting that you die here, among these other misguided rebels, and, of course," her gaze flicked toward Luma's back, "their would-be savior."

Ruvyn said nothing, and he wouldn't have had time to respond if he had wanted to, for with that last word, Vell sent a blast of battle magic hurtling forward. Ruvyn grunted at the impact but stood strong. His shield vibrated softly and absorbed the blast.

Vell did not look surprised. "Oh, you think I didn't

assume that Luma would put some kind of protection onto those shields? Of course I did, but no matter. They may be able to withstand regular battle magic for a bit, but not for long. And not from me."

Two more powerful blasts hit the line of shields in quick succession. Figg slid slightly backward on the sandy ground but quickly recovered, her jaw clenched and her eyes flashing.

Behind the line of shields, Luma's outstretched hands shook badly. This third stone had more resistance than the last one. The sweat at her temples trickled down the sides of her face and mingled with the droplets of crimson blood that seeped from her ears. *Halfway.*

Vell narrowed her eyes and leveled her staff again at the line of shields protecting Luma's back. "Time to end this."

Blue light burst with awesome intensity from the end of her staff and then kept coming. The five shields took the massive blast as one, vibrating and glowing.

Behind their shields, Corr, Aire, Elas, Ruvyn, and Figg strained their bodies, forcing themselves to hold the line against the onslaught. But Vell's battle magic just kept coming. All around the large cavern, sparks of blue flashed and crackled in the white glow of the light from the Four Stars.

Even in her semi-trance-like state, Luma could tell that something was not right.

Keeping her hands raised in front of her, she tore her eyes from the third stone and saw Vell's unrelenting flow of battle magic mercilessly pummeling the shields of her five guards. Cold panic hit Luma like a tidal wave. There was no way those shields would hold much longer, not under an attack like that. Heart pounding, Luma turned back to the third stone and, gritting her teeth, willed more starlight to fill in the crack. Time was running out.

Finally, she made it to the top of the third stone, and Luma dropped her arms, her entire body shaking violently. Her hairline was slick with sweat, and lines of blood from her ears ran down the sides of her jaw and dripped onto her collarbone.

The scars on Luma's palms burned as the chaos within her starlight flexed its power, pushing against the limits of the conduit rings. At the same time, deep fatigue clawed at her limbs and fogged her mind.

Swaying slightly, Luma glanced over her shoulder, squinting at the intensity of the battle magic that streamed unbroken from Vell's staff. Corr, Ruvyn, Figg, Aire, and Elas, their bodies trembling with exertion, were being slowly pushed back under the relentless barrage.

Gasping for air, Luma positioned herself in front of the fourth and final stone. But when her starlight burst forth, the burning in her palms was so intense that she had to clench her jaw to keep from crying out in pain. The resistance from this stone was the strongest yet.

Breathe in and out.

Luma began moving her palms up the stone. Slowly. Too slowly. From behind her, Aire screamed.

Desperate tears sprang to Luma's eyes and blurred her vision. This was taking too long. Vell's battle magic was too powerful. She'd never be able to heal the stone completely before the shields failed, and when they did, her friends would die.

Luma's hands shook uncontrollably, and her breath came in ragged gasps. More cries rang out from behind her.

On either side of Corr, Aire and Elas stumbled backward and fell. Their arms and shoulders were covered in burn-like wounds, and both of their shields bore long cracks across their surfaces. While still protecting Luma's back, Corr, Ruvyn, and Figg jumped forward, their three shields taking the blow that would have meant death for the wounded twins. Looking over her shoulder, Luma saw Corr, Ruvyn, and Figg struggling to keep their shields up to protect both her and their fallen comrades.

Vell advanced toward them, a smile on her face and a mad light in her eyes.

Deep fury coursed through Luma's veins to match the heat from the starlight power simmering beneath her skin. With a scream of defiance, she swung her right hand out toward Vell while keeping her left hand facing the stone. White starlight poured from Luma's palm and crashed into Vell's stream of battle magic just as Corr, Ruvyn, and Figg were blown backward, their shields destroyed.

Vell's eyes went wide at Luma's unexpected move, but then her face creased into a satisfied smile. *Luma will never be able to heal the final stone with her starlight power divided.*

Corr struggled to sit up. Slightly to his left, Figg and Ruvyn were both unconscious and badly wounded but breathing. Dazed, Corr stared up at Luma as she stood protectively over him, one hand facing the final stone, one hand facing Vell, white starlight streaming from both palms in opposite directions.

Panic and pain surged through Corr as he struggled to hold onto consciousness—there was no way she could keep this up.

"Luma, no!" His voice was hoarse, but Luma heard him. Keeping her gaze locked on Vell, she answered back through clenched teeth.

"I won't...let...her...hurt you!"

Vell could see Luma's arms shaking badly, and the sides of her neck were smeared with the blood coming from her ears.

In the bright glow from the starlight, Luma's eyes were bloodshot and puffy, the skin on her face and chest a patchwork of blotchy pink and ghostly pale. Her chest heaved as she gasped for air. Vell gripped her staff with both hands and forced even more power into her battle magic, smiling wickedly. Her victory was now all but inevitable.

A crash echoed from the passageway, and Luma's gaze darted away from Vell, searching for the source of the sound.

Vell seized upon Luma's brief distraction and sent an extra pulse of battle magic through her staff. Caught off guard by the intensity of the new attack, Luma managed to deflect the blast but stumbled backward and fell. Vell smirked and aimed her staff again.

One more blast is all it will take.

From the ground near Vell's feet, Figg's eyes fluttered open. Grunting in pain, she shifted her weight and, with a shaking hand, wrenched her short sword from the scabbard at her hip. Mustering all of what was left of her strength, Figg pushed herself up and swung out with the weapon.

Vell was forced to take her aim off of Luma as she dodged at the last second to avoid Figg's blade. She swung her staff down and fired a blast of battle magic toward the young elf. Corr grabbed the largest part of his broken shield and threw it across Figg's small body just before the blast hit her. The shield shuddered and cracked as the battle magic crashed into it, pushing Figg backward, the force knocking her unconscious once again.

A portion of the battle magic was deflected off the shield, and Corr threw his arms over his head, crying out as the blast burned into his forearms. Vell, grimacing at the distraction, swung her staff back up as Luma scrambled to her feet, her eyes wide with fear.

Just then, the cavern shook with a booming roar, and Ketu burst out of the narrow passageway in a shower of rock dust. Huge teeth bared, he launched himself at Vell. With a shriek, Vell threw herself to one side and rolled, narrowly avoiding the crushing snap of the dragon's jaws.

Jumping once again to her feet, Vell gripped her staff as Ketu positioned himself between her and Luma. All along his scaly neck and sides, the dragon bore deep scratches from raptera claws, but he didn't seem to notice the fresh wounds. His wide head level with his shoulders, the dragon bared his teeth again. A menacing hiss rasped from his throat as the spikes along the base of his jaw pushed outward.

"Luma. The stone. Hurry." At Luma's feet, Corr's voice was weak, his eyes were half-closed, and his face pale.

Catching her breath, Luma spun back to the final stone and raised both hands while Ketu faced Vell. Keeping himself positioned between Vell and Luma, his bat-like wings folded tightly against his body, Ketu swung his thick spiked tail. Vell jumped backward and, at the same time, fired a blast of battle magic from the end of her staff. The attack struck the dragon at close range, just below the shoulder. Ketu's roar echoed throughout the cavern as he stumbled backward. At the wound, blood began to ooze from beneath the scorched scales, and a vicious smile spread across Vell's face.

Still facing the stone, Luma's heart dropped at the sound of Ketu's pain. Panic, mixed with desperation, rippled through her as she willed her starlight to work faster.

Ketu, limping heavily, hissed at Vell and lunged. Vell dodged to one side but not fast enough, and the dragon's claws clipped the side of her torso. Grimacing, Vell put a hand to her side, then removed it to find a thin layer of blood coating her palm.

Ketu swung his tail once more, this time catching Vell hard across the chest. She was flung backward and landed in a heap on the sandy ground of the cavern a short distance away. With a low hiss, Ketu limped forward, teeth bared. Behind him, Luma, her jaw clenched in concentration and sweat dripping down the sides of her face, had passed the halfway point in the crack.

Vell lay still where she had landed, watching the approaching dragon through half-closed eyes, a cunning plan forming in her mind. Ketu took a few more limping steps toward her. One more step and Vell surged to her feet, her staff aimed at the center of the dragon's chest. The blast of battle magic mixed with Ketu's bellowing roar, followed by a ground-shaking crash as the dragon went down.

"Noooo!" Luma's anguished cry echoed off the cavern walls.

Tears streaming down her face, Luma spun from the

final stone to face Vell. With a scream that gave voice to her heartbreak, she threw both hands in front of her. A shockwave of intense energy, born of grief and fueled by rage, rolled through Luma's body.

The starlight that exploded from Luma's palms was more powerful than anything she had felt since putting on the conduit rings. It hit the very center of Vell's staff before the wizard leader could dodge out of the way. Vell shrieked as the polished wood of her staff began to blister, then to crack. Luma vented her rage again as another massive wave of energy rolled through her and out of her palms.

Desperately, Vell tried to pull her staff out of the direct line of starlight, but it was too late. The sound of splintering wood filled the cavern, and in a blinding flash, Vell's staff split in two.

A strangled cry escaped Vell's mouth as she stumbled backward, gasping, hands clutching the two broken pieces of her staff. Her gaze collided with Luma's—deep blue eyes wide with shock and disbelief. Her mouth opened as if to say something, but before the words could leave her tongue, Vell took another stumbling step and collapsed to the cavern floor. The pieces of her broken staff fell on either side of her limp body and disappeared.

****

Luma dropped her hands and stood as if frozen to the spot, her mouth agape. Her breathing quickened, and her heart raced as her gaze darted around the cavern, from Vell's lifeless body to Ketu's still form to her five friends, lying wounded and motionless beneath their broken shields.

And finally, to the stone. The last stone.

Luma sucked in her breath as a violent tremble rippled through her. It wasn't over yet. She still had to heal the final Sacred Stone, but now, all the strength seemed to seep from her body, to leave behind it nothing but crushing fatigue.

With one more desperate look at the carnage around her, Luma returned her attention to the last Sacred Stone and willed herself to remain standing. Grimacing, she raised her arms, only to drop them a second later, panting and trembling. The cavern spun around her, and she stumbled to one side as her knees threatened to buckle.

Hot tears burned in her eyes. She couldn't do it. She wasn't strong enough.

Luma stared down at the four rings that encircled her shaking fingers, their thin silver metal shining softly. She thought of the mage who had given her those rings to help control the chaos in the starlight inside of her. Without the rings, that chaos would have been too much for her to manage—it would have killed her to wield it for too long. Not that that mattered now. She was still too weak. Luma hung her head in shame.

I'm sorry, Eldamarr Rinn. I have failed you. I have failed everyone.

Luma's vision blurred as fresh tears flooded her eyes. She blinked and looked down at the rings once again. Then all at once, her vision and her mind cleared. *Chaos.* Maybe that was exactly what she needed now.

Almost in a trance, Luma pulled the four rings off her fingers one by one, letting each drop to the ground at her feet.

A deep tingle ran up and down her spine as Luma faced the fourth Sacred Stone once again. Taking a deep breath and exhaling slowly, Luma raised her arms so that her palms were level with the crack running through it.

Don't fight it. Nothing else matters now.

White light burst from the scars on Luma's palms as wave after wave of intense, scorching power rolled through her. Luma squeezed her eyes shut and kept her arms locked as she fully surrendered, allowing the raw chaos to burn, free and unchecked.

A second later, light began to beam not only from Luma's outstretched hands but from her whole body until it filled the large cavern with celestial radiance. The light streamed forward and poured into the crack in the final Sacred Stone, then crept steadily upward. As the light neared the top, Luma's knees finally buckled. Her eyes flew open and she staggered forward, gritting her teeth as she forced a final pulse of starlight into the crack in the stone.

The light hit the top of the crack with a brilliant flash that exploded outward. It streamed up to the cavern ceiling and then rained down in glittering sparks until it coated the floor around the base of the four monoliths in shards of flashing light.

It was a truly magnificent spectacle—beauty in its purest form.

But Luma did not see it, for the second the starlight had reached the top of the fourth Sacred Stone, the light coming from her body extinguished, her eyes rolled backward, and she collapsed.

Chapter 36

Figg's eyes fluttered open, and she groaned. Moving stiffly, she pushed the broken shield off herself as she struggled to sit up. Her head pounded, and blood ran from a wide gash along her collarbone. Fresh battle magic wounds overwrote the older scars along her arms and torso.

Slowly, Figg looked around the cavern, her eyes watering in the bright light. Clustered around her lay her fellow guards, unconscious but breathing.

Figg's gaze landed on Vell lying a short distance away. She reached for her short sword before realizing the wizard leader was no longer a threat. That could only have been Luma's work.

But where was the Daughter of Starlight?

Still seated, Figg painfully turned back and forth, searching.

Then, she saw her. Crawling forward as quickly as her wounded body would allow, Figg moved to where Luma lay crumpled at the base of the fourth Sacred Stone. Eyebrows knit together with worry, she placed a tentative hand on Luma's chest. Behind her came an agonized groan, and Figg turned to see Corr was also coming back to consciousness.

Figg's voice trembled with urgency. "Corr, help! Luma's not breathing!"

Gritting his teeth, Corr pulled himself up and

staggered forward, then dropped to his knees next to Figg. He reached out and cradled Luma's head in his hands. Her eyes were closed, and her lips were tinged with blue.

"Luma? Oh no, no, Luma, wake up." But Luma did not respond to Corr's desperate pleas. Corr's gaze shifted to Luma's hands, and his eyes flared. "Her rings! She took off her rings!" Panic edged into his tone as Corr began frantically looking around, searching in vain while still cradling Luma's head. "Where are they? She needs the rings. She told me they would keep her safe!" His voice caught in his throat.

One by one, the shards of light that glittered on the cavern floor burned out like so many sparks. Figg looked up at the Sacred Stones, tears blurring her vision. They loomed above her, their once gaping, jagged cracks now sealed with warm, white light, still softly glowing.

When Figg spoke, her voice was soft and filled with awe. "Corr. She did it."

Corr didn't respond. His broad shoulders trembled, and tears flooded his eyes. He shook his head, unwilling to accept that this was the price to pay for their victory.

Suddenly, a noise came from behind him: a low, guttural rumble.

Corr turned toward the sound, and his gaze collided with Ketu's large, black eyes. The dragon's breathing was labored, and dark purplish-red blood ran continuously from the deep wound in his chest, where Vell's battle magic had scorched away the thick scales. Still, Ketu inched forward to where Luma lay at the base of the fourth stone, and Corr shifted to one side.

Figg, still with one hand on Luma's chest, watched the dragon with wide, anxious eyes as he put his head down next to Luma's hand. Gently, Ketu nosed and nudged until Luma's limp hand rested directly on top of his wide forehead, her palm covering the four star-like markings that ran vertically between his large, black eyes.

For a moment, nothing happened. With a strangled sob, Figg hung her head. Then, she heard Corr's voice say her name, followed by a single word.

"Look."

Figg lifted her head and stifled a small, astonished cry. The underside of Luma's hand, where it touched Ketu's forehead, had begun to glow.

At first, Figg thought the light was coming from Luma, but as she continued to watch, she realized that it was the markings on the dragon's forehead that were the source of the glow.

A second later, little ribbons of light began to shine along Ketu's neck, running between his dark scales like thin rivers. The light flowed upward across the dragon's face and pooled under Luma's palm. Slowly, the light continued to build until Luma's hand was completely covered in a white shimmer. Then gleaming tendrils began to flicker up and around her wrist.

Corr, still cradling Luma's head in his lap, sat as if frozen, the glowing light reflecting in his wide eyes. The light flowing from Ketu continued to build, climbing up Luma's arm. Figg pulled back her hand as the glow concentrated on Luma's chest, slowly swirling.

Ketu made a low rumble deep in his throat as the last of the ribbons of light ran across his body, between his scales, and flowed upward into Luma. Then, a bright flash burst outward and reflected in the dragon's obsidian eyes just before they closed.

Ketu's head thumped softly to the ground, his breathing shallow. His thick tail twitched slowly back and forth, the spines along it scraping small grooves in the cavern floor before coming to stillness. Luma's limp hand slid from the dragon's forehead, where the four star-like markings remained but glowed no more.

Then, as the brilliance of the final flash of light faded into shadow, the Daughter of Starlight took a breath.

****

High above the cavern, the Four Stars once again formed a jagged shape in the inky night sky. The alignment was over, and along the eastern horizon, dawn was breaking.

All across the mountainside, the remaining wizards were disappearing, banished back across the bridge to Malicath by the Sacred Stones, their protective power once again in place.

A ragged cheer went up from the beleaguered elf fighters on the surrounding cliffs.

"Ediiiirrraaaa!"

The war was over.

****

Excerpt from the writings of Aire, Recorder of the Starlight Council:

It is only through the sheer power of my considerable will that I am sitting here at my desk, writing. The weather is lovely, warm, and cloudless, and below my office window here in the White Keep, the River Aque gleams in the morning sunlight. A more perfect day for the celebration I could not have designed.

The moon has been full six times since the four Sacred Stones were healed and Edira was saved.

All wizards have been banished from our world, well, all but one. Ruvyn remains. When the protection of the Sacred Stones was restored, it cleanly severed the bond between Ruvyn and his damaged staff, which allowed him to stay with us here on Edira. He joins Haryk, Corr, Elas, Izarre, Emalet, Figg, and myself on Luma's Starlight Council.

We wanted to make her queen, of course, but Luma would not hear of it. Instead, she formed the Starlight Council of Plains Clan and Forest Clan, and together, we strive to do what is best for all elves. Ruvyn speaks frequently of becoming the first ever cross-worlds ambassador, starting with Edira and Malicath. He seems convinced that wizards and elves have much to benefit from each other if only old stereotypes and prejudices could be dismantled and cooperation and trust built in their place. Figg actually agrees with Ruvyn about this, and to everyone's surprise, she has become his strongest supporter.

Emalet and my brother Elas have become virtually inseparable, and Elas is now even sporting a large, brightly colored tattoo on his arm in Plains Clan style. It closely matches one that Emalet also has on her arm. Elas tried to have me believe that the similarity was pure coincidence, but I think we all know better than that. I'm happy for him, but I still think the new tattoo looks ridiculous, and I am not about to pretend otherwise.

Luma remained unconscious for a full three weeks following the alignment, and Corr never once left her side.

As soon as the Sacred Stones were healed, the mage, Eldamarr Rinn, rushed to the mainland from across the Inland Sea, finally free from exile. He and Izarre cared for Luma night and day while her mind lingered at the gates of the Dark Forest between worlds. And when she did finally awake, something about her was different. She still wields the power of starlight, but it was as if the chaos within her had been burned away, and all that remained was peace.

In the days after Luma awoke, Eldamarr Rinn confided to all of us that with the Sacred Stones now fully healed, he had the power necessary to open a bridge to the far-off human world of Earth. If, that is, Luma still wanted to go home. Luma had thanked him but with a smile, shook her head, saying that she was, in fact, already home.

I thought Corr was going to pass out waiting for Luma to answer the mage, and when she did, he was smiling so much it looked like he had truly lost his mind. Izarre had to admonish him for gripping Luma's hands so tightly since they, too, were still healing.

When she was pulled from the cavern, Luma's palms were badly injured—the burned, torn, and blackened skin peeling away from her bones like the bark from a dying tree. Now gone are the crisscrossed jumble of dark scars that once marked Luma's forced passage to Earth, and what remains is a straight line of four star-like markings on each palm, much like those that adorn Ketu's forehead. Izarre believes that if it wasn't for the last-minute infusion of the dragon's starlight energy into her, Luma would never have survived after healing the fourth Sacred Stone. Which brings me to why we are celebrating today!

Today, we all gather for the Feast of the Dragon Statue. Carved directly into the mountainside above the cave entrance by the finest elven artisans, Ketu's likeness will be forever preserved.

Ketu himself will be in attendance, I am certain. It was also many weeks before we were sure he would live after the final battle, but Tsarra was utterly determined to save him, and as we all know, Tsarra's will is not easily crossed. Whatever starlight connection the dragon once had to the Four is now gone, but so is his ferocity and mistrust.

If anyone had told me before that elves and a dragon could live in such a state of harmony, I would not have believed it, but here we are.

Ketu is welcome everywhere and honored by all. He is especially beloved by the children, who, at Luma's laughing suggestion, have all taken to calling him "puppy dog." It seems a rather undignified nickname for a dragon, if you ask me, but Ketu doesn't appear to mind.

No elf, not even Eldamarr Rinn, knows how old Ketu is or exactly how long dragons naturally live, but I hope his years with us will be many. Perhaps, somewhere, in the far-flung corners of Edira, there are still others like him. No one knows that either, but everyone hopes.

And so today, we celebrate the dragon statue, but we also gather to dedicate the mural that Izarre painted along the narrow passageway to the Cavern of the Four, honoring the elven lives that were lost in the final battle.

Today is a day for celebration and joy but also for remembrance and gratitude for all those who sacrificed to make Edira free.

Trill and his owls are back in their homelands in the far west. Luma offered him a seat on the Starlight Council, but Trill politely refused (well, politely for an owl). He said now that the wizards are gone, and the alignment is over, elves should attend to elf matters and owls to owl matters. What exactly 'owl matters' are, I don't know, and quite frankly, I was afraid to ask. He promised to be here tonight for the celebration, though.

Speaking of which, I can hear from outside my office door that elves from all over Edira are starting to arrive for the feast. Oh, and on the horizon, I believe I see Trill and his owls coming this way. I'd better go and warn the others before Trill flies up and gives some poor elf a heart attack with his silent arrival. And so, for now, my duties as Starlight Council Recorder are satisfied, and I can join the celebration.

The war is won, Edira is free, and our long-lost Daughter of Starlight is home to stay.

A word about the author...

Molly's love of language and writing has been lifelong. She earned a degree in English and Communication and then went on to earn a second degree in American Sign Language Interpreting. An avid runner, Molly often gets her best story ideas while running and remains outraged that those ideas do not then present themselves, fully formed, on the page. When she's not running, writing, or interpreting, Molly can often be found taking an excessive number of photos of her dog, Bungee, and her two cats, Rose and Clover. Molly lives in the beautiful St. Croix River Valley of Minnesota with her husband and two sons, who bring her joy every day.

www.ingramcontent.com/pod-product-compliance
Lightning Source LLC
Chambersburg PA
CBHW072204030726
47501CB00015B/638